Cover Art by Paul Harmon

Front Cover: *Lady Of Shallot* - Oil on Canvas 48" x 36"
Back Cover: *Cinema Dreams* - Oil on Canvas 30" x 40"

Paul Harmon is an internationally exhibited artist who, from 1985 to early 1998, divided his time between permanent Studio/residences in Paris, France and Brentwood, Tennessee. Harmon's work is well represented in numerous galleries, museums, and major corporate and private collections in Europe, Asia, and the USA.

Paul's work hangs in the Tennessee State Museum, the Tampa Museum of Art, the George Bush Presidential Library and Museum, the Museum of The Principality of Monaco, and the city of Caen, France. He was chosen in 1981 to represent the U.S. in the Bienal de Arte, Medellin, Colombia, SA.

In 1994, Harmon had a major exhibition at the invitation of Caen, France. Curated by Galerie Deprez-Bellorget of Paris, this one-man exhibition was the official art show of the D-Day 50th anniversary.

Harmon is also the recipient of many major international painting awards including the Prix de la Ville de Monaco and the Prix de la Societe E.J.A. at the XXIV Prix International D'Art Contemporain de Monte-Carlo.

The painting *Working Man* from Harmon's exhibition/competition was chosen by Her Serene Highness Princess Caroline of Monaco for her private collection. In connection with the Prix de la Ville de Monaco, a canvas was commissioned by the Principality of Monaco for its permanent collection.

A comprehensive book, "Paul Harmon: *Crossing Borders*," is a 360-page color volume that showcases some of his work from 1961 to mid-2009. More than 526 paintings are featured in the book, along with on essay by Art Historian Robert L. McGrath, professor of art history, emeritus, Dartmouth College.

Harmon's work is featured in the Elmore Leonard movie *Pronto*, directed by Jim McBride and starring Peter Falk, Glenne Headly and James LeGros. Harmon lives and works in a 1793 farmhouse and studio in Brentwood, Tennessee, that is included on National Register of Historic Places. For more information, visit http://www.paulharmon.com

Black Orchid Night

A Novel Idea

H.T. Manogue

Other Works By H.T. Manogue

Novels

Bed Bosh & Beyond
ISBN# 978-0-9778130-6-3
2014

The Butterfly Ball
ISBN# 978-0-9778130-5-6
2012

Living Behind The Beauty Shop
ISBN# 978-0-9778130-4-9
2011

Essays

Short Sleeves Insights
Live An Ordinary Life In A Non-Ordinary Way
2010 Collection
ISBN# 978-0977-8130-3-2

Poetry

Short Sleeves
'Spirit Songs'- 2008 Collection
ISBN# 978-09778130-2-5

Short Sleeves- A Book For Friends
2007 Collection
ISBN# 0-9778130-1-0

Short Sleeves A Book For Friends
2006 Collection
ISBN# 0-99778130-0-2

Copyright Page

Special Thanks

The inspiration for this book came from several different sources. I know my dreams and inner senses helped form the concept of the book, but there were other physical and non-physical sources at work. Their input gave me added vision and intense clarity.

I want to thank Paul Harmon for allowing me to use two of his incredible creations for the front and back cover. Without Paul, this book would not have the appeal, pizzazz and quality of form that it has now. I am honored to call Paul my friend. Without him, this book would not have a face that perfectly displays the character of the work.

Special thanks to my friend Dia Sibert for organizing the interior of the book and my website. Dia has the unique talent of turning the ordinary into the extraordinary. Her interior design knowledge and friendship are appreciated.

I also want to thank Julie Lindy. Julie helped changed this book from a rough canvas to a sharp work of art. From day one, Julie was invested in this book. Her suggestions and edits made me think about the readers. I often get caught in the story, and ramble on about issues that are important to me and me alone. Julie reeled me back in and tightened the work so it flowed easier for readers. The material in this book can be challenging. Julie helped make it more understandable by her questions, comments, and an assortment of interesting notes. I didn't always take her advice, but thanks to her, this work will be read for decades.

Julie Lindy's information: www.editingforindies.com; https://www.facebook.com/thirdeyeediting; julielindyeditor@gmail.com. Twitter: @ThirdEyeEditing.

The Stanislav Grof paragraph is from his "Essential Shift" interview with the Institute of Noetic Sciences. The Interview is no longer available on the IONS site.

Doctor Grof's website: www.stanislavgrof.com/

Institute of Noetic Sciences Website: http://noetic.org/

The Unknown Reality quote in Chapter 17 is from the book, The Unknown Reality, which is part of The Seth Series written by Jane Roberts and Robert Butts, and published by Amber-Allen Publishing.

The Amber-Allen Website: www.amberallen.com/

The article in Chapter 17 was written in 1941 for the Louisville Courier Journal by David H. Bradford. The article was reprinted in the article: "The World War II Era and The Seeds of a Revolution." That article was reprinted on the website: http://www.pearsonhighered.com/assets/hip/us/hip_us_pearsonhighered/samplechapter/0205728812.pdf

The articles in Chapters 26 about the Tuskegee Airmen and black nurses were also part of that reprint.

To Lucas, AJ and Annabelle

I shall not commit the fashionable stupidity of regarding everything I cannot explain as a fraud.

Carl Jung

We are such stuff
As dreams are made on, and our little life
Is rounded with a sleep.

William Shakespeare

The best thing about dreams is that fleeting moment, when you are between asleep and awake, when you don't know the difference between reality and fantasy, when for just that one moment you feel with your entire soul that the dream is reality, and it really happened.

James Arthur Baldwin

What, if some day or night a demon were to steal after you into your loneliest loneliness and say to you: 'This life as you now live it and have lived it, you will have to live once more and innumerable times more' ... Would you not throw yourself down and gnash your teeth and curse the demon who spoke thus? Or have you once experienced a tremendous moment when you would have answered him: 'You are a god and never have I heard anything more divine.'

Friedrich Nietzsche

Foreword

I don't believe in happenstance, so to claim that I randomly met Hal Manogue while wandering among masses of people through the crowded exhibition hall at a major trade show would deny the power of auspicious coincidence. We found ourselves face-to-face, total strangers from different cities and states, drawn by a common interest: books. We spontaneously collided amidst throngs of people in search of other agendas. A conversation was inevitable: He is a writer. I'm a writer and editor, and we're both spiritual explorers who embrace the magic of universal mystery. Both of us are awestruck by the power of the written word and the under-manifested light and latent potential for brilliance in every human being. So we chatted. That chat led to a conversation, and not surprisingly, the conversation morphed into an enthralling and intense hour-long discussion – and of course, a connection. The relationship that resulted from that "random" encounter continues to thrive and evolve, and I never have a conversation with Hal Manogue without his gifting me with food for thought and inspiration.

"Black Orchid Night" not only will leave its readers with food for thought and inspiration, but with great storytelling as well. Hal Manogue is an expert in consciousness. Consciousness is an under explored field to which he's devoted his full attention and untold hours of study, as well as encounters with other masters in the field. His expertise on the many facets and faces of consciousness is reflected in his numerous works, and "Black Orchid Night" is a stellar example.

In "Black Orchid Night," Fiona, the protagonist, is Hal Manogue's emissary into one mysterious and under explored aspect of consciousness: lucid dreaming, whereby the dreamer is aware that he or she is dreaming, and with effort and intention, potentially can consciously direct the topics of dreams and influence their unfolding. Lucid dreams can occur in sleep states, in mediation, in intense "daydreams" – but always in that mystical and delightful Theta state where we teeter between semi-consciousness and the Delta state of deep and detached sleep.

The joy we find in Fiona is her committed use of lucid dreaming with the intent to find answers to enrich her personal power and her self-realization, to deal with and manage her demons, to drill for answers to the burdensome events and relationships of her past, and to discover answers to questions that seem impossible to uncover. Fiona, without question, seeks personal resolution and healing through her power of lucid dreaming. Fiona is special, but she's also *us*, whether we see ourselves as special or not (by the way, we are!).

Hal Manogue masterfully uses Fiona to demonstrate that we all have potential to uncover our unanswered questions, to resolve our pain-drenched traumas, and to begin uncoiling the convoluted mysteries of our own lives. We each can empower ourselves by deliberately and diligently undertaking our own versions of Fiona's persistent quest and by actively modeling her search to fill the nagging holes in the fabric of her psyche.

Through Fiona, Hal Manogue gives us tools to drill for the seemingly nonexistent answers to our own afflicted, unresolved mental and spiritual baggage, the stuff we've buried yet somehow still lug around, the long-ignored scars and harrowing heartbreaks that plague our everyday lives, the stuff we swear we'll never again talk or think about, and the painful questions we shrug off as "things we'll never know."

Among the some of the transferable tools that Hal Manogue employs through Fiona:

• Pursuing our personal passions and goals that bring us joy and make us *think*;

• Surrounding ourselves with friends and trusted, positive people;

• Protecting our homes and other personal sacred spaces with discernment;

• Confronting the difficult relationships, painful memories, and uncomfortable events of our lives with the courage to open our minds and put these burdens to work as tools for our own healing;

• Banishing toxic people and circumstances in our lives that sabotage our growth;

• Seeking objective, expert guidance to help facilitate our healing – people who, with the highest intention, safely prod us to those dark recesses of our minds that we invest great effort in avoiding;

• Giving ourselves permission to have fun – a necessary and non-negotiable healing elixir; and

• Courageously pushing us to open new windows of light and enlightenment into our own conscious minds – often with apprehension – so that we can move forward prepared to engage in the ongoing work of becoming our best selves, free of grudges and unhindered by burdensome emotional baggage that no longer serves us any useful purpose, while simultaneously preparing us to confront new and sometimes painful challenges.

And just as importantly, Manogue introduces Fiona to a colorful parade of people who are an integral part of her, people she's known all along without knowing that she knows them, who unwittingly shaped her current circumstances and help her discover the resolution and peace that eludes her for so long. He shows us that the best and the worst people come into our lives to teach us, but most importantly, we are all connected.

Through Fiona's committed persistence to acquiring clarity and resolution about the unresolved mysteries and traumas of her past, she's led (and willingly goes) to the most unexpected people, places, and eras of time that lead her to become the person she is now, and she draws on the people who support and guide her to help her become the person she wants to be.

With Fiona as his heroine and the delightful narrative of "Black Orchid Night, Manogue masterfully introduces us to transferable techniques that we can apply to our own lives, to our own quests for personal revelation, to our committed emotional and spiritual growth – and provides us with useful tools that can help us evolve unfettered as we navigate both the fearsome undertows and the soothing, joyous waters of our lives.

Julie Lindy
Third Eye Editing
October 4, 2015

Julie Lindy, Editor

JulieLindyEditor@gmail.com

www.editingforindies.com

https://www.facebook.com/thirdeyeediting

Twitter: @ThirdEyeEditing

Julie has ghostwritten and edited numerous nonfiction books and novels, including USA Today and Amazon best sellers. She landed her first professional writing gig at age 19 and has written professionally ever since. Her background is old-school journalism. Julie began her career at a newspaper owned by the New York Times. She spent several years in the newspaper business covering beats such as education, health, politics, prisons, agriculture, police and feature writing before moving into trade publications, and later, into freelance writing and editing. She continues to write and edit for global mass media and has won awards from the Associate Press, Gannett Co. Inc., the Newsletter Publishers Foundation, and state societies.

Julie's approach to editing is simple: the editor is the reader's advocate. Audiences begin books or magazines or articles because they *want* to read them. The writer's job is to keep them invested all the way through the final sentence. Why ask readers to start something they won't finish? Julie believes editor's job is to help writers lure readers to the final destination.

A few years after graduating from LSU, Julie completed a seminar in International Media Studies at the University of London. Later, she earned a master's degree in teaching secondary English education, and teaching 6th and 9th grades was among the most profound experiences of her life.

Julie loves travel and has lived for brief periods of time in England and Russia. She loves animals, community service, metaphysics, chilling out with good friends and family, exploring bookstores, and learning 'til her brain hurts, laughing 'til her tummy hurts, theater and movies. And she loves hearing from interesting people, so feel free to reach out to her!

Preface

As Shakespeare pointed out, we are such stuff as dreams are made on. We achieve so many things while dreaming, but we don't remember most of our accomplishments. For centuries, our dream reality has been a victim of antiquated beliefs and religious misconceptions. Hence, our dreams are shrouded in mystery. I've been studying the dream reality for the last seven years, and I've discovered some interesting facts about our dream experiences. The first fact is we don't understand the complete nature of our consciousness, so we say, "It's only a dream."

But dreams are not meant to be tucked away on the discount rack in our consciousness. We don't realize it, but we ignore part of ourselves in order to function physically in the ongoing expansion of the human species. We believe we are built that way. We fail to see we are in the process of becoming what we already are, and we certainly overlook the undeniable fact that dreams set the tone for that becoming.

Dreams exist in levels, just like this reality. Our wakeful levels of reality are measured in time sequences, but there is no time sequence in dreams, so it's difficult to make sense of them and put them in order. Dreams have their own sense of order. On one level, dreams mix wakeful experiences with other probabilities, and we experience a mish-mash of dream events. On another level our conscious beliefs and innate beliefs are homogenized, and we experience people, places and events in unusual ways. These dream levels help us with insights and artful expressions. On another level, we enter the spacious presence of consciousness where all experiences are formed.

These dreams experiences are a variety pack filled with waking probabilities that we lay out for physical manifestation. Some are manifested; some are not. Once we enter the fourth level, we wander through the hallways of consciousness and tap into the pulse of the soul. In this hallway, more levels of our dream reality are experienced. We live life as the soul lives it. We are the soul and all its counterparts. This consciousness journey takes us to the reality of the soul.

In dreams, the ego is dormant. We free ourselves from our waking focus, so we have the ability to function without a body as we wander through these vast never-ending dream realities. Our body remains in one place, but we still sense the sensations created by our body.

We remember some of these levels as we travel though them while dreaming. There are endless levels, and an endless amount of no time to experience them. Our dreams never end. We just move in and out of them, just like we move in and out of this reality. The interesting thing about dreaming is we sense that we don't just live one lifetime. We begin to realize how it feels it to live in multiple lifetimes.

Lucid dreamers have the ability to remember portions of dreams, and some of these dreamers also have the talent to dream at will. These people are not different than any other person in terms of psychic gifts or supernatural powers. What these people have is an open channel to other realities. They allow their consciousness to move multidimensionally using practice, a knowing attitude, and an open-ended belief structure. We all could remember where we go in dreams if we used those inner gifts. We rarely use them by objective design, but we always use them subjectively.

Black Orchid Night is the story of one of these lucid dreamers. She accepts what she experiences in dreams as another form of reality. Her waking world becomes a schoolroom filled with a new set of choices and probabilities. The lucid dreamer in this story discovers the connection we have with each other no matter what segment of the social ladder they represent. We all have been nasty characters, lonely and depressed individuals that make some really bad choices. The dreamer in this story is surrounded by the anguish of family dynamics and associations that can be considered sleazy and harmfully narcissistic. She begins to understand that she is more than one body and brain in one particular time. She finds another portion of herself living as someone with different skin color, and in a different time period. She realizes that skin color and ethnic backgrounds are choices that produce lesson for soul expansion. She interacts with this particular counterpart, and that connection influences present moment choices for both individuals.

It's not necessary to believe you are more than one individual in order to be another individual. We are wired that way by our multidimensional soul. We will still function and expand from the action of the soul regardless of our ignorance. Our mission as individuals is to experience our desires and expand from them. We are part of the creative activity I call the soul. The soul doesn't reincarnate. Reincarnation implies time. The soul creates without time. What we experience and what the character in this story experiences is one incarnation of the many incarnations that the soul expresses for creative expansion.

HTM

October 2015

The Musing

Yoga says instinct is a trace of an old experience that has been repeated many times and the impressions have sunk down to the bottom of the mental lake. Although they go down, they aren't completely erased. Don't think you ever forget anything. All experiences are stored in the *chittam*; and, when the proper atmosphere is created, they come to the surface again. When we do something several times it forms a habit. Continue with that habit for a long time, and it becomes your character. Continue with that character and eventually, perhaps in another life, it comes up as instinct.

Swami Satchidananda

Prologue

If you're really a mean person, you're going to come back as a fly and eat poop.

Kurt Cobain

Fiona remembered what her mother told her as she chased the pesky fly off her nose. She looked out her double-wide window in her orchid nursery. Her deceased mother, Olivia, came to her in a dream shortly after her death, and Fiona never forgot what Olivia told her. She heard the words again as the large fly played hopscotch on the bridge of her nose.

"Your life is divided into two worlds. You will encounter people and places that exist in a different time, and you will know them. Know that all you experience in those worlds is real. Everyone you meet and everything you do in dreams happens somewhere at some time."

Fiona smiled. She started to read a few words from her favorite book. But she was also looking through the north side window of her three-acre Williamson County property at three young does grazing on the lawn. She was still reading, but as she read and gazed at the does, her focus quickly changed. She was distract by the fly once again for obvious reasons. She reached for a sanitary wipe and put it up to her nose as she reminded herself that she couldn't stand the thought of fly poop invading her internal organs through her nostrils. With hands flying about like two paddles in a game of ping-pong, she tried to focus on the words she'd just read instead of her tiny nemesis. But as she gently touched her nose with the wet wipe, her ability to dream lucidly took her to another place. Instead of seeing the does running into the lush, green Harpeth River Valley woods, she remembered a recent dream. She was leaving Chicago in the 1940s. In the dream, she was riding on a bus to Nashville. She remembered the man in front of her on the bus, but she automatically snapped out of that dream. There wasn't time for that one now. The fly was back. Fiona put her hand through her hair, and then with the force of a tennis champion, she tried to swat the pest with the back of her hand. The insect reminded her that she could continue to fight, or she could run without moving, thanks to her ability to dream lucidly. She pushed herself up from the desk and went to her mini-fridge filled with bottled water. The fly followed her. She grabbed a bottle of spring water. The first cold swig gave her body an inner jolt. She went back to her desk and sat down. The fly was sitting on the desk. She put the bottle down, picked up her book, and tried to smash the winged annoyance, but the green-back fly was too fast. Fiona felt the frustration of missing the fly and the experience of the bus ride. Those thoughts made her a little queasy. Her nursery was her safe haven, and it was under attack. It wasn't the fly that was inflicting most of the damage: It was her endless daytime dreams. Fiona knew she was caught in two realities, and she tried her best to come to terms with both of them. Years of therapy helped, but her failed relationships and a strong resentment of religion made her a prisoner in her aging body. She thought about the recurring bus dream again. She thought about the people close to her that were in that dream with her. She had many recurring dreams through the years, but this one, the bus ride, changed her perceptions of life. She started to think that she was living more than one life. Her waking life and her dream life were so different. She thought about Dr. Krabb, her therapist. He called her dream adventures soul counterparts "excursions," and she liked that description. The bus ride to Nashville would come back time and time again, but for some reason, that dream was gone now. She saw three young kids playing football. She was a child of the 1960s once again, and she was in England. Her daydreaming mind turned to her childhood and her parents.

Fiona Adi Mistry was born in the small village of Raby Mere on the Wirral Peninsula just outside of the English city of Liverpool. Her dad, Roger, was a personnel director for a large oil company, and her mother, Olivia, was a French teacher at Liverpool Institute. Roger and Olivia were from two different backgrounds. Roger was part of a well-respected family from central India. His parents were doctors, and Olivia's parents were professors. Olivia's father, Stanley Evans, was an expert in Sanskrit literature, and her mother, Phoebe Altman Evans, was an ancient history and religion professor. Olivia met Roger and his family on one of their research trips to India, when Olivia and Roger were teenagers. Roger's given name in India was Chetan, but he quickly changed it to Roger when he began his studies at Oxford. His mother and father were Oxford educated, so it was the only school Roger cared about, plus he knew he could see Olivia more. He knew they would marry. While at Oxford, the pair got together every weekend and on holidays. Roger never went back to India to live. Oxford was only 172 miles from Olivia's home in Liverpool, so she would go to Oxford one weekend, and he would visit Liverpool the next. Roger spent holidays with the Evans, so he became the son they never had.

Fiona studied at the institute where her mother taught for a few years, but then fate took over. She didn't know what fate was back then, but she knew now. She was an attractive little tomboy. Her dark curly hair was shoulder length, and her almond shaped blue-green eyes sparkled in the sunlight. She was average height, but she was extremely muscular. Her dad said she got that physique from his side of the family. She could almost throw and kick a ball as far as her older brother, Geoff could. She told him that she would, when the time came, play football for Red, the Liverpool Women's Club. That dream never materialized. Fee, as the family called her, was back on the school's football field, but she was still at her desk thanks to her ability to dream lucidly at will. In this dream, she was watching her older sister chase the ball and then attempt to kick it. She heard Geoff shout, "Up the Pool." Geoff was a big Liverpool City Club fan. Sarah's young body was not as coordinated as Fee's, so she consistently missed the ball. Eleven-year-old Geoff laughed and called her a lump each time Sarah missed the ball. Sarah was the plain, non-athletic child with a very nervous attitude and peculiar tendencies. Geoff was a tall, skinny boy with sunken piercing eyes and a will to disrupt whatever the girls wanted to do. His troubling idiosyncrasies seem to exacerbate as he aged. Geoff's short black hair stood up at attention around his forehead, thanks to a healthy dose of petroleum jelly, as he ran after Sarah. His deep-set black eyes gave the impression that he was always thinking about something devious, even when he was playing. Fiona always thought he didn't like to play with them, and his actions usually confirmed her suspicions. He came off as angry and troubled, and he was. When the nervous twitch in his right eye started to flicker like the wings of a hummingbird, a wave of grief was coming for anyone in his line of fire. As Fee watched the daydream unfold, she saw Geoff come over to her as she positioned herself behind the ball. He grabbed her around the waist. She turned and looked at him with her piercing eyes. Fiona usually didn't miss when she focused on kicking the ball. She was a natural, and in this particular dream, she was about to show off her football talents, but for some reason, Geoff wanted to alter the outcome. As she turned, his right foot locked on Fiona's kicking leg, and she fell to the ground. She heard his angry, snarly voice in her ear.

"You've got to plan for all sorts of attacks, little girl. Everyone is an attacker in one way or another."

Fiona's focus quickly changed. She was back behind the oak desk. Thankfully, the fly was gone, but beads of sweat formed on her forehead. She didn't like to think about Geoff or Sarah, but she knew her lucid dreaming adventures could take her anywhere. Her relationship with her siblings was not the best then, and now at 50, her relationship with her older siblings was nonexistent. She knew early on that Sarah never liked her. But Sarah acted like she needed her, especially when they played. Fiona wasn't sure why her mind took her back to that particular moment in the past. She thought about that as she looked at a plump gray squirrel having lunch on one of her ten bird feeders positioned outside of her orchid nursery. She liked to watch these natural acrobats. They seemed to enjoy the challenge of finding food, eating it, or stockpiling it for another day. Not only were the squirrels acrobats, they were food bankers as well. She thought that was why her mind went back to that childhood scene. Brother Geoff was like a squirrel. He loved to take things from others. For years, Geoff would prey on younger kids, and then hurt them in some way.

She remembered how Geoff developed the habit of saving the spoils of his conquests in some demented way. He kept a journal, and if he took something personal from one of his young victims, he put those items in the old family footlocker that sat in his room. He always kept the chest locked with a heavy metal combination lock. Sarah and Fiona would ask him about the contents from time to time, but he would always tell them to "bugger off." He felt his vulgar vocabulary was one of his greatest assets, and he used it without regret on everyone. Including his parents. Roger and Olivia worried about Geoff's language issues, but they dismissed those thoughts rather quickly for some unknown reason. Fiona switched her thoughts to her church days and how she felt uneasy about God. The family, except for Geoff, went to church every week. She was taught that God was the doer and maker of her life. The thought of God being a man made her sick to her stomach, but she didn't know why.

Fiona's mind wandered again. Her move to the United States was front and center. The family moved to Nashville the year Roger was hired as the U.S. human resources director for a Danish pharmaceutical company. Olivia decided to stay home so the three kids could adjust to this small American city. When the family moved to Nashville, Geoff was almost thirteen. The move brought out the worst in him. Sarah and Fiona seemed excited about the move for different reasons, but Geoff rebelled. The family knew before the move that Geoff could have serious psychological issues. He trapped twelve-year-old Jiggy Didi in an old hay barn before they left England. Geoff kept Sarah's friend Jiggy in the barn for two hours. He didn't try to rape her, but he did cop a feel, and he scared her with threatening comments. Geoff let her go after she promised not to tell. Jiggy suffered in silence until she realized Geoff would do it again if he had the chance. Jiggy told Sarah before she told her own parents. Jiggy thought Sarah could help stop Geoff's threats, but Sarah knew Geoff would only make her life miserable if she did. Jiggy didn't want to tell her parents. She thought they might flog her for being with a boy in a barn. She was young, but old enough to know that it was the woman's fault in her native Maldives Islands when any sort of sexual acts occurred, and she believed it was probably the same in England. Jiggy decided to confront Geoff in front of Fiona and Sarah, but Geoff threatened all of them. Sarah encouraged Jiggy to tell her mum and dad. Sarah wasn't sure what Jiggy's parents would do, but it was her only solution. Sarah didn't want to tell her parents about Geoff. She was torn between her friendship with Jiggy and her fear and love for Geoff. Jiggy thought about Sarah's advice and decided she had no choice. It was a flogging or another attack by Geoff. So Jiggy went to her parents and told them everything. Fiona felt a twinge of sadness when she remembered that she and Sarah never told their parents what Geoff did to Jiggy. Maybe if they did, Geoff would have turned out differently.

Chapter 1

I melted into the dream as if I had always been there. I knew where I had come from; I knew where I was going.

Chelsie Shakespeare

Her thick, long black hair was soaking wet under her cream-colored, wide brim gardening hat, and the perspiration was slowly making its way to one of her crystal blue-green eyes. Her black Foster Grant sunglasses were beginning to fog from the moderate humidity and 70-degree temperature in her self-constructed backyard planthouse. Her white cotton V-neck t-shirt was beginning to show the outline of her braless 32C breasts, but all those minor distractions didn't matter. She was shivering with delight as she held one of her new potted purple Ophrys Apifera. She had several in her collection, but this group was the first group from the mountains of Sardinia. She was partial to this particular species because she remembered it growing wild when she was a child in Wales. Her mind began to race up and down her memory banks as she carried the first orchid in the group to its new home. Incredibly, the orchid reminded her of her first sexual fantasy. She was mentally experiencing a sex tape with her first love, Jude Pringle, in her inner theater. She never had sex with Jude, but she fantasized about it. She was scared to have sex with him. He was a big boy for his age, and she thought he had too big a penis for her small body. Even after all these years, her body felt a twitch as her mind played with her. Within seconds, her sexual imagination was in the full throttle position, but she quickly brought herself back to the task at hand.

She carefully put the first orchid in the new group in its designated plant box. Fiona was especially fond of this species because orchid aficionados like to call the Ophrys "the bee orchid." She called them savvy beauties since they had the ability to use trickery and deceit to attract male bees for procreation purposes. She also knew that this ingenious species gave up the need for male bees and turned to pseudocopulation to continue their long lineage. That was a fascinating concept.

"Funny," she whispered.

"Humans use several sexual tactics to keep the species alive, but few people understand the diversity and the beauty in procreation like plants do. Most people don't know that side of plants."

Fiona looked around the plant house as if someone heard her. But she was alone. She was always alone these days. She thought about the human drama she encountered through her life. Her relationship with her family as well as her interactions with the opposite sex left her feeling like a vacant house that was slowly deteriorating from neglect and abuse. Her parent's religion didn't help her justify the dreams and the visions she was having, and it certainly didn't help get a grip on her sexual disappointments.

Her mind switched back to the orchids. Her orchid business was her religion. It was her 21st century resurrection, she thought. She was on a mission of personal discovery. She methodically uncovered the sexual secrets of orchids, but her own sexuality was wrapped in the irony of her dreams. The thought of intercourse with a man was buried under the rubble of several failed relationships. She was a researcher and dreamer now. The only thing more important in life than orchids was her ability to dream. Her childhood dreams were typical dreams, but all that changed when the first tragedy took a slice of her life and devoured it. She thought she would have nightmares after her mother's suicide, but instead, she found the full flavor of the dream world. Her mother's suicide changed her in so many ways. Fiona's mother was her best friend all through her childhood. She was the only one who that understood her passion for being alone and her love of orchids. Fiona didn't know where her passions came from, and at times, she wished she could talk to her mother about them again. Her wish became a reality shortly after her mother's funeral. Olivia dropped herself in the white antique iron tub in the family's 1940s bungalow after taking a handful of sleeping pills and drowned herself. Sitting on the floor next to the white iron tub was a purple orchid and a note. Fiona didn't read the note, but she later learned through Geoff that the note simply said:

"Death by my own hand is a birth in another life. Look for me whenever you see an orchid bloom. Those new blooms are coming from a part of me, here, in this new life."

Fiona remembered her mother the night before she died. She sat quietly in the den reading a magazine. Fiona noticed the article she was reading. It was about World War II and how black soldiers helped win the war by flying missions over France. She remembered asking her a question.

"Mum, where were you during that war?"

Her mother looked up at her and smiled. Then her expression changed.

"Part of me was already dead when that war started, Fee. My sister committed suicide before the war, and part of me died with her."

Her mother looked back down and continued reading.

She remembered how shocked she was to hear her mother talk about a sister that night. Fiona never knew her mother had a sister. But Fiona knew why now. She found out after the bus stopped in Nashville, the bus ride in her recurring dream. She started to go deeper into her bus ride dream, but her phone rang, and she was back in the year 2012.

"Hi Fiona, Matt here. I need some orchids for the rectory. Can I come by in the morning and pick them up?"

"Hey Matt. I mean Father Matt. Sure, come after 9. That's when I'm on my second cup of coffee."

"Right. I don't want to come before that. I've known you too long. You can be a little grumpy in the morning, if I remember correctly."

"You know me too well, Matt. See you tomorrow."

Matt Ligon was her first high school boyfriend. He never tried to act out the role of a horny teen, and she never knew why until graduation. That's when he announced he was entering the seminary.

She never understood why Matt picked God over her until she started dreaming about "the bar". Now she knew seeing God was the not the final peg in the hole of death. But she had a little exposure to a new way of thinking when she saw an auburn-haired, blue-eyed, youthful version of her mother sitting on a wooded white bench one Sunday in August. Fee remembered falling asleep after her family birthday gathering. Her deceased mother was dressed in a white and purple linen robe. She was wearing her favorite silver-beaded house shoes. Olivia was surrounded by every color in the rainbow represented by phalaenopsis orchids that surrounded her. Not only did Fiona see the orchid's translucent colors, she smelled the difference in each color. Then, for the first time, she heard the orchids speak in what sounded like a British-accented voice filled with helium. Olivia smiled and immediately handed Fiona a delicate purple orchid.

"This is for you, my child. You are one of us and always will be. Your life is divided into two worlds. You will encounter people and places that exist in a different time, and you will know them. Know that all you experience in those worlds is real. Everyone you meet and everything you do in dreams happens somewhere at some time."

Her mother sat with her on that white bench surrounded by orchids night after night and would tell her, before she said anything else, that she was free. She heard Mother's voice as she opened her eyes in the morning:

"Fee, honey, you're an orchid dressed like a human now."

One night, her mother was standing next to the bench. A cluster of different colored Holcoglossum amesianum orchids were arranged in a row on the seat of the bench. Her mother's words came out slowly.

"Instincts and emotions move you through your life, child. Attract what you need from that world and discard the

34

frivolous senseless words, and people who hold you to a distorted form of righteousness. Resurrect your life using your imagination."

Suddenly Fiona flashed back to when she was twenty-one. Roger and new stepmother, Violet Simmons, felt it was time for Fiona to face life. Fiona told them about her dreams and her encounter with her mother and the orchids. They questioned her sanity.

The pair believed the same demons that took Olivia away were working on Fiona. They felt it was their duty to stop the madness before she harmed herself. She saw herself at breakfast one morning in June. Roger had decided to call his University of Liverpool roommate, Arthur Schuler, and ask for his help. Schuler was a well-respected but somewhat bohemian British psychiatrist who left England to set up a practice in New York. Roger and Schuler tried to reach Fiona with the tools of a democratic society, but she wanted no part of it. She liked Schuler and believed he knew what she was going through, but her father had different thoughts about her actions. The two men couldn't agree on anything when it came time to prescribe a solution. So Dr. Schuler dismissed himself from the case.

"Roger, your daughter has an unusual ability that we don't fully understand. I need time with her. I want her to come to New York and stay with me."

The message from Schuler was still on her mind, and so was Roger's face when she told him she was moving out. Roger asked why, then told her before she could answer that she was putting faith in the wrong person.

"Do you mean Schuler, Dad?"

"Yes, I do. He's twenty-three years older and a bit of a loon. I'm sorry I ever him involved him in this madness."

Fiona looked out the window and saw three young deer grazing in the woods behind the house. She felt the nerves in her hand twitch as she watched herself twirled around in the brown padded breakfast chair. She turned the chair toward her father. She looked at him and saw the pain in his eyes.

"I'm not going to have sex with him, Dad. I'm going for help."

As she relived the scene, she realized how alone he was back then

"I must go, Daddy. You know why."

Roger stared at her. He hesitated for a couple of seconds, and then nodded his head. He stood and looked at Violet as he quickly walked out of the room. Violet frowned at Fiona. She jumped to her feet and called for Roger to wait.

Fiona turned toward the window again. The deer were gone, but the iris and the honeysuckle in the garden seemed to be looking at her.

She smiled.

"The Earth does laugh in flowers", she thought to herself.

Chapter 2

Don't grieve. Anything you lose comes round in
another form.
Rumi

The sun was just coming up over one of the Tennessee
ridge tops as Fiona put the new Bucket Orchid in its place
one June morning. Fiona positioned her collection of
orchids by variety in her self-designed nursery. She cared
for more than a hundred varieties. She liked to call her
redwood plant house a nursery, because it made her feel
like she was caring for her babies. She told everyone they
were her children. This particular morning was like most
mornings. Her mind started to wander. Max Westwood was
on her mind. He was the man she chose to have children
with before she turned 30, but that relationship ended
tragically. Max was a churchgoer from a prominent
Nashville family that owned choice real estate on the west
side. The tall, handsome bodybuilder didn't have to work,
so he didn't. He lived for the thrill of it, and died because
of a thrill. He was 30 when his paragliding chute collapsed
while he was going for a world record in Draper, Utah.
Fiona remembered reading the report. He was thrown into
the hillside like a sack of potatoes. She cried because they
fought about church before he left on his final trip. He
wanted their children to be raised in his church, and she
didn't want them going to church. She told him she wanted
them to be lucid dreamers like her.

"You can't be serious, Fee. The only lucid dreamer I know is God."

"I didn't know you knew God, Max. Did he happen to tell you that dreamers see God differently?"

"Fee, I don't have time for this. I'm going to miss my flight. We'll talk when I get home."

She remembered the kiss he gave her and how strange she felt. She didn't want some man-made God teaching her children anything.

"Max's death was a fitting end, she thought. "He was a hard-headed rock in so many ways."

Her child birthing days were behind her, but she knew her mothering of orchids would continue for the rest of her life. She was still a beautiful woman at fifty. Her shoulder-length black hair had streaks of gray. Her olive complexion was riddled with age lines, but those lines seemed to be in just the right places. Her deep blue-green eyes were slightly covered by heavy eyelids, but that combination made her look intriguing and mysterious. She was aging like a fine wine.

Her bible, "The Complete History of Orchids," was open on the old English, six-foot oak picnic table she used as a desk and catch-all in the northern corner of the nursery. The table was positioned just below one of the massive wooden-framed windows. She stopped reading chapter six the day before, but she wanted to continue where she left off this morning. The Bucket Orchid needed special attention, and chapter seven would give her the answers she needed. She took a seat on the antique two-step wooden chair-ladder she used when she wanted to concentrate on her vast collection of orchid references. Her eyes focused on the first paragraph of page 120. Her perfectly shaped lips moved as she read the authors opening remarks:

"Somehow orchids managed to spread their beauty over six continents. They have successfully found a home in every conceivable terrestrial habitat. They earned respect in the botany world not only for their delicate beauty, but also for being the most diverse family of flowering plants. There are more than 25,000 species of orchids in 880 genres. The secret to their success in a word is sex. Not what we term normal sex. It is more like really weird sex. The Bucket Orchid is no exception. This pesky flower captures unsuspecting bees and uses them for its rather ingenious sexual ritual."

She was hooked. The plant sex thing aroused her in a way. She kept reading.

"The Australian hammer orchids are also cruel beauties. The wingless female wasps that become sexual prey have no idea what's in store for them. The flightless female wasp waits for a male wasp at the top of the stem. The male will pick her up and mate with her in mid-air. The hammer orchid effectively mimics the female wasp, and excites the unsuspecting male wasp to the point of ejaculation. The dupe male wasp is utterly fooled. He is so convinced that the orchid is a female wasp that he even extends his genital claspers into the orchid. The sexual scam is a double victory for the orchid. The natural deceit makes the female wasp reproduce asexually. That sexual behavior produces only male wasps. Female wasps are the result of actual wasp-to-wasp mating. When the male wastes his sperm on the orchid, more females become asexual, which means there are more male wasps to pollinate the hammer orchid."

Fiona thought about those words for a minute, and the sex puzzle started to fill her mind, but she soon drifted into the past. A subtle smile covered her face. She started to relive her first days with Art Schuler. Fiona had no concept of time when she went into one of her daydreaming trips. She was alive in another portion of her life once again.

She remembered that it didn't take long for Schuler to fall in love with her. Their work sessions escalated to sexual interludes almost immediately. Fee remembered the attraction she had for him as she sat in the nursery looking out the window. It was Schuler's mind that enticed her to have sex with him. He was the most attractive unattractive man she ever met. She knew he was a proper English gentlemen and celebrated doctor, and she knew he never married. Schuler was addicted to his work. Everything else was secondary, including women. Her mind formed a vision of him. His short, balding, overweight frame and downright obnoxious personality were turn-offs, so most women avoided him through the years, but she didn't. She knew the few female relationships he had were paid interludes with high-priced call girls. But all that didn't matter because he unlocked the secret of dreaming for her. He was a dream guru of sorts. She remembered her first session. His words were still fresh in her mind.

"Dreams don't begin or end, my dear. Only your awareness of dreams begins and ends. You begin to be aware of a dream, and then you leave it. The dreams you dream tonight may have been in existence long before now, but they begin when you become aware of them. You are fully aware of them tonight."

Fiona smiled. He was right, but she didn't really understand what he meant until she started going in and out of the dream that started with the bus ride to Nashville. She heard Schuler's voice again:

"In dreams, there are no physical objects, so there is no time as we know it. Time is actually the duration of physical objects."

She remembered her question. Her 21 year-old voice was front and center now.

"But how are dreams created, Art?"

"You create them, my dear, but you don't create them at any particular time. At the beginning of a certain level of dreams, you reach back into your other lives, of which you are not aware."

"I didn't know I have other lives."

"Precisely, my dear. Some of your dreams originated before the planet existed. Now I know that sounds strange to you but think this way: All consciousness exists simultaneously, so you are much more than you suspect. But in your dreams, you are an actual, durable, self-determined entity that projects the reality of several of your personalities. There is no conscious contact with these other personalities unless you tap into the stream of consciousness that exists within you. It seems you can do that without effort, my dear."

"Stream of what, doctor?" She remembered Schuler chuckling.

"The dream world, my dear, is a natural byproduct between your relationship with your inner self and the physical being you call, Fiona. It is not a reflection. It is a byproduct. Your energy is transformed from one state to another. Remember the dream world is a necessity for the survival of every physical individual."

Her mind suddenly switched to another interesting session: one that came a week after they had sex for the first time.

"Art, please tell me why I can remember my dreams so vividly."

"Yes. The art of dreaming is a natural talent, but remembering your dreams takes daring, exploration, spontaneity and independence. You are one of those people who are very conscious in the sleep state. You are sensitive to all the different subjective alterations that happen when dreams begin, unfold and end. Most people don't realize it, but dreams are inner meeting places for inner communication and commerce. You are able to recognize these inner places, and you become part of the reality that exists in your dreams."

"Interesting. So everyone can remember if they practice or something? Is that right?"

"Precisely, my dear. Most people must practice. The true art of dreaming is a science in itself. I don't have all the answers, but I do know there are people like you that don't need practice. You can, at will it seems, fall into the world of dreams and live them. Some may call this ability a dysfunctional part of your psyche, but you are not dysfunctional by any standards. The opposite is true. You use your inner senses more than others."

She remembered being relieved when she heard his words. Schuler made her feel special. She fell in love with his ability to put her in a category that few people understand. Fiona thought about how he ended that session.

"You know, my dear, the universe is a mass shared dream. It is a dream that presents reality in a certain light. But there are other lights where other realities are equally valid. Dreams are not based on chaos, as some might think. They are based on spontaneous order. Our dreams are spontaneous and have no reason to them. But there is order in the dreams we dream every night. We just forget the order and the spontaneity."

Fiona was back in the present. She looked at the small clock on the wall. It was almost 6 p.m. Time for dinner, but she didn't like to eat anymore. It was a necessary evil. Food was only fuel for the body. She used it to function; not to relieve stress and anxiety. She thought about Schuler again. Their love affair lasted for six months, but she stayed with him for almost two years. She stayed to practice dreaming. She was the perfect student and he was an understanding teacher. The last session with him was fresh in her mind again.

"You must understand, Fee. Value fulfillment and dependence are not based on permanence in dreams. Developments are possible that are not restricted to a certain time and place. Most of these developments you live are the result of actions that occur in many perspectives at the same time. They are not usually developments that occur within a set time period or series of moments."

"So are you saying my ego depends on time, but my inner self is not dependent on experiencing developments or occurrences in linear time?"

"Yes, precisely. Your physical growth depends on a series of moments for value fulfillment. That fulfillment is achieved by choices. In dreams, structure is not dependent on matter. Structure is the action of mental value fulfillment. You travel through perspectives of actions and you follow the actions and change with them."

Schuler didn't like to eat either. He didn't really like sex, but he was a compassionate and understanding partner. She remembered the day she walked out of his small office on Fifth Avenue for the last time. He was wearing his signature bowtie and off-white linen suit. His short, gray hair was neatly cut above his ears, and his reading glasses were dangling from the tip of his nose. The last words he said to her were forever etched in her mind:

"Remember Fee, whatever you lose will always come around in another form, especially in your dreams."

Chapter 3

With that, I took a deep breath and leapt; spreading my arms, pretending I could fly . . .

Chelsie Shakespeare

The next morning, Fee was back at her oak table in the nursery. She was reading, but not absorbing, her book until she turned to page 140. Her eyes dropped down to the picture of the fly orchid. She didn't have one in the nursery, but she immediately thought she should. She began to read the text.

"The fly orchid is at the mercy of flies for pollination. In order to lure flies, the fly orchid uses two types of trickery. The first tactic is a visual illusion. The orchid's flowers look like the abdomen of a female fly. But, the orchids complete the task by mimicking the scent of a female fly. The scent of the fly orchid is still considered pleasing, but it has a hint of unusual eroticism to it. Just like men who go wild for a sweet-smelling buxom blonde at a party, male flies go ape over the fly orchid's scent. Studies show that male flies are more attracted to the scent of the fly orchid than the scent of a female fly. They try orchid mating several times until they realize they are mating with something other than the real thing. The male fly is duped by a very savvy seductress"

Fiona smiled as she finished reading that paragraph.

"Just like the fly, my illusions are just as real as my reality," she thought. "He tries to mate without knowing what is real. But it must be real to him on some level."

She wondered if flies have dreams.

"Of course they do. They go through a metamorphosis. They are in a dream state when they do. The fly is not the maggot, and maggot is not the fly. They are different, but the same. Two worlds flow into one. Just like my worlds," Fiona mused.

She got up and started her daily orchid feeding process. She used Dyno-gro fertilizer, and spring water. As she went from bed to bed, her mind fell into her daytime dream state. Her body was performing a task, but her mind was years in the past. She and Sarah were discussing Sarah's choice to leave Nashville and go back to England.

"I can't take this bullshit anymore, Fiona. I'm not like you. I need to be with my own kind. I'm not a Southerner, and don't want to be. This place makes me feel like I'm a cracked Oreo cookie and I don't like it."

Fiona felt Sarah's anger. She understood.

"Going back to England won't erase your strange attitude and darker skin color, you know that, Sarah. Right?"

"You always thought I was strange, Fiona. I know my skin is darker than yours. It's not black, but I feel black somehow. I hear people talking behind my back at work, in the stores, and even in church. I've heard those voices all my life. The teenage boys that said: 'I would date you, but, you know, my parents want me to date a white girl.' And then there were the other boys and men that wanted to just bang me because I was different. They thought I was a cheap whore because I had dark skin. How can people be so ignorant? I want to go back to England. At least the people there know the difference between people from India and people from Africa!"

"I don't blame you, Sarah. I experienced that sort of treatment, but the difference between you and me is you convinced yourself that you were worthless and unlovable because of how you feel about yourself. All that stuff doesn't matter unless you think it does. Running away to England won't heal what ails you. We have dark skin, and we should own it without regret. I'm proud of my skin color, and you should be too. I too am drawn to black people, but I must say I'm fearful of black people for some strange reason. I've only been around one so I don't know why.

"So am I and I don't know why either. Where did you get all your confidence and bloody knowledge, Fiona? Did your precious orchids share their beauty secrets with you?"

"Yes, of course, but Jesse Alterman played a part as well."

"How so?"

"Oh, you remember him. He was that black bloke with the big black afro. I believe he was 6'1" when he was fourteen. The kids at school called him a freak because of his size. You remember? He walked with a limp and smelled to high heaven. I believe it was Jade East or Canoe or something."

"Yes, I remember him. Did you sleep together?"

"Well if you must know, no I did not. But he told me something one day I'll never forget."

"Yes, go on. What is it?"

"Jesse said he chose his looks. His height and unusual walk were challenges. They gave him courage because he realized there was only one him. No one else on the planet had what he had. He was proud of his uniqueness. After that, I looked at my body in a completely different way."

"Oh really, Fiona. You believe that crap? Well, I don't. I'm going back to a home that understands my skin color and my accent. I want to get away from the people who try to ruin my life. I don't need all the wishy-washy racial bullshit in this city; and the narrow-minded people in it. You know the Ku Klux Klan got its start just seventy miles south of here in that little place called Pulaski, Right? If I stay, I could be hanging from a hackberry tree in a secluded field just over the Maury County line."

"It's not those people you have to worry about, Sarah. It's your perception that scares you. You think everybody is against you because a few ignorant people have the balls to racially abuse you. I have had my share of insults about my looks over the years, but I know the people who make those comments are scared of their own shadow. They want everybody to be the same. That way, they don't have to worry about being different. They can blend in like a blade of green grass, and hide. That's a sad way to live, Sarah. You're not wired that way, and never will be. But I know you will do what you think is best for you, regardless of what I think"

Fiona's mind returned to the nursery, but her thoughts were still sifting through the past and her friend, Jesse. Her mind flipped back to Sarah. Sister Sarah went back to England and started to live a new life. Sarah never wrote, but Fiona heard from an old Liverpool friend, and she said Sarah met a man from an Italian family and they settled in Devon.

Fiona's friend told her the man was a few years older. She didn't know his name. She thought about how similar yet different they were. They had the same mother and father. They had the same childhood experiences for the most part, and off course, the same perverted brother. How could sisters be so different? How can I be so positive and alive, and Sarah be so negative and dead? But then Fiona realized Sarah believed she was a victim. Life was a war, and she battling the forces of evil with no weapons. Fiona started to whisper to herself as she went to next bed of orchids. She began to fertilize the Chinese Dendrobium Sinense orchid.

"That must be the root of Sarah's issues. Sarah must feel responsible for mother's death." Sarah was the last one to see Olivia alive. The pair had some sort of interaction after Mother finished reading that night, but Sarah never shared her conversation with Fiona. Sarah was trying to quit school, Fiona remembered that part, and she knew her Mother would deferd that action with her Father if necessary. Perhaps, Olivia didn't think it was a good idea, and they fought about it. That could be why Sarah fell in the hole of despair."

Fiona was moving through the nursery at a faster pace than usual. Her thoughts were in overdrive. Fiona's mind was free once again. She was agonizing over her sister's lack of communication about her last days with Olivia. She knew Sarah would never tell her the real story. Their childhood tolerance of each other was now adult deference. Fiona's daydreams brought up memories that made her uncomfortable. But her thoughts quickly turned to the puny-looking Holcoglossum amesianum orchid in front of her. It was one of her favorite orchids. The Holcoglossum had the ability to have sex with itself. It didn't need insects, scents, sticky fluids or birds to help fertilize it. The pollen-bearing anther of this orchid, which grows naturally on tree trunks in a particular province in China, uncovers itself, and actually rotates into the correct position. Once that process is completed, the anther inserts itself into the stigma cavity, and fertilization takes place. The ritualistic whispering started again.

Fiona smiled, as she took special care of her prized orchid. As she fertilized the rich soil around the orchid, she watched its violet beauty spring back to its grand form. She dropped her head so she could be closer to the orchid, and as she did, her words were clear and precise.

"I'm going to take a deep breath, spread my arms, and pretend I'm you."

Chapter 4

Yet it is in our idleness, in our dreams, that the submerged truth sometimes comes to the top.

Virginia Woolf

The Harpeth River was almost flowing over its banks when Fiona woke up the next morning. The river had flooded fields around her home over the years, but the water never reached her land, thanks to the limestone bluff the house was built upon. She dropped a raspberry-mocha coffee cup in her Keurig coffee maker as she looked out her bug-stained kitchen window. The fast-moving water set her mind in motion. The rain stopped, but the weather forecast called for more later that day. She loved the rain. It wasn't unusual for her to sit in the rain and watch each raindrop become one with the river. She felt like she was in church. Her church. The soaked natural rock formations and the dripping, broken tree line made her sense her spiritual under-presence. She felt a bond with the nature of God in a downpour. But today she didn't feel that presence. She just stood in front of the coffee maker, waiting for her first cup of java, and as she did, she began quietly reciting facts about the river. Her lips started to move slowly as she put on her red-framed glasses. Once they were in place, her right hand pulled the coffee mug away from the small coffee brewer, and her left hand pulled her white T-shirt down so it covered her brown braided belt, which held up her khaki shorts.

After her mother passed, Fiona spent hours sitting along the bank of the river under a bridge on Cotton Lane. That's when she decided to grow orchids and sell them. Her father wanted her to go to college, but the orchids took precedence. She searched for just the right place for almost 10 years. While she searched, she started growing Dendrobium, especially the phalaenopsis types, which are commonly sold in grocery stores and in garden centers. She also started to research the Paphiopedilum variety, and discovered they were easy to grow at home or in a greenhouse, so she began to cultivate them. When the early 20th century log cabin that sat on a bluff overlooking the Harpeth just off of Cotton Lane went up as a bankruptcy sale, she immediately called the bank's real estate agent. After several meetings, Fiona bought the house. She moved into the one-story, dilapidated house and began a remodeling project in June of that year. Her first project was the orchid nursery. She started with a 12 x 12 do-it-yourself redwood nursery kit she found at Home Depot. It took her ten years to transform the 1905 log cabin and the tiny nursery into an incredible 40 x 40 nursery, and an early 20th Century showplace. Her orchid nursery became the main attraction for local and out-of-town orchid lovers. People came from all over the state to buy orchids and ask for advice. Word-of-mouth business kept her busy all year. In a matter of a few years, the Orchid Lady was running a very profitable business.

Fiona's mind was still living in the past as she open the kitchen door and walked on her 8 x10 wooded deck. She took a seat on one of the black wrought iron chairs that circled her paint-chipped black table. As she sat down, she felt a twitch when she realized she never spoke to her sister anymore, and the twitch became stronger when she remembered swearing that if her brother Geoff called her again, she would report him to the police. In her mind's eye, sitting at that table, she saw him again. Geoff was about 35. He had the looks of a young Antonio Banderas then, and the personality traits of a Ted Bundy. Geoff still had a strong appetite for cruelty and crime. The picture of Geoff spending hours reading about successful criminals and how to get away with any crime was fresh in her mind. She flashed back to Geoff at 18. By that time, he had robbed two quick markets and stolen four cars. Fiona's parents were in denial about their first-born child. He was never arrested, so they believed his stories, which were completely different than the reality he was living. She remembered finding Geoff's diary one day when he was out. In his diary, he analyzed his atrocities and would try to correct any missteps he encountered along the way. He was always trying to better his misdeeds. He wrote: "There's always a better way to beat the system."

She knew Geoff viewed most people as a weak-willed group of back-stabbers who earned what they had coming to them. She called him 'the grim reaper,' and regarded him as everyone's worst nightmare rolled into one racially mixed misfit. She also knew his good looks and distorted, clever brain opened doors for him. But those doors closed quickly when his victims realized they were dealing with a sociopath. She tried to stay away from him, and she did until he called her several years ago.

Her lucid dream quickly switched to that year. She was back reliving the call once again as the river breeze played with her shoulder-length black hair.

"This is Fiona." Her Liverpool accent was slightly recognizable when she said those three words.

"Hey, Sis! How's the world of bitchy flowers treating you?"

Fiona was silent. She recognized her brother's voice.

"What do you want, Geoff? I must keep this line clear. I'm waiting for a call."

"Come on, Sis. It sounds like you're not happy to hear from me. I just want to say hello and tell you I need a place to stay for a couple of weeks."

"What is it this time, Geoff? Have you got your balls in a vise again?"

"Oh, I like that kind of talk, Sis. No, my balls are fine. I just need to get out of Atlanta for a while."

Fiona relived his move to Atlanta a year after Olivia passed. It was traumatic time for the family, but just another adventure for Geoff. He was caught robbing a woman in the parking lot of the Green Hills Mall by a security guard. Geoff pulled a knife on the guard and stabbed him in the stomach. The woman called 911, but Geoff escaped. When he came home that afternoon, he immediately went to his room, stuffed a dirty cloth gym bag with a couple of T-shirts and two pairs of jeans, and hurried out the door. The guard survived the attack. He was able to identify Geoff from a high school photo. The police came to the house the next day, and searched it. Fiona's parents finally found out what Geoff was really like when the police arrived. Geoff was long gone by then. She snapped out of her trance.

Fiona pulled her disheveled hair back and tied it with a hairband.

Her nighttime ritual of letting her hair down after a day in the nursery could take place in any of the six rooms in the house. The rest of Geoff's phone conversation came back to her.

"I don't have room here, Geoff. Call Dad and Violet, or someone else. You might be able to stay with a friend or two."

"I'm afraid I would smother that bitch in her sleep if I stayed there. You know how I hate her."

Fiona did know. When her dad married Violet, Geoff turned violent at the wedding reception. He punched Violet's son, Flip, and broke his nose. As he left the church reception hall, he urinated on the front seat of the wedding limo, and gave the driver a black eye. Fiona didn't care for Violet's son either, but Geoff's reaction to him was way beyond dislike.

"Why do you hate them so, Geoff?"

"Well, I'm not going to get into a long-winded conversation about her, but I will say she and her son pulled a fast one on me before the wedding, and I will never get over it."

"Fast one? I find that hard to believe, Geoff. What did they do? Rob a bank before you had the chance?"

"Very funny, Sis. No. Flip was running a small strip club in East Nashville. Flip would find young runaways in downtown Nashville and give them a place to stay while he turned them into strippers and call girls."

"I think that sort of thing would suit your needs. What's the issue, then?"

"I wanted to use three of the girls for a party. It was a party for friends who had connections. You know what I mean. They were bringing me some illegal stuff, and in exchange, I was supplying the girls for entertainment. Violet was the money behind the club, but I didn't know that then. I knew Flip, but I didn't know Violet was his mother. When Flip told me her name and who she was, I panicked. She had just started dating dad at that time, and she didn't want him to find out about her illegal activities. She made Flip renege on the deal, and he didn't tell me. The girls never showed, so I called that bastard and told him he was dead meat unless he gave me my money back. He told me the story about Violet, and that really got under my skin. I wanted to teach her a lesson. The wedding was the first chance I had to act on my words, because Flip disappeared right after he cheated me. I was surprised to see him at the reception."

"You didn't act surprised. You just lost it, and that wasn't cool. You embarrassed the whole family once again. Couldn't you wait until after the wedding to go crazy on him? You really pissed me off, you know."

"No! Violet was trying to hide something from all of us. She didn't want us to know she was the money behind a strip club."

"Geoff, you never cease to amaze me. How can anyone as smart as you be as dumb as you are? I really don't have time for your silly mind games. You can't stay here. I'm sure you'll find a bed somewhere. You don't need me for that."

"Shit, Sis. I'd ask Sarah if I knew where she was. I always liked her."

"Well I can't help you there. I'm sure you have friends that still live here. Ta Ta, Geoff."

Fiona hung up before Geoff could say another word. Geoff was always one step ahead of the law. He had Fiona's parents fooled, and almost everyone liked him because he could talk a good game and was handsome. After that phone conversation, Fiona realized Geoff's so-called luck was running out.

When the breeze started playing a familiar sound on her two Woodstock wind chimes, Fiona found herself sitting on one of the old white rockers on the front wraparound wooden porch. She realized she had been lucid dreaming and walking around the outside of the house at the same time. It wasn't the first time she snapped to and found herself standing or sitting somewhere different than she remembered sitting or standing. Her daydreaming episodes became more frequent as she aged, especially the one about "the bar". Years, ago, Schuler told her she was living another reality in her dreams. She stared across the river to the rock formation on the opposite bank. The sound of the river settled her. She felt relief as her thoughts moved to a more comfortable topic. A flash of sunlight made her squint, and when she opened her eyes, she saw her mother and father sitting on that distant rock formation. Her mother looked like a younger version of the Olivia that committed suicide. Her strawberry blonde hair was pulled back into a tight bun. Her long white cotton dress rested on the ground around her purple glitter slippers. She had a multicolored Cattleya orchid in one hand, and her other hand was on her husband's shoulder. Roger stood on a giant limestone rock, right next to a boulder. Roger's rock was about twenty-four inches lower than Olivia's. Roger was dressed like the young man who arrived in the States years ago. His blue Oxford cloth button-down shirt was opened at the collar, and it was immaculately pressed. His multicolored paisley ascot was tucked neatly between his skin and his open collar. His perfectly pleated khaki trousers touched the top of his perfectly polished cordovan penny loafers. His wavy, black hair was parted on the right, and his signature pompadour wasn't bothered by the southerly wind. His face had a two-day shadow, and his eyes were covered with aviator sunglasses. He had a book tucked under his right arm, and his left hand was in his front pocket. His brass button navy blazer lay next to the giant rock. Her parents looked like a proper British couple who happened to be from two different ethnic groups. Their appearance made Fiona a little nervous. They were smiling as the southern breeze blew Olivia's hair around in what Fiona called "a natural symbolic gesture." Fiona rose from the rocker and called to them. She raised her right hand and began frantically waving at them. She thought God had brought them back. Not the God religion talks about, but the God within her. The stream of energy that fueled her cells. Two minutes of waving didn't produce her expected reaction. Her parents didn't move. They just kept smiling, so she sat back down. The vision of her parents stayed with her as she sipped the third large mug of her favorite breakfast blend. Her lips began moving, and her voice sounded clear after the last gulp.

"They want to tell me something. I know they do, but what?"

Fiona took another sip of the black coffee and stared at them. She started a one-on-one conversation with them.

"Maybe I should have told you about Geoff years ago. I know you both loved him, but he's not capable of love. I should have told you. I'm so sorry."

She heard a noise behind her. Suddenly her eyes and body turned toward the back door. Nothing was there, so she turned and looked at the distant river bank again. Two doves were sitting on the two rock formations now. Her parents had turned into love birds. Her lips began to move again.

"Love birds?"

She started to smile as she rose from the rocker. She finally told her parents about Geoff. It was a little late, but they know now, she thought.

"Funny. I think the real message is nothing dies. Life goes on in another form, and we can choose that form. Like the orchids, we are forever in bloom."

Chapter 5

I don't think that science and the paranormal have to be at war; in fact, it's crucial that they work together. It seems naïve to believe that the world is exactly as it seems.

Chelsie Shakespeare

Fee was tending to her orchids one morning in June when one of her clients, Mimi Kenworth, casually mentioned Dr. Krabb while Mimi was putting several big, blousy phalaenopsis orchids in her colorful nursery basket. Mimi told Fiona her life story several months back, and she was replaying that story as she watched and listened to her new friend. Mimi was a native Nashvillian whose strong accent was a byproduct of her family ties to the city, plus her private school education. Her lean athletic body, long blonde hair, almond-shaped green eyes, and natural cream-color skin didn't give the impression of a woman who liked to get her hands dirty. She looked like a long-distance runner and an energy bar eater. Mimi's mother, Martha Lipscomb Kenworth, was the daughter of David Lipscomb, one of founders of Lipscomb University. She was an avid gardener, so Mimi learned to love flowers and the Church of Christ early in life. As she aged, her orchids became more important than the church. When she graduated from Lipscomb with a teaching degree, she immediately moved into a family-owned, two-bedroom 19th century Green

Hills rental. There was a small climate-controlled garage attached to the house, so she started growing different varieties of orchids in her self-made hothouse. She had enough room to grow several different varieties. She decided to visit Fiona's nursery after she heard about it from a church member. Mimi fell in love with the nursery. She would make the twenty-minute drive to Franklin every two weeks not only to buy orchids, but also to watch Fiona care for her collection of orchids. She arrived at the nursery earlier than usual on this particular day. All her past conversations were short point-of-sale pleasantries with Fiona. Mimi was quickly moving from one aisle to another. When she started up the third aisle, she came face to face with Fiona. She pushed her Lipscomb Mustang ball cap a little higher on her forehead and took her tortoise shell sunglasses off so she could see Fiona's eyes.

"I had a dream about you the other night, Miss Fiona." Her old Nashville accent was in high gear. "Now, I don't usually dream about women, so please don't get the wrong idea. My therapist, Gabriel Krabb, said I was trying to contact you so we could discuss my orchid dream. That might sound strange, but it's true."

Fiona was still fertilizing as she listened. When she heard the words 'dream' and 'orchid,' she put the metal watering can down and smiled at Mimi. Fiona hesitated for a moment.

"Oh my God! Another orchid dreamer! I bet I was holding a bouquet of purple Bombay Dendrobium, right?"

Mimi was speechless. That was sort of her orchid dream.

"What? Wait? Did you have the same dream, Fiona? Is that possible? This conversation is starting to scare me right now."

"Oh, please. There's nothing to be scared of, Mimi. I have these kinds of dreams all the time. This particular dream was a message telling me a new friend was coming into my life. This new friend came to me in that dream as a bouquet of orchids, but that's not unusual for me. My dreams are sometimes filled with orchids. I remember all my dreams."

"I never had dreams about flowers or orchids before, and I never have dreams about women. I do dream about men every now and then, but that's another story."

Mimi put her hand over her mouth and laughed.

Fiona ignored the comment about men. She had her own man issues, religion issues and political issues, but she wanted to know more about the doctor.

"Oh, right, Mimi. I know."

Fiona realized it was game on. Her mind was fully engaged now.

"Your Dr. Krabb sounds interesting. Tell me about this Dr. Krabb. What do you know about him?"

Mimi put her flowers on the table in front of her.

"Well, as I mentioned, Dr. Krabb is my therapist, and I would like to date him, but I know that's a no-no."

Fiona leaned on the table behind her.

"Yes, that could raise some eyebrows. Is he from Nashville?"

"Here's what Gabriel told me. At the ripe old age of 10, he wanted to know exactly how the mind worked. His father, Dr. Milton Krabb, had a family practice in Smithville, Tennessee, so he spent hours talking to his dad about the brain and the mind. By the time he reached his third year of high school, he was convinced that the medical profession was his calling, even though he showed promise as a young painter. He attended Vanderbilt University for undergraduate work, and completed his medical studies at Duke University."

"Gabriel loved Tennessee, and that brought him back to Nashville after interning at Johns Hopkins. Gabriel didn't want to be a typical psychiatrist. He wanted to reach deep into the human psyche and find the real answers to questions that his textbooks and professors answered in a very limited way.

"Gabriel told me that he decided to immerse himself in metaphysical work when he returned to Nashville, so he opened a practice in Belle Meade."

Fiona listened to Mimi without moving. She thought Dr. Krabb was trying to combine the known with the unknown elements within the psyche. That was what Schuler did.

"Dr. Krabb also told me that he was especially interested in dreams and past lives, and how they impact human behavior. He liked working with patients who had issues dealing with what was considered real, and what was a dream. He called his dream exploration 'the unknown reality.' He also said he was one of the first doctors in this part of the country to recognize dreams as more than fictitious episodes created by unresolved thoughts, waking beliefs and latent behavior."

Mimi took a breath.

"I didn't consciously think about this at the time, but part of me was attracted to his long curly hair and piercing blue eyes. He reminded me of my favorite cousin in a way, and that made him feel very familiar to me."

Fiona thought Mimi was finished talking, so she pushed herself away from the table. When she did, Mimi started again.

"His office is on Harding, across from the Kroger in Belle Meade. As I mentioned, he specializes in past lives and dreams. I started going to him about 10 months ago. Some of his statements don't register with me right away. I must think about them for days. My beliefs seem to get in the way. You know what I mean, Fiona? We all have these social and religious truths, and they become habit-forming. Dr. Krabb opens another door in me when I see him. He sort of plants mental seeds in me, and they begin to grow in one way or another. Does that make any sense to you?"

Fiona smiled and nodded. She knew Mimi was telling her about Dr. Krabb for a reason. But Fiona didn't know that reason.

"I may give Dr. Krabb a call. He sounds like he might be able to answer a few question I have about my dreams," Fiona replied.

"I'm sure he could help in some way, Fiona. I'm happy we had a chance to talk this morning. Funny isn't it? I've been coming here for a couple of months, but this is the first time we've really talked."

"Yes, it's very funny, Mimi. Everything happens for a reason. The orchids brought us together for a reason."

"I'm not sure I know what you mean by 'a reason,' Fiona. Do you think the orchids knew we would have this conversation before we did?"

"I believe the orchids can communicate with us when we allow them the opportunity. The dream world is the perfect place. In dreams, we can put our egos to rest and let the rest of us understand and relate to these other forms of life."

"Wow! I must tell Dr. Krabb more about you, Fiona. He'll be able to explain what you just said so I can understand it."

Fiona smiled.

"Yes, I'm sure your Dr. Krabb will put what I said in a simple frame for you. You started coming here a couple of months ago because of the orchids. They brought us together. But we weren't ready to exchange thoughts back then. We had other issues. It seems Dr. Krabb may be the common denominator in this exchange of ideas. How amazing is that?"

"That's amazing and crazy at the same time. I will talk to Dr. Krabb about all of this stuff. How much do I owe you, dear?"

"Twenty dollars should do it. I know you'll enjoy that colorful phalaenopsis, the Ophrys eleonorae and Ophrys lupercalis. You know they trick bees into pseudocopulation. If they can do that, you can just imagine what else they're capable of."

Mimi started to laugh.

"I don't like to talk about sex even if it's as harmless as bee and flower sex."

Fiona chuckled.

"Oh, so sorry. I enjoyed meeting you, Mimi. I'll see you in two weeks?"

"Yes, Honey. I want to hear what Krabb says about us."

*****

"I see you love the Paphiopedilum and Cypripedium varieties, Doctor. And I love your paintings and decorations."

"Yes, orchids, art and furniture are some one of my weaknesses."

Fiona finally made the Dr. Krabb appointment and kept it. She sat in the black leather recliner and looked around the room. Several diplomas were on the wall to her left, and when she looked over to her right, she saw a sleek black 1940s credenza and original pieces of art near the window, which faced the right side of the building. On top of the credenza were three orchids: a moth, a lady slipper and a boat orchid. She immediately felt at home. She turned to Krabb.

"Oh, I like to say that orchids are my strength, but I also like your artwork. Are they the works of local artists?

"Thank you. I do collect art from local and international artists, Fiona. Do you collect?"

Fiona looked at his collection as she answered.

"No, but I would like too. I'm here because one my friends, Mimi Kenworth, is one of your patients. Anyway, she said you kind of interpret dreams for her. She said you told her we have a bond, and I want to know why you said that to her."

"Yes, I remember that conversation with Mimi. I don't want to go into too much detail about Mimi's last session, but she said you have an orchid business. She explained one of her dreams to me, and she wanted to know what the dream meant. You were in the dream, and orchids were in that dream as well."

"Yes, right, that's what she said. Do you see a lot of people that dream about orchids?" Fiona asked.

"No, but I do have patients who communicate with other things. You know firsthand that your dreams are interesting experiences. They have no beginning or end. The only thing that ends is your awareness of a particular dream. If you have a dream, you live it just like you do a waking experience. The only difference is you have the freedom to move about the dream without ego restrictions. The images, people and other forms in your dream have the same freedom. Not all dreams have messages, but all dreams are real experiences. Some dreams contain messages about your waking world. Not everyone can communicate with life forms that are focused in another reality. You may be able to do that, and I think Mimi can be if she does a little work. You both have a strong connection."

Krabb looked at his credenza and then looked at Fiona.

"As you see, I have a connection with orchids as well."

Fiona looked at the orchids again. The Lady Slipper was the same color as the one in her dream. She stared at the soft pink and yellow flower and thought: "Could that one be the same as the one in my dream?" Fiona looked at Krabb once again.

"Yes, I understand. I was a patient of Art Schuler several years ago. He told me the same thing about dreams. Did you know Arthur?"

"Well no, but I did read some of Dr. Schuler's work. I must say he helped me in my quest to somewhat understand the dream reality. None of us fully understand it, because it is so personal, but at the same time, it can be very social as well. You know, orchids are social aren't they? They do communicate, you know."

"Are you inferring that your Lady Slipper told you about Mimi and me? Can you understand the language of orchids, Doc?"

Fiona smiled, and Krabb started to chuckle.

"Yes, in an unusual way. All forms of life communicate through chemical emissions, frequency vibrations, and in some cases, ultrasound. The study of plant communication is still in its infancy, but scientists now know that plants do communicate with one another above and below the ground. Human to plant communication is still considered impossible by most people, but there have been some case studies that show humans can pick up vibrations from plants, and translate them into words. I don't claim to be one of those people, but I don't doubt the fact that some people can pick up some sort of signals from plants."

"Can we get these vibrations or signals in dreams, Doc?"

"Yes, but I don't think most people are ready to accept that ability. I did have a patient that said he communicated with trees on his property. Studies now show that trees do have consciousness, but they are not wired the same way as our consciousness. This particular patient is able to pick up the vibrations of his trees, and he understands them. Trees have feelings, but don't express them the way we do. Trees can detect insect attacks and other natural villains that cause them harm. They communicate with other trees in same area so those trees can defend themselves with chemical substances or other means. Other plants have that same ability."

"Well that's why I'm here. I think am able to communicate with my orchids. Wait. Let me rephrase that. I think my orchids are able to communicate with me, but they don't do it while I'm awake. They do it when I dream. Is that crazy or what? Schuler said my inner sense of communication was open. I also have another dream that seems to be taking over, but let's talk about the orchids first."

Dr. Krabb smiled and looked at the orchids for a second.

"Well some folks might say you're crazy Fiona, or you've lost touch with reality, but that's not the case. Here's why. Our physical reality is the focus of our energy and our attention. But, understand, sleep is not a byproduct of our wakeful life. You might say the dream world is a shadow image of your waking world. It functions according to the possibilities within it, just as we carry on according to the possibilities inherent in our physical world. We are just as awake while we're sleeping. When we are in the dream world, most of our energy is focused on that world. Our awareness is turned in another direction, so to speak. Only a small amount of energy is available physically. That energy sustains the body while we sleep."

Fiona listened without making any facial expressions. Most of what Krabb was saying was old news, compliments of Schuler. Nonetheless, she didn't take her eyes off the guy who looked like a 1970s hippie but spoke like a doctor.

"Now, we remember only vague and disconnected portions of our dreams, so they appear to be meaningless and chaotic. The ego censors most of the information within our subconscious. The censoring process is important for most people, but some of us are equipped to handle the censored information and focus on it. My guess is that's what you do. You are able to understand the distortions and live them as they happen. Your consciousness can translate the language of the orchids and use it to create experiences in your waking world."

Fiona's lips opened, and she moved her butt around the seat of the chair. Her mind was absorbing Krabb's last statement. Suddenly a light came on.

"Do you mean my subconscious becomes part of the consciousness of orchids in my dream, Doc?"

Krabb liked her question. He knew consciousness has the ability to change and blend with other forms of consciousness if a person has expanded his or her awareness of reality. Fiona's question was deeper than she realized.

"Well Fiona, that question is difficult to answer, but the best way to answer it is to say yes. Under certain conditions, your consciousness becomes one with the consciousness of the orchids in your dreams. You are no

70

less human because of that phenomenon. You are living and remembering more than one reality at the same time. Most people can't do that."

"Okay. I think I understand, but what about my dreams when I'm awake?"

Krabb smiled.

"Do you mean daydreams, Fiona?"

"Yes, daydreams. I relive past experiences with my family, and I also see dead members of my family. They look alive and happy. My daydreams last a very long time."

Krabb looked at the Blackberry phone on his desk and realized the session had ten minutes left. He wanted to see Fiona again. He wasn't completely sure why, but his inner voice let him know this wasn't the end.

"Daydreams are another form of the dream world, Fiona. Time has no meaning when you daydream. Daydreams relieve stress, foster creativity, and invigorate the body, mind and spirit. You leave your immediate world behind and ponder the past, present and future without your ego hindering your memory. In the daydreaming state, you can see a world filled with expectations or a world locked in worry. Whatever that world is to you, it will become some portion of your waking world."

"When I daydream, I start in one place and end up in a completely different place," Fiona said. "I move around and don't know it. I could wind up in the river one of these days. I even saw my dead parents in one of my recent daydreams. What do you think is up with that, Doc?"

"We often visualize parents who pass on, Fiona. We see them as we remember them in the good times and in the bad. We see them dressed the way we like them, and we watch them go through the normal process of being alive in daydreams. Those apparitions are real to us, and in a sense, they are real to your parents. Most of the time, they are sending us a message through our subconscious. Some of us accept the message, and others ignore it. What do you think they were trying to tell you?"

Fiona looked at the credenza and the orchids. She smiled and turned to Krabb.

"They want me to know there is no such thing as death. And there's no such thing as one true religion. They want me to use my inner senses and create my life. They also want me to know that my religious beliefs and nurturing ways came with me when I was born."

Krabb nodded his head.

"Interesting thoughts, Fiona. I'm afraid our time is up today, but I would like to continue if you are up for it."

Krabb stood and extended his right hand.

"If the money is an issue, you can always pay me in orchids."

Fiona laughed as she pulled herself out of the recliner. She thought she was daydreaming for a second. She put her hand out and touched the soft hand of the interesting character standing in front of her.

"Are you sure about that? The bartering system is not dead here, Doc?"

"Yes, indeed. I think we can explore new dream territory together if you're willing. I promise I'll be an interested companion rather than a dull, unconnected doctor."

"Do you make this kind of arrangement with all your patients?"

Krabb laughed as he gently pulled his right hand from Fiona's.

"No, I don't, Fiona. But with your permission, I think your experiences will help me finish my book, and that is worth something. I've been writing it for the last fifteen years."

"Must be a long book."

Krabb laughed again.

"No. I'm writing it in my dreams."

"Does that mean you haven't started it in your awakened state?"

"Exactly. It's in the note stage at the moment, but I think you will help me bring it into this world if you come back."

"Sounds like a deal, Doc. I will call for another appointment."

Fiona turned and quickly walked toward the reception area. She didn't know why she told him she would call, but she did. Maybe the Lady Slipper asked her to.

Chapter 6

All the things one has forgotten scream for help in dreams.

Elias Canetti

Fiona dressed in a bright yellow shirt and khaki shorts the following Sunday morning. Her black Teva sandals were covered by the body of her cat, Simon. He was her protector, and his closeness was a sign of his loyalty. She was in a lazy frame of mind that particular morning. It was 50 degrees at 7 a.m. The sun was just showing its mighty face, so she knew today would be another milder-than-normal day. Just a night had gone by since her visit with Gabriel Krabb, but she wanted to make another appointment. She sat on her porch and wondered about that change. Krabb brought up some interesting thoughts about her dream world. It was another reality, and as he said, there were many realities in that world. She thought about her daydreams, and as she did, she realized she was daydreaming. As her eyes focused on the riverbank, her mind was surfing her present netherworld. Reality, she thought, is one big daydream. Even though her parents never came back to the limestone rock formation across the river, she knew they were around her all the time. She turned her head and looked at the oak and hackberry trees at the beginning of the woods. The woods extended for miles behind her house. She looked down at her black

Movado watch. She had another hour before she had to start her nursery chores. She hadn't had her morning coffee. No need for caffeine today. She felt her body roar with energy as she began her daily yoga routine. Simon immediately raced away from her. He understood his time with her was over. She was going into another world, and he completely understood. He felt her need to stretch her body and mind.

As Fiona went into her first torso bend and stretch, her mind went back to the year she first met Violet Simmons. Her father was still recovering from Olivia's death, but somehow, Violet managed to get more than her fair share of his attention. She saw her dad sitting in his favorite chair. He was telling her and Sarah about Violet.

"She's a breath of fresh air and a wonderful listener. I can't believe how much she cares about me. It's only been a couple of weeks, but I feel I've known her all my life."

Roger's British accent was still as strong as the day he arrived in the States.

"Well you never told us how you met her, Dad. Did someone at work introduce you?"

"Oh I thought I mentioned it, Fiona. We literally ran in to each other at the grocery market a couple of week ago. Violet came around the corner of the condiment aisle full throttle and slammed into the bloody basket with such force that my English tea jumped out and landed in her buggy."

Roger was smiling as he continued his story.

"Violet apologized for her lack of consideration and offered to give me another package of Earl Gray, since mine was crushed under her watermelon when our baskets collided.

Of course, I declined her offer, but I did ask her to have tea with me. Don't know why I did that. Maybe I noticed she was not wearing a wedding ring."

Fiona watched her mind's video as Sarah spoke.

"Why would you want to get to know someone who was so inconsiderate, Dad?"

Roger didn't answer immediately.

"Well, my dear girl, Violet's face reminded me of my mother's face when she was much younger, and I was caught in the moment, I guess. Of course, her skin was lighter, but she had the same mannerisms or something."

As Fiona relived the conversation, a vision of a young Violet appeared. Violet did have a beautiful round English face, and she did resemble her paternal grandmother in a strange way. Her dynamic gray eyes sat in perfect symmetry with her thick brown eyebrows. Her shoulder-length auburn hair was cut Cleopatra style, and her slim nose filled the space between her slightly Asian shaped eyes perfectly. Her bangs gently touched the top of her eyebrows. Her kiss-me shaped lips were covered with thick red lipstick, and her two-carat diamond earrings barely saw the light of day due to her hairstyle. She had the body of a runway model, but Fiona's vision was a body that was 20 or so pounds heavier. The extra pounds made her look like a full-figure clothes model. On the outside, Violet was put together like an antique car collector's dream, but on the inside, Fiona thought she was a strange mixture of savvy businesswoman and street-smart working girl. Fiona looked at her watch again. Half past seven. She quickly finished her 30 minute yoga routine. She didn't remember what poses she did when the alarm on her watch went off, but her body muscles told her it was a good workout as she bent over and touched the porch. Violet was still on her mind. She had to stop thinking about her. Her workday was about to begin. Every day was a workday for her. The orchids needed her, and she needed them. Fiona opened the screen door, and then she pushed the old walnut back door open with her right foot. Both sandals were in her hand. She grabbed a banana and opened the fridge. She reached for the fresh cut fruit she bought at the store the day before and pulled a bottle of spring water from lower shelf. That was breakfast this morning. But a low-level mental uncertainty was pulling her away from her objective world as she sat at her oval oak kitchen table. Violet was still in her thoughts. Suddenly, eating the fruit became automatic functions as Violet's life story started to play in her mind. Violet had a very troubled life.

Fiona was in the nursery when her mind returned to the present. Her thoughts about Violet didn't upset her, so she began to feed the orchids as usual. Sunday mornings were slow at the nursery. Most of her customers went to church, so she didn't expect anyone to arrive until noon or later. She knew why she hated church so much. She didn't like the control or the politics. God didn't either, she thought. She stopped at her desk after she gave the orchids their usual breakfast. Breakfast, of course, depended on the species. Different varieties were fed according to their needs. The Lady Slippers were fed a high nitrogen fertilizer once a month. They only needed watering every 7 to 10 days. They had to stay moist; sogginess could impact their ability to survive. This particular Sunday was feeding and watering day for that Paphiopedilum group. She also had to make sure the temperature was in the 75-degreee range. Her individual climate control system was a vital part of the well-being for her orchids. Some varieties required more heat and humidity than others, so she had mini-dome built out of clear plastic. Each cover had a door and light attachment in order to control the amount of light they received. When one of her customers came to buy for the first time, she said that the nursery looked like Fiona was growing human pods under clear plastic mini-domes. The customer also said the domes reminded her of the 1950s movie, "The Invasion of the Body Snatchers."

Fiona walked to her oak desk and looked at the open orchid book. She started to turn the pages to another chapter. She wanted to get Violet and church out of her mind. When she turned to page 175, she immediately stopped and read the title: "Plant Talk: Orchids Can Heal The Soul Without Making A Sound." She looked out the window and immediately thought about her session with Krabb. She began to read more.

"Over last 15 years, the notion that orchids can communicate is becoming more fact than fiction. Orchids have the ability to use different elements within their molecular structure to communicate. The remarkable conclusions from various studies are revealing the complex ways orchids exchange information with each other. Researchers have unearthed evidence that orchids are far from unresponsive organisms. They engage in regular conversations with each other. In addition to warning their neighbors about attacks by herbivores, they also alert each other to impending droughts and threatening pathogens. They also recognize each other, and they adapt to the information they receive from orchid neighbors. Moreover, orchids "talk" in several unique ways. They use airborne chemicals and the soluble compounds that are exchanged

by their roots. Some species are capable of using networks of extremely thin fungi to exchange information, while others can use ultrasonic sounds. Orchids have their own version of a soul, and they create a social system that researchers are just beginning to understand. Soul-to-soul contact with orchids is not science fiction. Their souls and our souls are connected by a web of what some researchers call a complex connection of consciousness."

Fiona stopped reading, stood, hurried toward the door, and almost ran toward the house. She knew she had to make another appointment with Krabb. She wanted to know more about her reoccurring dream and orchid talk. When she reached the kitchen wall phone, she stopped and remembered it was Sunday. She looked around the kitchen and saw a black marker sitting on top of her "things to do" note pad. The pad was on the dirty countertop next to the electric stove. As she wrote the note about calling Krabb, her mind started to wander again. Violet was back for some reason. It seemed that Krabb, the orchids, and Violet dangled in front of her like white California grapes hanging on the vine. They weren't related, but in some strange way, they were. As she moved out the kitchen door, her mind projected a vision of herself sitting with Violet years before. The past suddenly became her present. She stumbled to her porch swing and fell into it. She saw herself asking Violet about her life. She heard Violet's voice in her mind once again.

"You know, honey, I was in three foster homes before I was 18. I can't tell you how bad some of those folks were to me. I never knew my parents. They left me with my father's cousin, Miranda, when I was a week old. She adopted me, and I became a citizen. My parents were English. Miranda

called them English runaways because they came to this country to get away from the law. When I was 12, Miranda died of a drug overdose. I was sent to a state facility until another family came along. My new family had two foster boys, and they were wild. I was beaten, sexually abused and tortured by these teenage delinquents for four years. I finally ran away. I was caught a week later trying to steal some food from a grocery store. I went back to that nasty state home and waited once again. This time, an older couple took me home and tried to make a house servant out of me. Funny thing was they were black. I guess they wanted to give someone white the same treatment they got when they were younger. I stayed there for four years. But they did help me learn how the system works. They had a discreet escort service, so they taught me how to talk, dress and get what I wanted while I did all the dirty work. At 18, they let me do some escorting. I started to make my own money. A lot of money. I used my looks and body to get what I wanted. By the time I was 21, I had my own service. I was living the good life in downtown Philly until a john turned out to be a cop. I spent two weeks in jail. When I got out, I moved south. I got married to a farmer named Will Pooker. We were married for two years. He wanted children, so in a moment of weakness, I told him I did too. That was a big ass lie. But we had a boy, and that farmer wanted to name him Junior. I lost my temper and said 'Oh, hell! Why not just call him Flip? At least he would have a chance with that name.' Will tried to keep me there, but I hated farming, so when Flip was about a year old, I left that farmer with nothing but a jar of peanut butter and a stale loaf of bread. I took everything I could carry and then some. You know, when I first saw you, I thought we'd met somewhere before, but I knew that couldn't be right, you

being so young and all. I know you never worked for me,
but then I thought I might have dreamed about you before
we met. Strange, honey, but I feel like I've known you a
long time. "

Fiona's mind was back in the present. Violet's last statement was fresh in her mind. Somehow Violet was still very much alive in her. Violet was becoming an important piece of her recurring dream puzzle. She began to whisper.

"I don't how or why, but Violet hasn't left me yet. She has some kind of hold on me."

Fiona wasn't hungry, but she was tired. It was a busy day, and she was ready to relax. She sat in her recliner and turned on the 6 o'clock news. She heard the young newsman say something about the shooting death of the young black boy in Florida back in February, and then she fell into one of her dream states. She was watching a scene develop on a Greyhound bus. She was on her way to Nashville.

The Counterparts

The wise grieve neither for the living nor for the dead. There was never a time when you and I and all the kings gathered here have not existed and nor will there be a time when we will cease to exist

Anonymous

Chapter 7

I'm trying to bring you on board because I've never lived a life without you. And I don't want to start now.

Molly Ringle

The handsome black man threw an issue of Life magazine on the empty seat next to him. The cover image showed a big-busted woman in short-shorts pulling on an airplane propeller. Fiona wasn't interested in flying across the country in one of those prop airplanes. But the cover did remind her of some of her mom's old photographs. Then she noticed the date on the cover: September 16, 1940. She heard the man whisper to himself.

"This bus ride is turning into a bulging nightmare in more ways than one. Shit! I should have gone into that nasty washroom before I left the terminal in Chicago. Man, I can't understand how anyone would think I could make that dirty washroom any dirtier. Hell, those 'colored' signs really bug me."

The man looked out the window with his hands between his legs. Fiona saw the corn sway in the fall breeze as the bus rolled through the farmland between Chicago and Indianapolis. Suddenly, the bus slowed down. She heard the driver say, "There's road construction for the next 40 miles." The man looked around, and Fiona saw his blue eyes. He mumbled again.

"I might pee my pants if this is how it's going to be. I should have never sold my old beat-up '36 Chevy coupe."

The man rose from his seat and looked around. He started to walk toward the back and then stopped. Fiona felt like he was standing over her now. He was dressed in black tweed pants, long-sleeved black collar shirt open at the neck, and black high-top, Converse All-Stars. The shoes looked a little strange on a guy she believed was well past 20. He didn't look like a basketball player, but his long curly hairstyle and his almost white facial features made Fiona think about the Virgin Islands, a place she had never been. Then Fiona's dream took her to what appeared to be a hospital in Harlem, New York. She was putting an oxygen mask on a man, but she suddenly snapped back on the bus in true dream fashion.

Suddenly, the scent of Old Spice cologne tickled Fiona's nose. She felt herself tap the man's shoulder, and then she heard her voice. It wasn't her voice. The voice was deeper, and her sentence structure seemed different, but the words felt like her words.

"Excuse me, sir. Are you any relation to Jackson G. Smith from Harlem? His daddy was from Jamaica, and he had that same aroma floating round him. I fell in love with that spice, and for a little while, I started to use it myself."

The man jumped when he felt her fingers touched his right shoulder. He showed his straight white teeth when he answered.

"No, never been to Harlem and don't have kin there. Glad you dig the scent."

His smooth Caribbean accent made his words sound rhythmic.

"Yeah, Old Spice. You know, it brings back memories. Guess smells do that."

She felt her fingers pull away from his shoulder in this dream.

"Lord, you sure remind me of him. Thought you might be a cousin or something. Your eyes, nose and mouth are the same as his. Your skin is whiter, but he wore his black hair curly, a little long like yours. His hair was so thick."

Fiona saw herself almost touch the man's hair as she continued.

"He loved me, and I loved him until I really got to know him. His mama was white, and his Jamaican daddy was a cotton picker down South."

"Oh, yeah. Young love. Guess you'll always remember him, right?"

She looked down and noticed that her purple cotton dress outlined robust nipples and a thin waistline. The 1940s looking pump on her left foot hung slightly out in the aisle, and her beautiful light chocolate hands rested comfortably on her knee. She watched as the man picked up the magazine. He looked out the window and then stood.

"Mind if I sit next to you? My neck is not cooperating with my body. I'm in a little pain. Gotta go, if you know what I mean."

Fiona felt herself smile.

"Yes, please do. I mean sit, but don't go. I know what you mean, and I hate that feeling."

Fiona's right hand was in the air as the man took his new seat. Fiona heard her deeper voice again.

"My name is Jayla Thackeray. Looks like we have a few hours of sitting before we arrive in Nashville. Are you staying in Nashville? Do you have family there?"

Fiona's head moved to the other side of her pillow. She didn't know why she called herself, Jayla.

"I'm Myles Dunbar. Nice to meet you, Jayla."

The bus driver interrupted their conversation.

"Folks, there's a gas station a half mile ahead. I'm going to stop. If you want to get off, you can, but please be back within 15 minutes."

Myles smiled at Jayla. She felt his interest in her as he gently embraced her right hand. She felt a strange connection as he quietly whispered.

"Don't worry. You're helping me forget about the pain. I'm on my way back to Nashville to paint."

"Oh really? You're an artist? Did you go to art school down there?" She felt her eyes light up, and she felt her heart beat.

Myles barely heard her soft voice, so he leaned over so his face was closer to hers.

"Yeah, Fisk."

She began talking before the name Fisk hit her ears.

"I went to Meharry. I always wanted to be a doctor, but I became a nurse instead. Those were the years, I must say. It was my first time away from my home in Humboldt, Tennessee. I was free from small town gossip. I wanted to explore the world, and Nashville was part of that world. But, I didn't really appreciate Nashville back then. Too many rednecks around town."

She felt herself quickly looked around to make sure no one was close enough to hear her. She looked straight into Myles's eyes.

"Those ignorant fools reminded me of some of the folks in my town, so I stayed on campus most of the time, even though my skin was lighter than most black folks' When I did go off campus, I went with a group of white friends. You know, slavery was still alive in those good ole boys' minds. Those ignorant white men had no idea that skin color wasn't a sign of inferiority. Hell, being born a Negro in the 20th century is a sign of strength and conviction. It takes courage to face a world of bigotry as a Negro person. You know what I mean, don't you, Myles?"

Fiona heard herself talk in this dream about Negros and slavery like she knew what she was talking about.

Myles answered quickly.

"I did have a few scary episodes when I was in school, but for the most part, I knew where not to go. There were invisible boundaries, and I knew I couldn't cross them even though half of me was as white as the people in those places. I learned to deal with my racial challenges. I stayed alert when I was off campus, and I watched what I said in public."

Fiona focused on the sound of the man's voice as she processed his words. His voice had a gentle strength to it. She could tell he was proficient in the art of communicating.

She heard her voice again.

"I'm not sure I follow you, Myles. Do you mean you fought back racism with words?"

Myles's big smile appeared once again.

"Well, in a way. I learned to rationalize situations and to defuse them with humor or with other tactics, like changing the subject. I always had a sketch pad with me, and I would use it if I had to.

She felt herself laugh.

"Wait. What? You're crazy!"

"I didn't get into that kind of situation often. As I said, I knew where not to go, but if I did run into that kind of trouble, I used my knowledge of social statistics. I would throw out facts like the white population is going to be the slowest-growing ethnic group over the next forty years, and the Negro population will be the next-slowest growing ethnic group. I'd tell them that Asian and Hispanic groups are going to increase. More Asians and Hispanics mean more bigotry unless we work together to celebrate our similarities rather than our differences. Persecuting or eliminating the Negro is not the answer to increasing the white population. The natural movement to homogenize the world is under way. Skin color is not a curse or a reward. It is a natural choice and a personal way to experience life."

Fiona's dreaming eyes looked at Myles.

"I bet that speech made them soil their pants, didn't it? You must have met some really rational bigots around town. The bigots I came across had a hard time keeping their ass crack from showing 'cause their brain was up in it somewhere."

Myles laughed as he pulled his face away from hers.

"Enough of that stuff, Jayla. Why are you going to Nashville?"

Suddenly, the sound of metal pressing on metal filled the bus. The bus pulled into the Amoco service station and stopped. The brakes woke up Fiona. She looked around. She didn't know where she was for a second. The dream about the bus ride was still fresh in her mind. She had never dreamed in such depth before. She went into the bathroom and sat on her makeup bench. As she sat, she wondered why she was talking to a black man on a bus in the 1940s. She sat on the bench for 20 minutes. Her dream life was changing, and she didn't understand why. Everything in the dream seemed very real: the bus, the man and the woman he called Jayla.

Chapter 8

There was a bright flash of brilliant white light, like the midday summer sun reflecting off of a freshly cleaned mirror.
And then it was gone.

Raymond Rice

Fiona jumped off the bench. She turned the spigot on and felt the warm water slip through her fingers. She looked in the mirror and saw she was still Fiona. She quickly walked into the kitchen and pulled a bottle of water from the bottom of the fridge. Fiona walked to her small table, and she pulled out one of the red vinyl-covered chairs. She started to think about her meeting with Krabb. She remembered him saying dreams don't end. Your awareness of them ends. She looked out the window and noticed the fiery red sun dropping in the sky. Why was she on a bus in 1940? Why was she Jayla instead of Fiona in this dream? The dream felt like more than a dream to her. She had to go back and get on the bus. The answers were there, she thought. She looked at her wall clock. It was almost 7:30 p.m. She took another swig of water and pushed herself away from the table. She had to go outside. Dusk was a special time for her. The day was creeping away, and the night was tiptoeing in. The humid air began to turn cooler. She sat on her bench and wondered why her dreams were so detailed. If what she just experienced was just a dream, then what she was doing right now on her porch was also a dream. She sat for an hour and relived every part of her dream experience. She had to go back to that bus and find out what she was doing on it and why she was talking to that handsome man Myles. She finally went inside and sat on the bed. She set a glass of red wine on the nightstand.

The first sip hit her body with the force of erupting lava rushing down the hillside to a beach. She wasn't a drinker, but she wanted to pass out as quickly as possible so she could get some answers. She took another sip and slipped under the down comforter. Three minutes later, thanks to her ability to dream at will, she was walking through a large, solid walnut door with a black orchid hand-painted on it, and the words Black Orchid were written below the orchid. She noticed a short black guy in his 50s standing at the end of the hand-carved walnut bar. His full gray beard looked like a sparsely grown field of cotton, and the Ray-Ban aviator sunglasses sitting atop of his balding head had tape holding the arms together. He immediately pulled his black and white wing-tips away from the brass footrest under the bar and started to walk toward her. She stopped. She pulled her white clutch closer to her breasts when she saw the man's eyes focused on her off-white, below-the-knee cotton dress and her perfectly shaped breasts beneath it. The strange Negro man had a half smile on his face as he held out his right hand. His black and white orchid print shirt was open and revealed his scraggly gray chest hair and round beer belly.

"Hey there, baby. You must be Jayla. I'm Shorty Longsleeves. Tyrone said you would be in tonight. Are you ready to have a few drinks?

Fiona felt Jayla's eyes. She was having a hard time focusing in the dimly lit, strange smelling room. Fiona thought the bar had an odd energy as she looked around. There were eight black men sitting at the bar, and four black women were standing behind three of the men. Mr. Longsleeves made Jayla uncomfortable, so she quickly said:

"Hello Shorty. Where's Tyrone? He's the owner, right? He said he would be here tonight."

"Tyrone had to meet a guy at another location, so he's out for the night. It was kind of sudden. He told me to take care of you."

Shorty put his hand on Jayla's arm and gently pulled her closer to the bar.

"Come on. Jake, get this lady a drink."

Shorty's left hand was pointing at Jake as he guided Jayla to the end of the bar. Jake, the bartender/bouncer, immediately acknowledged the request by nodding his head as he put a Beefeater and tonic in front of a middle-aged, overweight man who had his elbows on the bar. The intoxicated man's head was firmly planted next to his new drink. The strong smell of alcohol that surrounded him seemed to act as a human shield. None of the girls at the bar paid attention to him.

"Okay, Jayla. What's your pleasure? Scotch?"

"No, I'm not drinking tonight, but I appreciate the offer."

Jayla's annoyance with him really started to show as Shorty moved his face closer to hers.

"I bet you were something back in Harlem or wherever you've been. I see you have the goods. No wonder your brother-in-law, Tyrone, wanted you here. He's tired of that sister of yours, you know. She's got some sort of brain disease. He says she has some crazy-ass dreams."

Shorty put his arm around her waist, grabbed her leather belt and said:

"Tyrone does things a little different than me. I like my sweetness fast. You know what I mean?"

Jayla's eyes focused on his bloodshot brown eyes, which were slightly crossed and barely noticeable due to his drooping eyelids. She tried to move her body away from him, but his hand was wrapped tightly around her belt. Her short temper got the best of her.

"Are you serious? The last thing I want is an old smelly ass like you around me. I'm not who or what you think I am, but I know what you are. You're a piece of shit."

Jayla dug her long nails into his arm as she moved toward the door. As she did, Jake quickly slid under the opening at the side of the bar and tried to stop her. Jake had seen this scenario play out many times before, especially when Shorty was as drunk as he was tonight, so he knew what he had to do. Shorty watched him jump in front of Jayla.

"Ah hell, let her go, man. We don't need another bitch around here that thinks she's got high society ass. That's for sure."

Shorty looked at his bleeding arm as Jake slide back under the bar. As he did, Jayla turned toward Shorty and gave him the finger.

"Screw you, man. I came in her to talk to Tyrone about my sister-- not to be insulted by a small, overweight, drunk."

Jake looked at Shorty and laughed.

"Never heard you described like that before, Shorty"

Jayla could tell Jake didn't really like Shorty. Fiona thought she recognized him, but she couldn't place where she knew him.

Shorty looked at Jake, then he glanced at the customers at the long bar. They all were smiling at him. He didn't know what to say, but he knew he had to say something. The bitch couldn't get away with disrespecting him in his own place. He had to save face.

"Tyrone said you were a whack job witch. Get your ass out of my bar, and don't come back. I don't give a shit who you know. You're not welcome here."

As the door slammed behind her, Jayla saw a telephone booth on the right side of the building. She pulled a nickel from her jewel-covered white clutch and dialed her sister's number. The phone rang four times before a deep voice came through the 1940s telephone line.

"Yeah, what's up?'

"Laquisha, Honey. It's Jayla. Tyrone's manager just tried some shit on me. I thought you and Tyrone were going to meet me tonight. Are you okay? Tyrone said you were having some problems sleeping when we talked on the phone last week. I'm here to help you. I'll come by tomorrow night and we can talk about it, okay honey?"

Laquisha was silent for a few seconds.

"Oh, hell. I'm going crazy, Jay. I think I'm white when I'm dreaming. Now don't get me wrong — I kind of like that, you know. I am sick of being colored."

Jayla went silent for a few seconds. Jayla did know. She thought Laquisha was always self-conscious about being a Negro. Tyrone was her first Negro husband. The first two husbands were products of a white father and a black mother. That's what married white men did for fun in Humboldt, Tennessee.

Fiona's mind was still in dream mode. She was now a young Jayla talking to a younger Laquisha. They were in the small town of Humboldt, where everybody knew everybody's business. Jayla was asking Laquisha not to drop out of school. She didn't want her to marry that crazy first husband. But Fiona felt Jayla snap out of her daydream, and she was back on the phone.

"What did you just say, Laquisha? This silly phone cut out."

"Well, I'm happy you're here, Jay. I feel alone. Tyrone works all the time, and he's unhappy. I don't blame him though. I don't like my life right now. I want to be somebody else, and for some reason, I can't change what I've been thinking about, Jay."

"I know, Quisha. I can help if you let me. I'll come by and see you, and we can work this out together."

Laquisha thought for a minute.

"Okay. Come by around nine and we can discuss it a little more."

Chapter 9

Have you ever met someone and felt like you've known them forever?

Michelle Madow

The next morning, Fiona showered as soon as she awoke. She thought the hot water would wash away the bad feelings she picked up from her dream. As she closed her eyes and moved her washcloth around her well-toned body, her mind's eye flashed a picture of a Holcoglossum orchid. She didn't know why, but she loved to think about orchids in the shower. She quickly turned the water off and reached for her towel. As she walked toward her bed, she gently patted her body. She picked up the phone from her nightstand and pressed Dr. Krabb's number. Within a few seconds, she heard Krabb's secretary's voice.

"Hello."

"Dr., Krabb, please?"

"May I tell him who's calling, please??"

"Oh, it's Fiona. Sorry to call so early."

"Yes, of course, Fiona. One minute, please."

Linda passed the call through to the doctor.

"My dreams are really getting interesting."

Krabb smiled into the phone. "Yes, in what way?"

"I'm riding a bus in the 1940s and visiting a bar called the Black Orchid."

"Well that sounds like more than a dream doesn't it, Fiona?"

"I think it sounds crazy, Doc?"

"No, not at all. Why not make an appointment? We will discuss what may be happening to you."

"Yes, I will. I'll call your receptionist a little later. Thanks Doc."

"Sure, Fiona. See you soon."

But Fiona didn't call Krabb for an appointment that day. Another dream took her back to the 1940s that afternoon. Fiona was watching Myles think about Jayla. The image of Jayla was plastered along the walls of his mind, and Fiona was feeling it in this particular dream segment. Myles was daydreaming in her dream. Fiona saw him stand in front of his bathroom mirror. He wasn't the 20-year-old flamboyant artist of yesteryear anymore. He was a 30-something, racially mixed, artist who went through the school of life in his own way. One by one, he went through his mind's catalogue of his life and work. Jayla was the woman he always wanted to paint, and now he had the chance. He thought he could paint her and maybe do much more. Fiona knew she wasn't in the scene, and Jayla wasn't either, but she was watching this man live his thoughts as if she was having a conversation with him.

Myles was sweating profusely as he continued his self-analysis.

"I don't even know Jayla, but somehow, I'm sure I do. I'm sure I've painted her in my dreams! Here I go again! I'm dreaming of dreaming!"

Myles snapped out of it and looked at his gold-plated Timex: 8:30 Time to eat dinner. His shabby apartment was just off Gallatin Pike in East Nashville. It was the perfect place to paint. And it was close to the Black Orchid. Fiona heard him say, "The Black Orchid must be my new canvas."

As he put on his signature black outfit, he thought about his meeting with Jayla. He walked outside and opened the driver's side door of his newly purchased 1938 Dodge. For the first time in a very long time, he had purpose. He had a new woman to paint and a place to paint her.

Burrus Filling Station had outdoor service for people like him. He could order food there and never go inside. He went there many times while he attended Fisk. Myles ordered a barbeque sandwich, fries and a coke at the outdoor window. He pulled a dollar out of his pocket when the girl told him he owed 55 cents. He grabbed the warm bag from the young woman and stuffed the change into his shirt pocket. He popped the clutch on the Dodge as he pulled away. Myles munched on the fries as he turned the wheel, changed gears, and kept his foot on the accelerator. The three stop signs he encountered on Broad Street made his blood boil. "These damn signs are making my food cold. This city is getting too big for its own good. Hell, what's the point of making people stop every ten yards?"

He heard the horn blast as he stuffed three fries in his mouth. The man in the car behind him kept his hand on the horn. Myles quickly released the clutch and stepped on the gas. Remnants of a half-eaten fries stuck to the steering wheel when he opened his mouth to vent his frustration.

"Hell! I know that asshole is not from here. Folks in this town never use their horns."

Totally annoyed and still hungry, Myles kept going until he pulled into the dimly lit parking lot off Third Avenue. He found a spot at the end of the lot under a street light. Even though it was almost 10 p.m., the temperature was still in the 80s. He kept the car running as he stuffed the cold, messy barbeque sandwich in his mouth. As he downed the last swig of Coke, his mind told him not to go into the club.

The voice in his head said, "You're late. Maybe she's gone. No. Hell, I'm going in."

He opened the door, and as he did, he accidently dropped the remains of his barbeque bag in the parking lot. A pickle landed on the white tip of his right shoe, but he didn't notice as he made his way to the huge walnut door. The music hit him before he could adjust his eyes to the dark crowded room. He didn't like the blues. The song that filled the room sounded like a bunch of Memphis drunks on illegal mash. But there were beautifully dressed Negro women everywhere. They were all sizes. There were at least ten men in various positions around the bar. The four booths that hugged the black walls and windows were also filled. The blaring Memphis beat hit his eardrums like a jackhammer, so he quickly went to the corner of the room, where a restroom sign hung over a paisley-draped entrance. The soiled table in front of the entrance had an empty beer bottle and a shot glass teetering on its wobbly edge. He pushed the nasty debris with his forearm to the other edge. He looked down at the armless wooden chair before he decided to stay for a few minutes. Just as he put his butt on the narrow seat, he heard a man's voice from behind the paisley drapes.

"Hey, man! That's my table."

Myles looked up and saw an old, overweight gray-haired man coming through the drapes. He jumped up and wiped his butt with his right hand.

"Sorry, man. Thought this spot was empty. I'm not staying. I'm just looking for someone."

"Maybe I can help. I'm Shorty Longsleeves, the manager, and this table is my front office. Who you looking for, man?"

Shorty's attitude was cordial. He rarely tried to piss off his new customers.

"Well, I'm meeting a friend here."

"Does she have a name? Does she work here? All the girls are local, and they don't travel much."

"No, but she knows the owner."

Shorty smiled. The gap between his yellow front teeth made him look older.

"You mean Tyrone?"

Myles turned his head toward the bar.

"Do you know a woman named Jayla?"

"Yeah, I know Jayla. I told her to keep her ass out of here last time I saw her. She got some tongue on her."

"Sorry to hear that. She didn't strike me like that. She's a friend of mine."

Shorty put out his hand.

"What's your name, again?"

Myles hesitated but he put his hand in Shorty's.

"My friends call me Myles. Jayla said she would be here around 10 tonight, so I'll just wait at the bar."

Shorty nodded his head and pulled back his hand.

"Whatever, Myles. We'll be here. Have been for the last six months."

Myles wanted to make a move toward the door. Before he could take a step, a tall young woman dressed in a yellow, low-cut blouse and bright blue short-shorts stepped in front of him.

"Hey, sorry to bother you, but I heard your conversation with Shorty. I think I know the woman."

"Is she a friend of yours?"

The woman stood still as she threw her long black hair back on her shoulders. She smiled and put both hands in her back pockets.

"Not really, but I saw her here the other night."

Myles looked into her black eyes.

"Have you seen her tonight?"

"No, last week. I was in the club the night Shorty and Jayla had a big fight. I heard her say she just got in town, so I figured she is the woman you're looking for. Women don't come in here unless they have been here before. Don't think she'll be back, but I bet Tyrone knows how to get in touch with her."

"She told me she would be here tonight."

The girl put her mouth up to his ear.

"Tyrone will be here at midnight. That's when Shorty usually passes out. Maybe your friend is coming with him."

Myles saw a flash of innocence in her deep-set eyes. His eyes and hers were inches apart. She quickly put her mouth up to his ear again and tried to say something, but she kept moving her weight from foot to foot. Her mouth moved with her feet.

"My name is Nyla. I came here with a friend. Well, actually he's my cousin. We're tight. We were raised together, so he's like my brother instead of my cousin."

Fiona's dream images were clear. Their voices sounded like she was standing right next to them.

Myles nodded his head. He listened and thought he knew her, but then he remembered he painted a woman in Chicago who looked a little like her. Nyla reminded him of her.

"I'm Myles. Have you done any modeling?"

The girl nodded her head affirmatively. She handed Myles a flimsy, hand-written card.

"I model clothes for my sister when I work there sometimes. She has a small store in East Nashville. Are you in the advertising business?"

Myles quickly read the name and number: Nyla Paige, (615) 555-9754.

"No. I'm a painter."

Nyla dropped her head and moved closer.

"Okay, Myles. If you need a model call me, okay?

Myles started toward the door with her card in his right hand. He waved it as he pushed the door open with his left. "I'll call you, Nyla."

Sunlight started to fill Fiona's bedroom. Her eyes opened slightly as she rolled over and pulled the comforter to her neck. This dream was too real. She wasn't in it, but she heard every word and watched every move of the characters in it. Nyla was familiar in a strange way, and Myles seemed familiar too. But both of them lived in the 1940s and were dream characters! She wondered how they could be so familiar and yet be so foreign. Today she would call Krabb for an appointment, but she remembered it was Saturday. The call to Krabb would have to wait until Monday. She went to the sink, looked in the mirror and began to talk to herself.

"Really? What the hell? In these dreams, I'm another person! Does everyone turn into someone else in their dreams?"

Chapter 10

People don't just live one life. They keep coming back until they get it right.

C.R. Strahan

The dream was real, just like all the others. But this time, Fiona's brother, Geoff, was at it again. He was behind the bar at the Black Orchid offering watered-down drinks to unsuspecting customers. She felt his negativity as she turned from side to side in her queen-size bed. Geoff didn't look like himself in this dream, or in any of the dreams she'd had since she last saw him. His skin was much darker, and he was much taller. His British accent had turned Southern, and his high-pitched voice was now deeper. Last time she checked on Geoff, he was living in Las Vegas. But appearance aside, Geoff was the same old Geoff. She immediately noticed his lack of empathy and his strong will to cause destruction of some kind. Age didn't show on him in this dream. A 30-something image of this version of Geoff made her dreaming mind want to speak to him.

In this particular dream, Fiona was trying to convince him to get help. She was sitting at the bar with a woman who looked like a younger version of her sister, Sarah. Geoff kept calling the woman, Amber. This dark-skinned woman was wearing pink and cream shorts. The words, "DON'T DO IT" were written on the bar napkin in front of her.

When the woman turned the napkin over, Fiona saw the words: "IF YOU DO, WE ARE DONE."

The dreaming Fiona stood up and pointed to Geoff.

"Geoff you need help! You're going to jail again if they find you here."

Geoff ignored her, but the woman beside her turned her head as she downed a shot of Scotch.

"He's not Geoff. He's my husband, Jake. He almost threw you out the other night, remember?"

Fiona stared at her and then looked at Geoff. This Amber person was right, in a way. The guy behind the bar was different, but she knew Geoff's energy when she felt it, especially in her dreams.

"And who might you be, then?"

"Lord have mercy, girl! Look at me. I'm Sarah! I'm your bloody sister, but you can call me Amber!"

Fiona looked at the smile on Geoff's face. Then she looked at Sarah, who now claimed to be Amber and was married to her brother. What? How? Sarah married to Geoff? Fiona's face almost turned white in her dream.

"How could you marry her, Geoff? You know how perverted that is? And you, Sarah! I expected more from you. How could you be shagging your brother?"

Fiona's British accent was stronger than it had been in years.

Amber threw another Scotch down her throat and slammed the shot glass on the bar top.

"He's the only man I ever loved. You know I like women!"

Fiona felt the anger. Her body was perspiring, but she kept the dream intact as she turned on her back.

"You must be joking, dear. I'll excuse your foul mouth and silly comments. I know this is just a dream."

Fiona spent hours learning how to remember her dreams, but this one was shaping up as not worth remembering. Plus, there wasn't an orchid in sight. She watched as Geoff came closer. He yanked her torso closer to the bar. His hot, alcoholic breath sent a chill down her dreaming body.

"I don't usually let my customers upset me, but you are dangerously close to pushing my destruct button. You know Shorty doesn't want you here. You better get your ass out of here before I lose my temper. Ain't that right, Jiggy?"

Fiona was surprised to hear Geoff refer to Amber as "Jiggy." Was Sarah, Amber and Jiggy in this dream? This dream was filled with associations that didn't make sense. Jiggy was Sarah's best friend when they lived in England. Now Sarah was Jiggy and Amber at the same time, and Geoff was Jake.

Jiggy watched Fiona pulled her coral cotton blouse to her waist as Jake let her go.

"That's right, Jake. We don't need her, do we?"

Fiona watched the pair as she turned and walked toward the door. Other people were in the bar but their faces were distorted by the low lights and smoke in the room. As she walked out of the bar, Fiona saw a painting of a black orchid on the door, just below the peep hole.

Suddenly, Fiona's eyes opened. She heard Van Morrison singing "Brown Eyed Girl." It was 6 a.m. when she pulled herself out of bed. Then she sat on the edge of the bed with her phone in her hand and matter-of-factly whispered, "I must be starting a new chapter in my dream world, and I have no idea why."

She immediately dialed Krabb's number. A pre-recorded message asked her to leave a message.

"Doc? This is Fiona. Please call me back."

Something was happening to her in that dream. Why was Geoff back in her life looking like a completely different guy? What about Sarah saying her name was Amber and they saying it was Jiggy? She hadn't thought about Jiggy in more than 30 years. That dream was a nightmare of epic proportions. The dream was too strange, but she knew it was real on some level of her being. She remembered Krabb's words:

"Dreams have a personal validity to them. Your dreams are a byproduct of your existence. Your dreams contain concepts that will, at some point, transform your field of physical knowing. So your dream world is not a shadow image of reality. It is its own reality. You experience certain dreams to understand that developments are possible because they have matured in other perspectives, which are not tied to time."

Those words didn't mean much the first time she heard them. Krabb gave her too much information in that first meeting. She needed to hear and absorb more of his wisdom. She realized that Geoff had become an enigma of sorts. He was Jake too, and that sent a bolt of fear down

Fiona's spine. If Geoff was somebody else in dreams, then there were others enigmas there too.

"Maybe we all are enigmas. I guess we just don't know it. Somehow, we live more than one life. Just like orchids, we are more than just one flower. That's crazy! But dreams don't lie. Geoff is Jake somewhere in time, and Sarah is Jiggy and a girl named Amber."

Fiona grabbed her phone and coffee mug. She opened the screen door and smelled the honeysuckle. It was a beautiful May morning. The porch thermometer told her it was already 70 degrees, and there was not a cloud in the sky. She sat on her swing and thought more about the dream. She faded into a daydream.

Fiona was back in the bar reliving last night's dream, but she quickly snapped out of it. Mimi's name raced across her mind. She tapped her phone. Three rings and then silence. A few seconds later, a low voice pushed words through the phone.

"Hello?"

"Mimi? Did I wake you? This is Fiona."

"Hey, Fiona. It's okay I have to get ready for work. What can I do for you?"

Fiona wanted to jump right into her dream, but she hesitated.

"I didn't know you worked. What do you do?"

Mimi didn't answer right away. It was too early to go into a long-winded conversation about work, especially today. She pulled her legs up to her waist and grabbed her black-rimmed specs from the nightstand.

"Oh yes. I work. The company I work for is actively involved in criminal rehabilitation."

"Interesting. You'll have to tell me more. Can we get together and have lunch this week?"

"Well, I don't know, Fiona. I might be able to get away tomorrow. I'll look at my schedule, and I'll call you later. Puckett's at noon tomorrow might work, if that's okay with you. My office is across the street."

"Yes, I love Puckett's, Mimi."

"Is there something special you want to talk about, Fiona? New orchids, maybe?"

"Well, in a way, yes. But it's more about a dream I had. You still see Doc Krabb on a regular basis, so I thought you could help me before I make another appointment with him."

"Yes. I will if I can, Fiona. I'll call you later.

"Right. Sorry to call so early, Mimi.

Fiona hung up the phone. She felt better. Mimi could help her decide how to handle her meeting with Krabb. She needed support right now.

Mimi relived her phone conversation with Fiona as she soaked her body under the hot shower. The steamy water and fragrant shampoo gave her a burst of energy. She really liked Fiona. The orchid connection was one reason, but the dream connection was deeper, and that interest kept drawing them to each other. She thought about Dr. Krabb and his dream therapy. She knew more than she did a year ago about her dreams, but she knew there was much more to learn. Fiona was involved in that knowing in some way.

As she stepped out of the shower, Mimi heard her phone ring again.

"What the hell? Two calls before 7? This is going to be an interesting day."

She quickly wrapped the oversize towel around her toned body and tried to reach to the phone before the fourth ring.

"Hello, this is Mimi."

There was silence on the other end and no message light. She looked at the number and didn't recognize it.

"Oh hell." She tapped her phone, kept it in her hand and went back to the bathroom. Getting ready for work in the morning was a ritual she didn't like. The hair, makeup and clothing decisions took more time than necessary most days. Her mind wasn't present as she went through the inane process of making herself presentable. Trying to solve the enormous social problems that exist in the justice system was a life-long personal challenge for her. She spent years studying the lives, habits and mental anomalies that exist in hardest of criminals. These men and women do the unthinkable and some of them consider it normal. The amount of money spent on some hopeless cases went through her mind. The return is virtually nonexistent. She thought about a letter she wrote to her boss:

"The system is like a strainer. Hard-core criminals can't get through the tiny holes of rehabilitation. They block the strainer because no one treats the cause. The system punishes instead of educating."

As she styled her hair, she remembered one of her case studies, which somewhat explained the reason for the justice system debacle. Pablo Cordova had been in prison most of his life. He was one of the few that managed to turn his life around. Pablo's raspy voice was in her mind:

"I'll tell what you already know, Miss Mimi. Most first timers believe they can't get a decent job because they made a mistake. Their crime record acts like a stop sign. Because of that, they resort to more petty crime to pay the bills. We all got to eat, have some kind of shelter and a little recreational fun from time to time. The system, because of its lack of empathy, makes them feel like no one cares. Most of them lived without caring all their lives. Broken homes, abusive or absent parents, and early exposure to crime, which they believed was justified, puts them and keeps them in an abnormal state of mind. If you ask 10 criminals about their childhood, eight will tell you about situations that no child should experience. They live like wounded animals. They are absorbed with fear. They fight anything and everything that seems sane. They want to make a difference, and they chose crime as the vehicle. The more arrests, the more conditioned and violent they get. The system desensitizes them, and it continues to degrade them. The only way to change hardened cons is to recondition them with education, effective mental tools, compassion and understanding. We all make different choices, but we all wind up the same way."

Mimi thought about Pablo at the right time. Her morning meeting was with the Nashville Corrections Department head. She knew he heard stories like Pablo's many times before, but his department didn't have the mindset to react in a different way. Her job was to formulate a plan that he would accept and help implement it in a small controlled test. Her company, TimeServed, was commissioned by the governor to study and then incorporate test solutions that will reduce the prison population and rehabilitate the tough cases. Mimi knew it was an uphill battle, but she constantly dreamed about an anti-prison community and its successful rehabilitation programs.

Then her thoughts turned to Fiona.

"Maybe my friendship with Fiona and my obsession with criminal rehabilitation are related. Orchids may not be our only connection. Maybe Krabb will find another link between us."

Mimi walked into her meeting that morning with a pink orchid in her hand. She figured out how Fiona might be connected with her work when she had her first cup of coffee. The flower was sitting on her kitchen table as she quickly looked over her meeting notes. She looked up, grabbed it and smiled.

"You're going to be my prop today, and I thank you for your service."

Mimi made it to the meeting in record time. She had 15 minutes to spare, so she chatted with the receptionist about orchids before the young woman had a chance to ask her the routine office question.

"Would you like coffee, Miss Kenworth?"

Mimi followed the woman into the large conference room. The personable 20-something office worker put the orchid on the conference table and asked Mimi to have a seat. Mimi sat and looked at the orchid as she waited for Martin Lutz, the head of the Nashville Corrections Department, and his assistants, Peter Wakefield and George Bandy, to appear. When they arrived and took their seats, Mimi stood and pointed to the orchid. She didn't believe in small talk.

112

"Good morning, gentlemen. Wouldn't it be nice if we all had more than one life, just like this beautiful orchid? There are five distinct flowers on this one stem. Each one is experiencing a life, a life filled with proper nourishment and light. The flowers may look alike, but each one has different markings, and each one experiences light on that stem in a different way. One is not better than another. They live to express their uniqueness in unity."

The men looked at each other as they sat across the table from her.

"I mean, look at these incredible creations. Each bloom expresses uniqueness with the right sunlight and nourishment. Perhaps our prisons would look a little different if we thought about prisoners in a similar way. They may not have known how to blossom with rightful expression the first time, thanks to family, social and economic issues, but they never stop blooming. They bloom in prison, but those blooms are restricted by a system that hinders rather than educates. We don't provide the kind of nourishment and sunlight that prisoners need to blossom correctly. Most prisoners return to prison. Right, to them, is what they know from what they experience. The orchids know they will blossom and thrive in their environment. We don't tell them how to thrive. We don't tell them how much light is enough. They are wired to know. So are we, gentlemen. When that wiring is short-circuited by abusive or oppressive situations, we believe that the circuitry is permanently damaged. So we create programs that foster the broken circuitry. We never fix or rewire it. We just hope we do. Prisoners need more than hope. They need the same nourishment as orchids. Our program is designed to do just that. Here are the details of that program."

Mimi passed out her report.

"Give us a chance to prove to you that prisoners can lead productive lives in prison as well as when they return to mainstream society. The governor believes in this program, and he thinks you will too."

The men looked at each other once again. Martin, the boss, was a large man with a white, short-sleeved shirt and red bowtie. He looked at her. "People are not like orchids, Miss Kenworth. We only live once and die. I don't understand your analogy."

The two other men nodded in agreement. Mimi stood and looked at the men.

"And therein lies the problem, gentlemen. We think we are so much more than a flower, when in reality, we are the same. I don't expect you to agree right now, but please read my report."

Martin touched his bowtie and nodded.

"No one has started a meeting like that before. I want to talk to the governor. I'm sure we'll have questions once we read the report and hear what he has to say," he said.

Mimi stood, shook hands with the three men and started for the door.

"Miss Kenworth, do you want your orchid back?"

Mimi turned and smiled.

"No, the orchid is for y'all. Every time you look at it, you'll see the unrestricted beauty in life. Then you might think about the restriction we put on prisoners. Maybe that will help you find the courage to change a system that has been broken for years. Orchids have a way of talking without saying anything."

The men chuckled. Martin looked at Mimi.

"Guess we have to learn to speak and understand flower instead of Southern then."

Mimi opened the door.

"You already understand flower, sir. You just don't believe you do."

Chapter 11

No one, good or evil, ceases to exist; life is energy and energy cannot be created or destroyed; it is recycled.

Patricia Cornwall

The call from Krabb came around 2 that afternoon. When Fiona saw his name on the caller ID, she was excited. There was something intriguing about him. She liked men with character, and Krabb had plenty of that. The orchid connection was another plus. She tapped her phone after the second ring.

"This is Fiona."

"Hi, Fiona. Doctor Krabb here. How are you?'

"Oh, hi, Doc." She acted surprised to hear his voice. "How are you?"

"Well, thank you. Fiona. What can I do for you? Do you want to come in and talk?"

"Yes, please. I need your help. My dreams are changing, and I'm concerned. I'm starting to see familiar people I know in my dreams in an unfamiliar way."

"Yes, that could happen. It happens to me sometimes."

Fiona laughed.

"Well, I'm seeing people I know or have known, and they are somebody else now. They look like strangers I've known forever. I know that makes no sense."

"Oh, right. Yes, let's talk about it. When do you want to come in? I have a 9 a.m. tomorrow. Can you make that?"

"Yes, tomorrow. I'll be there. Thanks, Doc."

"See you tomorrow, Miss Fiona."

The phone went dead. Krabb didn't waste time on the phone, and Fiona liked that. She made the note in her phone calendar and went back to work. Her plants needed her, and she needed them. As she fertilized the new Cymbidium, better known as the boat orchid, her phone rang again.

Mimi was returning her call.

"Yes. Let's do lunch at 11 tomorrow, Fiona. That way we'll miss the crowd."

"Well, I have a meeting at 9 with Krabb, so I might be a little late."

Fiona quickly returned to her boat orchid. The boat orchid was one of her favorites. She remembered what she read about its 2,000-year-old history. This pink beauty was in full bloom. She felt its aged, stately elegance as she carefully changed the water and cut back the bottom of the spike. But her focus started to fade. She quickly moved to her desk and sat. Her head dropped, and her mind went into the past. She opened the email program on her laptop and started typing.

"Dear Sarah, It's been too long. I miss you and your small taradiddles. As you know, I have an insatiable appetite

when it comes to knowing the truth. I saw you in a dream last night. You said you were Jiggy and somebody else. Do you and Jiggy still stay in touch? Do you know a girl named Amber? Write me when you can. Love, Fiona."

Fiona pushed the send button. She thought about her message to Sarah. She knew Sarah didn't see Jiggy. No one had. Jiggy disappeared decades ago, but Fiona had to be sure. Dreams don't lie. There was some sort of connection, and she had to turn over every stone on the path to the truth. She knew Krabb would help, but she hoped to hear from her sister before tomorrow's meeting. Fiona looked at her watch. 2:45. The phone calls and email made her forget about eating lunch. She went to her bedroom slipped the wooden clogs off her feet, and put her head on the down pillow. Within minutes, she was back in her dream world staring at the walnut door with the black orchid on it. She opened it. The smoke-filled room made her gag, but she moved toward the bar. Five men sat at the head of the bar. The bartender wasn't Geoff this time. She heard one of the men call his name.

"Hey Shorty, hit me again."

The bartender wore aviator sunglasses and a scraggly beard.

"Just a minute, piss-ant. I'm fixing your buddy a sidecar."

Fiona remembered her dad drinking a sidecar when she was 12. He told her the drink was cognac, orange liqueur and lemon juice in a sugar-rimmed glass. It was a popular drink in the 1940s. Fiona looked at the five men again. All of them wore suits. Their suit jackets had wide lapels, and their ties were extra wide with bright floral prints. As she watched, the fat man at the end of the bar yelled in a high-pitched voice.

"Well, make me another dirty Shirley while you're at it, Shorty." The man laughed.

Fiona knew that drink too. She had her first dirty Shirley when she was 18. The vodka, ginger ale and grenadine concoction made her sick. The only thing she liked about it was the cherry. She never touched alcohol after that episode. In a flash, the short bartender turned around, and put the two drinks on the bar. He looked at Fiona through his oversized glasses.

"Oh, it's you again. I thought I told you to stay out of here."

His voice was filled with mucous. Fiona was standing next to the man drinking the dirty Shirley and smoking a cigar.

"I'm looking for Jake. Is he here?"

Shorty smiled and looked at the first man.

"You hear that big dick? Rocco, she wants to talk to Jake."

Shorty turned his back and started to walk toward the other end of the bar. Fiona followed him.

"Do you know where he is? I need to talk to him."

"He may be at the morgue, sister. I heard someone put a bullet in his head last night. Why do you think I'm behind the bar? I got better things to do with my time."

Fiona felt the tears run down her face as Shorty gave her that news. Suddenly, everyone disappeared. The loud ring was familiar. She quickly opened her eyes and reached for the phone.

"Hello?'

"Fiona, its Mimi. Sorry, but I need to change our meeting time tomorrow. Can we meet at 1:30?"

Fiona quickly looked at her phone. It was almost 5 p.m. She was still groggy from her dream.

"Hey, Mimi. Sounds good. I have to go now. See you then."

Mimi could tell that Fiona was in an altered state, so she simply said, "Bye for now, Fiona."

Fiona was in shock. Her dream world just informed her that her brother might have been killed in the 1940s. She couldn't stand not knowing what her dream was telling her. She had to find her brother. Maybe the dream was telling her that Geoff was going to die. Maybe someone shot him, and she didn't know it. She wouldn't be surprised if that was the case. As her feet touched the floor, her phone rang again. It was Krabb's office.

"Hi Fiona. This is Linda at Dr. Krabb's office. Sorry to call so late, but the doctor has been called away unexpectedly. Can we reschedule your appointed for the 27th at 9 a.m.?"

"Well, yes. Thanks."

Fiona looked at her phone. Geoff was in there somewhere. As she scrolled down the list, her mind played back her dream. She wondered why Geoff was Jake in her dream, and why Jake could be dead now. She tried to remember the faces of the men at the bar. All except for one were wearing a hat of some kind. She did remember the hats. The guy sitting on the first stool, Rocco, had a high-pitched voice. Shorty called him "big dick." He was wearing a black fedora with a blue silk band. The contoured brim covered his eyes. The large man sitting next to him wore a gray felt Homburg with a black Petersham ribbon band and binding on the brim. The hat sat on the back of his head so he could see Shorty. All the men were black. The third guy wore a brown Porkpie hat with a matching thin leather band. Fiona thought about his profile. His face was familiar, but she couldn't remember his name. The thin man on his right didn't wear a hat. He had a pencil mustache, jet black hair slicked straight back, and a large cigar. The smoke from the cigar still annoyed her sense of smell as she remembered her dream. The young man sitting on the end looked Middle Eastern, but he wasn't. His tan trilby hat had a solid black band with a flat black ribbon fastened on the left side. A small feather stuck out from the ribbon. She remembered seeing this man's face as she followed Shorty to the end of the bar. He was the spitting image of a young Max Westwood. Fiona's forehead was wet with perspiration. Once again, someone from her distant past was front and center in her dreams.

She had to snap out of it. Her dream didn't make sense. She found Geoff's last known phone number and quickly pushed the send button. After the first ring, a recorded message told her the number was no longer in service. She threw her phone on the bed. Her stomach started to ache with anxiety. Her dream world was taking her to a place she couldn't understand, and that bothered her. There were no loving orchids in this dream world, just a dark, dirty little bar with black men from the 1940s. The loving orchids were now a group of men. She picked up her phone and sent another email to Sarah.

"Sarah, have you heard from Geoff? Please call me or email. Love, Fiona."

She thought about the word 'limbo' as she moved to her brown leather recliner. Maybe Geoff was part of limbo now. Fiona knew he never wanted to be part of this world because he thought it was distorted beyond belief. Fiona turned on the TV. The seasoned weatherman with the well-fitted but obvious toupee was explaining the unseasonably cool weather. She vaguely listened to his weather forecast for the next week. She whispered to herself as the weatherman smiled at the camera. Then she watched the DIY network program that showed her how to remodel her old house. She watched three episodes, even though she'd seen them all before.

Fiona pushed the remote buttons as she went on a mental escapade about good and evil. She always thought Geoff was evil. *"Maybe that's why he might be dead in her dream. Maybe that's why the orchids were gone."* Then she thought again. The orchids weren't completely gone. There was a black one on the walnut door. She thought that door was a sign or message of some kind. She walked to the kitchen. She had to stop thinking about her nightmare.

But she wanted to go back to this dream before she met Krabb. She looked at the white clock on the gray plastered wall. "Oh hell, time for bed." The sun just made its way to the horizon. She didn't care. Her dream world was the most important one now. She wanted answers, and she believed she could get some sort of satisfaction if she went back to that dingy bar. She checked her computer for a message from Sarah but found none. Fiona wrote another message to her.

"Hey Sis, Have you heard from Geoff? I think something happened to him. Let's talk please!! Love, Fiona."

She turned off the lights and moved toward the bedroom. Fiona stood in front of her bathroom mirror and looked at the lines on her aging face. She had grown accustomed to her mature look. The warm water and liquid soap felt good, and the Aegean lotion brought her skin back to life. She pulled the hairpins from her bun. She let her long hair drop to her shoulders. The brush moved through her thick mane with ease. Her head felt each vigorous stroke, and she began to relax. She slipped into her bedtime T-shirt and jumped into bed. The day was over, but night was the only day she was interested in. The orchids could wait. Her clients could wait. She had to solve the mystery, and the only way she knew how was to live it again. As she pulled the down comforter to her neck, she picked up her phone. Still no message from Sarah. She dropped the phone, inserted the charger line and closed her eyes. Within five minutes, part of her was in bed, but another part of her was free in her other world.

Chapter 12

I recognized you instantly. All of our lives flashed through my mind in a split second. I felt a pull so strongly towards you that I almost couldn't stop it.

J. Sterling

The low-cut, blue sequined dress that covered most of her toned, dark legs fit her like a scuba suit. Every inch of her body was on display as she moved closer to the man without the hat at the bar.

"I didn't think I'd see you again, girl, after I missed you the other night. I don't want to go through that again, you know what I mean?"

Fiona watched Myles stand. She felt him kiss her on the cheek. His arms closed around her body, and she felt the affection in her dream state.

"You said you would come tonight, but I know how it is when you lose someone."

Fiona was confused. Was he talking about Geoff? Her mind tumbled through this scene as the handsome man's face drew so close to hers that she could smell the Kentucky bourbon on his breath. He suddenly let her go and gave Shorty a hand signal.

"What's your drink, Jay? You want a bourbon and soda? I heard about your sister from Shorty. I didn't know it was your sister until Shorty explained why he was talking about two deaths with the guy next to me. He said they found Jake's body, and Tyrone wife's killed herself. I jumped into the conversation when Shorty mentioned the girl from New York. I knew he was talking about you."

Myles took a long swig of his bourbon.

"Jayla? Are you okay?"

Fiona looked around the bar, and then she looked at her body. It wasn't her body. She looked into mirror behind the bar. The black face looking back at her was Jayla's. The blue straw tilt hat with the cock feather spray was not her style either, but she was wearing it. She suddenly realized she was someone else. A black someone else with blue eyes. She heard herself say, "God. I look good."

Jayla pulled a perfumed handkerchief from her blue gator clutch. Fiona thought she was dressed like she just came from a 1940s theme party.

"*My name is Fiona.*

She tried to say those words through Jayla, but Jayla was silent.

Myles smiled and asked her again.

"Jayla, are you okay? What can I do, Honey? You got to talk to me."

Fiona stared at the man.

"*Krabb, is that you?*" Fiona recognized the smile and the voice. Her head turned from side to side in bed.

Perspiration soaked her body. The man in her dream was another version of Krabb! It was Gabriel Krabb with dark skin. She smiled as she looked at Myles's clothing. This black incarnation of Krabb was wearing a blue sharkskin suit and blue and white spectator wing tips. His yellow floral tie, tied in a double Windsor knot, was attached to his blue cotton shirt with a gold tie clasp. His gold cuff links matched the clasp.

"Come on, Jayla. Let's sit and talk. Hell, I'll just listen. I'm a good listener."

Shorty jumped into the conversation.

"Hey, I heard what Laquisha done. I told you about Jake the other night, and now the cops have his body. It don't make sense. This place might look like a den of killers, but it ain't. It's a respectable place, you know.

"Myles and I are just trying to have a little time together. What do you know about all of this?"

Shorty shook his head, and as he did, his aviator sunglasses flew off the top of his head and landed on the dirty floor in front of Jayla's white baby doll pumps. Shorty was annoyed.

"Can you pick those damn things up?" His curt attitude angered Jayla. Myles reached down, picked up the cracked glasses and put them on the bar.

Jayla looked at Shorty. She didn't like him the first time she met him, and now she thought she knew why. "*Shorty is a snoop and a gossip. Bartenders can be that way*," she thought.

126

Fiona opened her eyes and touched her forehead. She quickly fell back asleep, and she was living another dream. She was talking to Violet about her son, Flip. She didn't know where they were, but she vividly saw the scene unfold. Violet was telling Fiona that she wasn't the kind of mother who passed on anything positive while Flip was growing up. She had her own demons to deal with. In fact, Flip moved in with a friend when he was 13 because, as Violet said, "he couldn't stand my nagging." Flip began acting out his frustrations in high school. He was constantly in trouble with the law. When the police caught him trying to steal a car at 18, the assistant district attorney prosecuted him, but the judge offered Flip an alternative: Join the Marines instead of serving jail time. Flip took the deal and barely passed the height requirement.

Six months later, Flip was walking about 20 feet behind a tank during Operation Desert Storm. When a missile hit the tank, Flip was knocked unconscious and stayed in a coma for two weeks. He went into a German hospital and was later discharged. He was diagnosed with a mild traumatic brain injury and post-traumatic stress disorder. Flip didn't want to see Violet when he returned, so he found an old girlfriend and moved in with her. Flip married the girl, but the marriage didn't last long.

Flip's deep emotional problems were exacerbated by his service, but his issues started long before the war. His war injuries gave him the opportunity to take advantage of the system. He turned into a narcissistic, cunning and conniving psychopath who cared only about his image and the money he artfully hoarded from his second wife and two kids. His abusive, neglectful and alcoholic behavior went on well into his 30s. His only friends were service buddies who drank with him as he told lies about himself and his achievements. His distorted view of life made him feel special. Violet knew he was an exaggerated male version of herself, but she was too busy weaving her own lies and taking care of her ego to care what Flip did with his life.

Fiona watched Violet tell her, "Flip is sick, and I guess he got a little of it from me, but it was that no-good farmer father of his that ruined him. I hated that man. He abused the fire out of me, and I guess I passed a little on to Flip, but I'm not going to admit that to anyone but you."

Fiona's eyes opened again. She put her feet on the floor, and for some reason, she thought that Shorty may have influenced Flip's behavior. That didn't make sense to her, but it did make her think. She began to think about the other people in the bar. All of them were familiar in some way. She thought each one might have a Caucasian counterpart who played a part in her life. Schuler told her about counterparts.

She reached the bathroom and threw her clothes on the chair next to the door. She was immersed in deep thought as she showered.

"I'm living another life and watching it on my mental screen. I must tell someone. I know I'm not losing my mind."

Fiona turned the water off and grabbed her towel as she stepped in front of her full-length mirror. She grabbed a pair of jeans and a fresh T-shirt. She was still thinking as she put her Teva sandals on her moist feet.

*"My skin is a little dark. Maybe I have some black genes
and don't know it. Hell, anything is possible. I guess we all
have black in us. They say the human species started in
Africa, so that might be the answer."*

Fiona was anxious as she went through her usual morning
and mid-morning routine, but she constantly looked at the
clock. That was a little unusual. Her lunch meeting with
Mimi was playing with her mind. She wanted to tell Mimi
about the dream. She checked her phone. No message from
Sarah. Fiona shook her head and said, "I'm okay. I just
need some answers."

She steered her car on to Cotton Lane. It was time to have
a real conversation with a real person. Her nerves tingled as
she thought about what she would say. As she crossed the
Harpeth River, she saw an albino doe standing on the right
bank of the river.

"Cool! Those protected creatures don't show themselves
very often," Fiona thought.

Fiona pulled into the parking garage across from Puckett's
at 1 p.m. Mimi was already seated. Each table was covered
with a red-and-white checkered tablecloth. The walls
around the country-style restaurant displayed food and
other soft goods like a grocery store. That was the
ambiance of Puckett's: part grocery store and part country
cooking. Fiona smiled as she walked toward Mimi's table.
Mimi stood and opened her arms.

"Hey, Fiona. You look great! It's so good to see you."

Fiona felt the love as Mimi's arms wrapped around her.

"I'm so happy to see you, Mimi. It's been over a month,
hasn't it? How's work, and how are your orchids?"

"The orchids are thriving. I have them sitting on a table that faces west. They seem to love the amount of sun they get. I don't know what I would do without them. They show me the delicate beauty in all living things, and I began to use them in my work."

Fiona nodded happily.

"I know, Fiona. I'm amazed by their energetic sensual expressions."

"Oh, you're so right. I only wish humans could express their senses in the same way. It seems we use too much or not enough energy to express our thoughts and beauty. Orchids know how to express beauty delicately."

Fiona nodded again. She wanted to discuss her dream, but she wanted to do it gracefully.

"So what's going on at work, Mimi? I've never asked you about your work before. You're a teacher right?"

"Funny you should ask. I have a teaching degree, but I work for a company that works on social issues for the state. One of the issues is prison reform. I recently presented my prisoner reform proposal to the Nashville Corrections Department"

"Oh, wow! That sounds important. How did you find that job?

"Well, I wanted to be a teacher, but for some reason, I have always had a fear of bullets, bombs and guns, so I decided to face my fear in a somewhat unusual way. I decided to help the people who use weapons and other things in the wrong ways. There is no right way, you know, but the people we call criminals need more help than we give them."

"Interesting reason, Mimi. I like it. So how did your clients like your presentation?"

"They didn't know what to think at first. That's the problem. Our representatives are tied to the old school way when it comes to prison and prisoner reform. If it was up to them, we would still have chain gangs and hangings. They believe most prisoners can't be brought back into mainstream society unless they are physically and mentally punished in some way. Their motto seems to be, 'Treat violence with violence. An eye for an eye.' But that narrow-minded thinking doesn't work."

"Tell me about your proposal, Mimi. I'm interested in anything that will shake things up politically."

A tall blonde waitress with a beehive hairdo and a big smile interrupted Mimi's answer.

"Hi y'all. Do y'all know what you want for lunch or should I come back?"

The waitress filled the water glasses as she went through the list of daily specials. Fiona and Mimi ordered salads and grilled cheese sandwiches. The waitress smiled as she walked away.

"So, tell me about your proposal, Mimi."

"Well, as you know, our prison and our prisoner reform systems are broken. No one wants to spend the time or money to fix them for several reasons. My company was hired by the state to come up with a manageable solution to both issues. Two-thirds of the prisoners released reoffend within three years. Our prisons are overcrowded now. If we don't change the system soon, the system will completely fall apart. We are in for a rude awakening in the near future if our penal system breaks down before we make the necessary adjustments."

"So what is the solution? Let all the low-level drug offenders out for time served?"

"That's an idea, and we are looking into the mechanics of that proposal. But the real issue is do we continue to punish offenders, or do we educate and rehabilitate while we restrain them. We believe we should restrain and rehabilitate, not simply punish them. My proposal is to change the prisons into functioning communities. These communities would provide every form of therapy available. Substance abuse, psychological analysis, medical and dental assistance, work training and other social needs, as well as the same educational training we offer to a functioning law-abiding community. Achieving some sort of educational degree in prison is the only program that has been 100 percent effective in preventing repeat criminal activity. We believe they should earn what we call a prison degree. They would graduate when they learn how to cope with themselves. We believe all prisoners should be treated with kindness and respect so they learn firsthand what it feels like to be part of the solution rather than the main problem."

"Bet the boys in cheap suits don't want to spend the money to start that kind of program, right Mimi?"

"Well, I didn't get into the details on my first meeting. I just talked about orchids. But you're right. Money is always the issue, but if we don't make a change soon,

Fiona, the whole system will collapse. Norway has a community-type program in place, and the results tell the story. They have the lowest recidivism rate of any country in the world. It's not perfect, but we can make it near-perfect with the resources we have available."

Fiona realized Mimi was right. Rehabilitation is the answer, not bars and punishment. She was so engrossed in the prison conversation she forgot about her dream during lunch. As soon as Mimi finished her lunch, she looked at her watch.

"Oh darn. Its 2:30, Fiona. I have another meeting. Please forgive me, but I must go."

Mimi grabbed the check and stood to hug Fiona.

"Let's get together in the next couple of days. I'm sorry I talked your ear off today."

Fiona didn't have a chance to say much. She thanked her friend for lunch and returned to her car. It was good to listen to someone else, but she was a little frustrated. She drove on to Main Street and immediately pulled over. She felt herself going into lucid dreaming mode. Jayla was in the Black Orchid talking to Myles. A woman stood at the other end of the bar with a drink in her hand.

The woman faced her. Jayla recognized her features. The woman was black, but the long blonde wig and her well-proportioned body reminded her of Violet. Jayla stared as she heard the woman say, "Just because we're married doesn't mean you can touch me like that. You know how sensitive I am, Shorty."

The woman's voice sounded like a black version of Violet's voice. Violet was in her life once again. But this time, she was married to Shorty who Fiona realized was Flip. He wasn't her son now. They were married.

Suddenly, she was back in car, and back in the present. Her dream world was expanding, and the people in it were different but all too familiar. She put the car in drive as the light turned green, her right foot hit the petal with force. She had to get home to her orchids, and she had to see Krabb before she lost touch with what was real. But Jayla was real, she thought. She was her own person. Fiona was watching another life being lived. Maybe it was another one of her lives. Krabb might help her figure that out.

The Pain

Everything is connected, like a delicate web.
Ever growing, ever changing. New silvery
strands come together every day, and once the
strand is formed, no matter what superficial
circumstances may sometimes keep you apart,
it is never broken. You will meet again, perhaps
in another lifetime. The connection is
unbreakable, lying dormant in your
subconscious.

Chelsie Shakespeare

Chapter 13

**He walked out of the cottage and into the night.
He was stark naked.**

Max Ehrlich

The two cockroaches running up the unpainted drywall in
the kitchen seemed to be playing a game of tag as they
approached the greasy wood table where a bowl of cold
black beans and six empty bottles of Coors were scattered
across the table. The bugs ran around the bottles like mice
in a maze, but the beans seemed to be their final reward.
Every night at precisely 10 p.m. at least two roaches would
follow the same disgusting path to reach their feast. But in
their world, disgust was nonexistent. The race for the beans
was the pinnacle of success. Food was their source of
energy and life. The ultimate gift of survival lay before
them, thanks to a man who lived like one of them. The
bowl of beans was Geoff Mistry's dinner two weeks before
the roach competition began.

Geoff didn't remember dinner two weeks ago. Most of the
time, he didn't remember where he was or how he got
there. All he knew was the high he felt from the crack he
scored from the guy who lived in the same distressed
building. Geoff had a deal with that bloke. Geoff would
make his way out of the basement of the almost-vacant
building on 14th Street in downtown Las Vegas every

morning, and he walked down Freemont Street until he found a tourist he could con. Even though Geoff was an old broke addict, he still had a knack for petty extortion. He carried an old kitchen knife in his belt, just in case one of his marks tried to resist his request. The belt was covered by an oversized T-shirt. It wasn't oversized by design. It was oversized because of his weight loss. His body was covered in scabs, but the shabby fatigues and dirty long-sleeved T-shirt with the words "The Reds" on the front and "Up The Pool" on the back hid most of them. His stubbly face was the face of a junkie with nothing but his next fix in mind. Most tourists who saw him coming their way on Freemont Street quickly ducked into a casino, or they crossed the street to avoid him. But not everyone was that savvy. Some tourists would stop when he approached them. They listened as he told them how he lost everything in a fire the week before, and how he needed a few dollars to hold him over until the insurance check came. The story was unbelievable, but most of the people who listened gave him loose change or a few dollars just so he would go away. Most days, Geoff would make $40 or $50 without much effort. He would stop at the quick market and buy a six-pack of beer and a stick of beef jerky around 4 p.m. each day. He drank two bottles and ate the jerky as he walked back to his flop-pad to hit the pipe again. His next stop was the bloke's apartment on the first floor of his run-down building. His mission was to smoke some crack compliments of the bloke and his woman. Geoff just called her 'The Bitch."

The bloke, Chance Hansen, wasn't always into selling junk. At one time, he was a young, surfer-boy turned ambitious, high-dollar real estate salesman in Los Angeles. The money flowed endlessly back in the 1990s, but the dawn of the

21st century changed that scenario. The cocaine and weed parties didn't help either. Chance was aging and spending more than he made. As the market spiraled out of control, so did Chance. His beach boy looks faded, and the birthmark on his cheek darkened. The trips to Vegas and the money-hungry women he showered with gifts became his full-time obsession. When the LA market started to crack, thanks to the greed that fueled it, he was caught with no savings and a highly mortgaged house in Santa Monica. He had a few thousand in cash, so he gave the house to the bank and moved to Vegas. He moved in with his stripper girlfriend, Bitsy Taggart. Bitsy worked in a seedy bar off the strip, so she cultivated several drug connections. Bitsy agreed to let Chance sell some product using her connections. She thought he could help sell product, and she could make more money.

Bitsy was more than a stripper and drug dealer. She was a 27-year-old con artist. Her soft-spoken manner, wholesome looks, and fit body fooled a lot of people. She liked Chance, but she didn't trust him. She didn't trust anyone. Money and power were her only allies, and she used them wisely. Bitsy and Chance set up a small drug operation in the vacant apartment building on 14th Street a few months after they met. Bitsy and Chance didn't live there. They just used the place as a drug store. The owner of the building didn't care what they used it for as long as he got the $300 rent each month. The arrangement worked. Chance never sold drugs to strangers, but Geoff was an exception. Chance called him 'the English dude living downstairs.' Bitsy didn't like him. When Geoff knocked on the door, she never answered. She made Chance open the door. Geoff always yelled something when he knocked, so there was no doubt who was at the door. Chance always let Geoff in. He liked the old English bastard. He would greet Geoff the same way most days.

"Hey, you old English bastard! What the hell are you into today?"

Geoff usually walked right passed Chance. On this particular day, he immediately looked for Bitsy as he unleashed his urge to bullshit.

"Found me two old bitches on Freemont that really wanted to help me. They hit the slots and gave me $100 in quarters. I went into the Golden Nugget to exchange them, but two security guards wouldn't let me get near the money window. Here's fifty in quarters."

Chance nodded and went into the bedroom. He grabbed two small packets and handed them to Geoff when he returned.

"This is some good shit. It will rock your world, dude."

Geoff stuffed the two small packets in his front pocket and smiled as he walked around the apartment looking for Bitsy. Chance noticed Geoff's decaying front teeth as he tried to block his path.

"Where's that woman you live with, mate?"

"Oh, she's getting ready for work. You know how these show girls are, dude. Takes them forever to get ready to get ready."

Geoff shook his head in agreement.

"Yeah. I guess it takes a lot to look good when you're naked."

Chance laughed.

"You got it, bro. She's got to dress up before she takes it off."

"Yeah, you're lucky, mate. You get to see her in the flesh all the time. That bitch has some body. You think she would show me her tits sometime?"

"I don't know. Why don't you ask her next time you see her?"

Chance knew there was no way Bitsy would show Geoff anything, except the Derringer she carried.

"I'll ask her to get you a ticket for the show. How does that sound?"

"Yeah, mate. I'd be in tit heaven, I reckon."

"Right. I'll let you know. See you tomorrow then."

Geoff was satisfied. As he walked down the steps to the basement, he mumbled to himself, "Next time I'll find that bitch and ask her myself."

The beer buzz was in full bloom when he reached his front door and tripped on a package.

"Damn! Bloody hell! I'm going to give that landlord something he won't forget! "

Geoff didn't pay much rent. The old landlord let him live there for $50 a month since there was no heat, air or hot water. Geoff didn't like the old bastard, but he didn't cause any trouble, although he wanted to.

Before he looked at the name on the label, Geoff grabbed a foil packet, a lighter and small pipe from his pants pocket. He began smoking. Five minutes later, he looked at the label on the package. It wasn't his name. He opened the package, and when he saw it was just a box, he immediately threw it across the room. The nesting doll in the box hit the beans, and the box landed on the table next to the dirty bowl. He picked up the label from the dirty floor and looked at it. The package was addressed to Bitsy Taggart. He didn't know a Bitsy Taggart. He tried to take another hit, but he couldn't find the lighter or the pipe. He slowly walked to the faux leather recliner in the center of the room, took off his clothes, and dropped himself into it. Geoff grabbed his left shoe. He reached for his right shoe but he couldn't reach it, so he rested his head on the arm of the chair and passed out. He was naked except for the shoe on his right foot.

"We usually get the package this time every week, Chance. Something is wrong. Go down the hall and see if that asshole delivery guy put it in front of someone's door."

Chance didn't feel like running all over the four-story building for Bitsy, but he nodded his head.

"Sometimes, those guys get the first floor and the basement confused. I'll try the guy downstairs first."

"If that old prick got our package and somehow figures it out, we got problems, Chance."

Chance knew Bitsy was right, so he quickly put on his sandals. Chance was knocking on Geoff door two minutes later. No answer. Chance knew Geoff was passed out, so he decided to check with the other five residents of the building. One lived on the second floor, two lived on the third, and two lived on the fourth. He didn't know any of them. Chance walked up to the fourth floor and started there. No one answer the door in either apartment. He got no response on the third floor either. Floor two was different. After two knocks, a short, old woman cracked the door open.

"I don't want any damn magazines."

The woman's voice was soft and raspy.

"I'm not selling anything, ma'am. Did you get a package today?"

"I haven't got a package in the last ten years."

The old woman slammed the door. He shook his head and walked down one flight of stairs.

Bitsy was standing at the door when he opened it.

"So? Did you find it?"

"No. This place is like something out of a horror movie. I think the building is filled with zombies."

"What about the old prick downstairs?"

"He must be passed out. I'll try him later or in the morning."

"You better. My ass will be fried if I don't find that stuff. You know how much is in there, don't you? Two grand worth. I'm not taking that kind of hit, so we need to find it."

"Don't worry. If it's in the building, I'll find it."

"I'm telling you, if that son of a bitch on the first floor got the package, we will never see it. You better go down there again and check him out now!"

"Right. I'll try him again."

Chance was outside of Geoff's door five minutes later. He decided to use the same tactic Geoff used when he knocked on his door, so he knocked and yelled, "fire", as loudly as he could. No answer. He beat on the door. No answer. He turned the knob to see if the door was locked. It wasn't. He opened the door and saw Geoff passed out naked on a nasty recliner. He looked around the room and felt sick. The stench, along with the complete turmoil he saw in that three-room basement apartment, was sickening. He walked toward the chair and touched Geoff's shoulder with a cane he found on the floor.

"Dude, you still alive?"

Geoff grunted. He was alive. Chance looked around the room. Trash was everywhere. Plastic cups and papers littered the room. Whiskey bottles were strewn on the floor. The kitchen table was covered with dirty bowls and bottles. Chance didn't see the doll's box on the table. It was upside down, and it had black marks on it from the collision with the black beans. But the doll inside the box was intact. Chance felt sick again. His eyes began to water from the stench as he stood over Geoff, so he quickly moved toward the door. As he did, he thought he heard a voice. He turned around and looked at the old man, but he was still in the same position. Chance whispered to himself as he pulled the door closed behind him.

Bitsy was dressed for work when Chance opened the apartment door.

"Well, did you talk to him?"

"He's out cold. That place is not safe for humans. The apartment smells like dirty ass."

"I'm going to work. He'll wake up in a few hours. I think the package is down there somewhere. It has to be. I called UPS, and they said the package was delivered at 4 this afternoon. It's in this building somewhere, and my guess is the old prick has it. You have to find it now, Chance."

"Right. I'll stay on it."

Bitsy left the building. The package was like gold to her. She and Chance could turn $2,000 worth of product in less than three days. That's why she kept Chance around. He was a good salesman. Their relationship wasn't about love. It was about money.

Chance put his head on the big white pillow on the weathered red leather sofa. If the old guy in the basement had the package, he would find it in the morning. Going back into that rat's nest of an apartment was not on his to-do list tonight. It was almost 9:30 p.m. He decided to go to the Golden Nugget for a nightcap, and then sleep in his apartment a few streets away. He pulled out a small vial from his pocket and dumped some white powder on the coffee table in front of him. He sketched out four fat lines with an old business card. He pulled a dollar out of his front pocket and rolled it into a straw. The first line went into his nostril, and his eyes began to water. His body chemicals recognized the surge, and they immediately responded. The second line reinforced the first hit as he put his head back on the pillow. Line three and line four sat on the table. His mind wanted more, but the loud thumping and scratching on the door interrupted him. As he walked toward the door, he heard mumbling on the other side of it. When he looked through the peephole, he saw Geoff. The old man was naked except for a shoe on his right foot. He was weaving back and forth and holding something in his right hand. Chance opened the door. Before he could say anything he smelled the breath of a dragon.

"You got a beer, mate?"

Chance looked at the old bastard in front of him. His eyes focused on Geoff's right hand. He was holding a dirty beer glass.

"I'm on my way out to get some. Do you want me to bring you a six pack later?"

Geoff began to move through the doorway. Chance thought about the package.

"Hey wait! Did you get a package today? My girlfriend ordered a gift for her niece, and it was delivered to someone else by mistake."

Geoff put the beer glass over his penis and began to laugh as he pushed past Chance.

"I'll go with you, mate."

"Dude, wait. No. I'm meeting someone. You need to go downstairs and put some clothes on."

"Clothes? Bloody hell! This is my shagging suit, and I need a beer."

"Okay let me check the fridge. Maybe I have a beer for you."

Chance raced toward the kitchen, and Geoff went into the bedroom. Chance heard a slurred English accent once again.

"I thought I could show that bitch what she's missing."

Chance grabbed a bottle of Coors and took it to Geoff, who was pissing in a flowerpot by the window.

"Hey, wait. We have a bathroom if you need it."

Geoff shook his junk and looked at Chance. He pulled the bottle out of Chance's hand and poured the beer into the dirty glass. His shaking hand spilled half of it on the rug. Chance was losing patience.

"So did you get a package today?"

Geoff looked at him without answering. He gave Chance the finger as he walked past him.

"Thanks, mate. Tell the bitch to come get it."

Geoff was out the door and down the steps before Chance could stop him. Chance decided to wait an hour or so before he went back to Geoff's. Chance locked the door behind him and went for the other two lines. Cocaine never left him alone.

The appearance of the old man, made Chance think twice about his current lifestyle. He didn't want to look like that old mess in twenty or thirty years, but that thought didn't stop him from snorting two more lines. He justified his actions by telling himself he wasn't a heroin addict. Weed and cocaine were tamer bedfellows.

Bitsy walked in the door around 11 the next morning. She was pissed. Chance was asleep on the red sofa. She walked over and kicked his foot.

"Chance, get the hell up. I want to find that package."

Chance didn't move. Bitsy kicked him harder. Her right shoe connected with his left calf.

"What the hell is wrong with you? We've lost a lot of product, and you're sleeping? I've been trying to call you all night. What are you doing? I'm getting tired of this shit, Chance! Get the fuck up and find that package!"

Chance finally opened his eyes and stood up. All the cells in his body were stuck to the top of his head, or at least he thought they were. He couldn't feel the rest of his body. He pulled up his khaki shorts as he watched Bitsy walk around the room in a panic.

"Don't worry. I found the package last night. The old man has it. It took me all night to find it. That's why I stayed here," he lied. "The old man was strung out. I had a hard time with him, but he has it. I'm going down there this morning."

"Okay. I'm waiting. When are you going?"

"Hell, Bitsy. I need to piss first."

Chance was sick. He was sick of drugs, and he was sick of Bitsy. Then he remembered the money as he stood over the commode. He had to get back what he spent, and selling drugs was the only way.

The hot shower helped Chance pull himself together, but his head was still pounding as he put yesterday's clothes back on. He slipped into his sandals when he reached the front room. Bitsy was sitting by the old window.

"Don't come back unless you have the package. I'm sick of this shit."

Chance felt his blood boil, but he just shook his head and slammed the door behind him. He stood in the hallway for a few minutes. He wanted to go back and give Bitsy some shit, but he walked downstairs and stood in front of Geoff's door instead. He let himself in. He looked for Geoff but didn't see him. Then he saw it: The smashed nesting doll lay on the floor beside the old recliner, and about 19 big cocaine rocks were on the floor. Somehow Geoff, figured it out.

"Hey, dude Are you here?"

No answer. Chance saw a closed door next to the kitchen. He opened the door and found naked Geoff face down on the floor with a lighter in one hand and a piece of paper with a phone number in the other. The pipe was still in his mouth, and his shoe was still on his right foot. Chance felt his face. It was cold. He pulled the note from his stiff fingers and read it: (615) 555-6511. Shaking like a leaf, Chance suddenly screamed, "The old prick is dead! He found a way to leave the world just the way he came in: Naked! Except for that shoe."

Chance was in a crime scene and started to think about the consequences. A wave of fear overtook him. He could do nothing but run.

An hour later, Chance was at the bus station. He had enough money stashed in a locker at the bus station to buy a ticket to anywhere. The 19 rocks, plus the two grams of coke in his pocket, would help him get started in another city. He wasn't sure where he would go, but a country music poster in the bus station helped him decide. The phone number on the poster had the same area code as the dead Englishman's note. He bought a one-way ticket to

Nashville. He wasn't a country music fan, but he could become one. It was time for him to change.

The police found Geoff's body two days later. The old woman on the second floor called them when she smelled the rotting stink coming from the basement. The cops figured it was a drug overdose. They questioned some of the residents, but they were no help. The police were especially interested in the first floor apartment, but when the building owner opened it for them after a couple failed attempts to locate the resident, they hit another dead end. The apartment was empty. The owner told police it was never rented, and the building was for sale. The four remaining tenants were leaving at the end of the month, he said, and old guy in the basement must have been a poacher. He never rented the basement area. It was not safe. The police didn't believe him, but after checking the owner's records, they had no proof. All Geoff's transactions were cash and never recorded.

The police never identified the body.

Chapter 14

Beneath my armor lies a heart more fragile than glass. Like water kissing sky forming clouds, like desert meeting wind that echoes sadness carried for a thousand miles, we shall embark on a journey shared when our paths cross each lifetime. The moment I met you again, your eyes became the windows of eternity.

Tia Guo

Sarah's computer screen came alive as she pushed the start button at 7 a.m. the last Saturday morning in May of 2012. The computer was her life. It was her work, her connection with others, and her fantasy world. The window in her small downtown apartment was half a mile from the river, but she had a bird's eye view of the debris-filled but rapidly flowing Cumberland River. She stared at the river as her computer went through its wake-up routine.

She thought about her life as her eyes watched a flock of tiny birds fly in perfect formation. She knew little downtown Clarksville wasn't Nashville, and Nashville wasn't the same city she left a few years after her mother died. She didn't believe she would ever come back to the States, but she did. She always thought England was her real home, but she had to leave or suffer in silence the rest of her life. Her mind took her to her first marriage, which lasted eight years. The verbal and physical abuse wasn't in her marriage vows. Her second marriage was supposed to be the start of a new life, but that one ended after 10 more abusive years. She didn't know why she attracted these angry men or even why she was attracted to men at all. The computer was a kinder husband now. She could turn it off if she felt any stress. Her job as a computer programmer gave her the flexibility she needed to daydream during certain parts of the day. When the screen was finally ready for duty, Sarah began another day behind the two large screens that connected her to the world. Her inbox indicated she had 16 messages. She believed most of them would be notes from retailers trying to make a buck or some foreign dude telling her $20 million was waiting for her if she would only click. When she opened the program, she noticed five trash emails that her filter didn't catch and 10 emails from clients. The last one made her look out the window. She had to think again before she opened it. It was from her sister, Fiona.

Sarah's mind painted a vivid portrait of Fiona. She loved Fiona and Geoff, but she didn't like them. She felt pain in her stomach when she thought about her younger sister and how Fiona could do so much more than she could. Fiona was prettier, smarter, and her personality opened doors and opportunities that Sarah never had. Sarah saw herself as the plain shy one. She had to work harder for what she achieved, and that work included receiving respect from her siblings. Fiona was the superstar, the main course. Sarah was the stiff green beans, and Geoff was the cold, dried mashed potatoes. She heard her inner voice say she should hide her feelings, but she didn't want to. That's why she moved back to Clarksville, not Nashville. She didn't want to see Fiona, so she never told her she lived in Clarksville. Her mind switched to Geoff. After all these years and the dreadful acts he committed, she still felt family love for him for some reason. Even though Geoff wandered across the States for 35 years, he kept track of her. Contact in the last 10 years was sporadic at best and non-existent at other times. Sarah knew Geoff served 10 of those 35 years in a Kansas prison for robbery. She knew he was accused of stalking a young woman in Denver 10 years ago. She still had contact with him when he moved to Las Vegas. He stopped communicating with her a year ago. Sarah looked at the screen and opened Fiona's email.

"Dear Sarah, It's been too long. I miss you and your small taradiddles. As you know, I have an insatiable appetite when it comes to knowing the truth. I saw you in a dream last night. You said you were Jiggy and somebody else. Do you and Jiggy still stay in touch? Do you know a girl named Amber? Write me when you can. Love, Fiona."

Sarah looked out the window again. She began mumbling.

"After all these years, this is what I get? A question about a girl I haven't seen in years, and some girl named Amber? What in the world is she thinking?"

Her fingers hit the keys, and the reply screen was front and center.

"Hi Fiona. The last time I saw Jiggy, I was with you. Remember? Amber who? Ta ta for now!"

That was all she could manage to type, but she didn't send it. Her stomach started to growl. She put on her favorite jeans and, grabbed her favorite T-shirt. The Reds were still her favorite English football team, and her shirt attested to that fact. She bought the same shirt for Geoff and sent it to him before he made the move to Las Vegas. Love for the Liverpool team was one of the loves they had in common. For some reason, she went back to the computer. There was another message from her sister.

"Sarah, have you heard from Geoff? Please call me or email. Love, Fiona."

She thought about Geoff again, but she didn't answer the email. She went into the bathroom and looked into the full-length mirror. She went back to the computer once more. Another message was in her inbox.

"Hey Sis. Have you heard from Geoff? I think something happened to him. Let's talk please!! Love, Fiona."

Sarah had enough. She turned the computer off. Fiona didn't care about her. All she wanted was an update on Geoff and Jiggy. How thoughtless can one person be? She left her small apartment. Denny's was just a half-mile away. Three days a week, at around 8 a.m., Sarah went there for a cheese omelet, three strips of bacon and wheat toast. Denny's tea wasn't English tea, so she always had a glass of orange juice instead. Today was one of those days. She wanted a shot of Jamison Irish whiskey instead of tea, but that urge faded as she slowly slid behind the wheel of her Mini Cooper.

*****

When Chance Hansen finally reached Middle Tennessee, he didn't know what to do. The bus made an unexpected stop in Clarksville at 12:30 a.m. on Saturday, May 27, 2012, so he decided to get off and stay there. It seemed like the kind of town someone could get lost in. Downtown

Clarksville looked like a ghost town. The one-man bus station looked trapped in the 1950s. The plastic red seats, stark white walls and the pungent smoke reminded him of an old movie he saw when he was a kid. Marlon Brando or James Dean was sitting on one of those red chairs smoking a Lucky Strike waiting for a bus out of town. Chance sat on one of the chairs against the wall and closed his eyes. The old English dude appeared behind his eyelids and startled him. He jumped up and went out the front door. The old red brick buildings had the charm of a small town, but they were ravished by the winds of time. He reached in his pocket and pulled out a $10 bill from his roll of stashed money.

Chance grabbed the overnight bag he bought in Kansas City and walked to the crosswalk. The Denny's sign on the opposite corner screamed at him. If Denny's was here, then the modern world wasn't too far behind. He quickly crossed the deserted street. The Clarksville Denny's was like any other Denny's except it had never been remodeled. A sleepy-eyed young waitress with bright red hair poured his water as he sat at the counter.

"Hey, welcome to Denny's! Would you like coffee, honey?"

Chance wasn't a big coffee drinker.

"How about a Coke?"

The waitress nodded her head and walked away. Chance looked around. Two young men sat in the booth to his right were having a disagreement. He turned to his left and saw four young men in uniform. He remembered seeing the Fort Campbell sign a few miles down the road.

"So, do you want something to eat?"

"I'll have a ham and cheese on white."

The waitress smiled and bent over the counter.

"You want fries with that, baby?"

"No, but I would like your number."

"I can't do that, baby. I got a boyfriend. He's in the military. You know what I mean, don't ya?"

Chance was sorry he asked. He was bored and needed company. He turned his head again and noticed two young women in a corner booth. They looked like weathered versions of the Two Broke Girls on TV. Maybe he could work some of his old magic on them. He turned his head and looked at the well-endowed waitress again.

"Do you have a sister?"

"Yeah, but she's married to a hard ass."

Chance laughed out loud. He liked her. She was honest and to the point. Two character traits he forgot he had. He stood and looked for the restroom as the waitress walked toward the kitchen window. It was time for another hit. He had to stay up all night. As he walked past the two girls, he smiled, and they smiled back. The one with the low cut T-shirt said, "Hey."

As he opened the stall and reached in his back pocket for the vial of coke, he thought about the phone number the old prick held in his hand. The coke vial had an automatic release, so he put it to his left nostril and took a hit. The powder did its job. He blasted both nostrils. He was ready for action. He had his invincible helmet on. He knew that's what it took for him to find a place to start over. That phone number was the key. He thought about the old dude once again. He didn't know why Geoff had the number in his hand while he was on the pot, but he imagined he was going to try to call the number for some reason at that particular time in his drug induced reality. Chance thought he could talk his talk to the person on the other end of that number and get some answers or a little help finding a place to stay. He thought he could even make Clarksville his new home base. No one would look for him in this strange city. Bitsy and her criminal friends don't know shit about Tennessee. He stopped at the girls' booth and showed them some of his rusty California charm.

"Hey, I don't want to interrupt, but I just got to town and I need a place to stay tonight. Is there a cheap motel nearby?"

The girls looked at each other and smiled. The girl with blonde hair and low cut T-shirt picked up her coffee cup, sipped, then put it down. She whispered to the other girl.

"He's all we got tonight. Maybe we can make a deal, Kaci."

The other girl put her mouth to the first girl's ear.

"Yeah, let's see what we can get out of him. But I'm not fucking this perv."

The blonde pulled her head back and looked at Chance.

"We know a place, but it will cost you."

He thought the blonde's accent was Midwestern. She didn't sound like the waitress.

"I might be able to handle that. Are you interested in something better than money?"

"What you got?" Kaci perked up.

"Yeah. You got what I think you have?"

Chance knew he had hit a mark.

"You know it. Do we have a deal?"

"You'll have to leave before 8 in the morning if you have what you said you have."

"I can handle that. Is it in walking distance?"

"Yeah, we'll take you there when you're ready. Don't get any other ideas, dude. We're just trying to help, that's all."

Chance had heard those words before. The more he looked, the more they looked like working girls.

"Sweet! I'll be ready in ten minutes. Do you two have names? My name is Chance."

"I'm Dori, and this is Kaci."

"Nice to meet you."

He smiled and saw the waitress put his sandwich on the counter.

He walked to the counter and quickly ate his sandwich. The waitress dropped his check in front of him.

"Be careful, now. It's a small town, but we got big bullshitters round here."

"I'm use to bullshitters, but thanks anyway."

Chance left her a $5 tip and walked out the door. The two girls were right behind him. As they walked down the partially lit street, behind Denny's, Chance noticed two men behind him. They were the same men who argued in Denny's. They kept their distance, but he didn't like what was taking shape.

"Did you two notice the guys behind us?"

Kaci, the tall one with the dark hair, looked at him but kept walking.

"They're our friends. They share a place with us and watch over us sometimes."

"Hey! All I want is a place to stay for a few hours, no strings attached. I'm not the violent type."

Dori looked at him as her platform shoes clattered on the sidewalk.

"We know. We'll keep our part of the deal."

Chanced smiled.

Dori stopped at an old storefront. There was a wooden side door next to the front door. The side door was for the upstairs apartment.

"Here's our place. Let's make the trade inside before we go upstairs, dude."

The tree-lined street was deserted, and Chance was a little nervous from his last hit. He knew he was outnumbered. The men were standing fifty feet away. Kaci had her hand in her purse. Chance slowly opened the unlocked door and reached into his shoulder bag at the same time. He pulled out a folded piece of paper and handed it to the blonde, who was standing on his right shoe.

"That's my foot, sweetie."

Dori moved her foot.

"How much you got there?"

"It should be a little over a gram."

"Cool. Follow me."

Dori opened a second door with a key that hung around her neck and started up the steep stairs. Chance felt dizzy as he climbed to the top floor. Dori hit the light switch when she reached the top. There was a mattress and box springs on the floor. A brown reclining chair, small wooden table and a floor lamp with no shade were in front of the only window in this small smoky room. Chance looked around and noticed a door next to the window. It was a bathroom with a sink and commode, but no shower.

"The store opens at 8:30. You can't be here when it opens."

"What kind of store? I noticed the windows were blacked out. Are you staying here too?"

"No, we use this place sometimes, but not tonight. Remember, be out of here by 8:00. You don't want to be here after 8:00, I promise."

Chance looked at his watch. It was almost 3 a.m. Dori didn't say another word as she turned and almost ran down the stairs. He noticed several unused condoms on the table. He pulled his powder-shooter out of his back pocket and snorted. He felt the rush immediately. He sat, and the room became a jail cell. He thought about his old real estate days.

He was somebody then. He was nobody now, just another guy running away from himself. Depression set in. "You have no friends, no wife, and no kids. All you have is $1,629.45 and a bag filled with dope. He closed his eyes and the next thing he heard was his own voice. You gotta go, man! Go back to Denny's."

All he could think about as he walked back to Denny's was that he needed another hit of coke. When he reached the restaurant, it was just past 8 in the morning. He felt sick. Too much dope and no real sleep made his hands shake. A woman sat alone at the counter. From behind her, he could only see her black hair and the back of her contoured figure, but that was enough. His mind was racing.

"I need a friend. Maybe this woman could be a friend," he thought to himself.

Sarah sat on her usual stool at the counter. She didn't know that this day would change her life. The middle-aged waitress, Millie, smiled as she wrote Sarah's order down from memory. Saturdays were always slow days for her. Most of the offices downtown were closed, and the retail stores didn't open till 10. Today was the start of the long weekend, so it was especially quiet and a slow-tip day. Sarah sat at the counter, and three men sat in booths reading The Tennessean. The waitress knew the men. They were shitty tippers.

Chance sat on the stool next to the woman. He vaguely recognized her from somewhere. Sarah quickly looked his way. She thought he might be high, but she didn't react.

Millie smiled at Chance "Coffee, hon?"

"Ah . . . well . . . maybe . . . no, water. Water with ice?"

"Do you know what you want to eat, hon?"

Chance looked at Sarah and the plate in front of her.

"I'll have what she has."

He smiled at Sarah and turned toward Millie.

"Ah . . . better . . . better . . . add a couple of strips of bacon too."

Chance was trying to feel better, but his head was pounding. He reached into his front pocket and pulled out the paper the old dude held when he met his maker. His inner voice spoke to him through the pounding. "Call that number," it said. He put the paper face up next to his water and stared at it while he ate.

Sarah tried to finish eating as fast as she could. The man's body odor was making her sick. She was ready to ask for the check. She fumbled through her designer hobo bag, found a $10 bill, and set it on the counter next to Chance's scrap of paper. She knew the total would be $6.50 before tipping. Millie picked up the cash and Sarah's check. "I'll be back in a flash with your change, dear."

Millie rang the sale and returned in record time. She put the change in front of Chance's piece of paper. Sarah was checking her phone for messages.

"Thank you, dear. I'll see you next week."

Sarah smiled and nodded her head as she read Fiona's latest message.

"Hey Sis, Have you heard from Geoff? I think something happened to him. Let's talk, please!! Love, Fiona."

Sarah shook her head as she picked up the first quarter and put it on the top of the bills. As she picked up the second, she couldn't help but read the scribbled phone number.

It was her phone number! She stared at the guy. He looked like he should be in a 12-week rehab program.

"Excuse me," she gasped. "Where on Earth did you get that number?"

Chance didn't like her tone, but he recognized her Liverpool accent.

"Got it from a guy who talked like you."

He was anxious and annoyed. He fidgeted.

Sarah thought for a minute. She knew no one had her phone number except her family and a few close friends and several business associates.

"That's strange. I don't remember giving my number to anyone around here. Where do you live?"

Chance stared at Sarah. He liked her face. She was talking to him, and that felt good. He felt like part of society again, even if it was only for a couple of minutes. He tried to talk coherently.

"Got it . . . got it . . . in Vegas."

Her words, "my number," suddenly registered with him.

Chance slowly pushed himself up. Somehow, the person he was here to find was sitting beside him.

"Are you . . . do you . . . I mean . . . This is your number? Do you, I mean do you know an old British guy who lived in Vegas?"

162

Sarah changed her tone and stepped back a couple of feet.

"My brother lives there."

Chance moved closer to her. His eyes focused on her T-shirt. She was wearing the same shirt the old dude wore every day.

"His name was Jeff, but I just called him the English Dude. He . . . he liked that. He gave me this number and said I should call this number if I ever came to Tennessee. But . . . but . . . he never told me whose number it was."

Sarah immediately knew he was talking about Geoff.

"Is he okay?"

Chance started to feel better. He didn't want to blow this opportunity. He hoped Sarah could help him. He could tell she was straight, and she seemed genuine.

"Uh ... um ... Is there some place we can talk in private? I'll tell you what I know about him. I think it would be better if we talked somewhere else."

Chance was putting his sentences together better. He knew he had to in order for her to believe him.

"I'd rather talk about it now, please." Sarah pointed toward the booth behind them.

"Let's sit here. I want to hear about my brother."

Chance knew he had to be careful. He couldn't expose the circumstances of the English Dude's death. He needed Sarah, and he had to convince her she needed him. Chance took a seat at one end of the booth, and Sarah walked over to the other. Sarah's heart pounded. Chance put his head on the table for a few seconds. When he slowly looked at her, she felt a twitch in her stomach.

"Now, what can you tell me about Geoff?"

Chance put his head down again. His hands were in his lap. Suddenly, he picked his head up and put his hands on the table. He looked out the window. He knew he had to weave this tale in the right way.

He sighed. "Your brother would go into town every day and do something. We didn't know what he did, but he always had money. He would come home around 4 p.m. every day and knock on our door. He just wanted to talk to me and my girlfriend for a few minutes. He seemed to like soccer, and I played a little when I was a kid, so we would talk about it. He knew more than me, so I just listened. About a month ago, I heard a commotion in front of our building, so I went downstairs to see what was going on. When I opened the front door, I saw two squad cars and four cops with their guns drawn. Your brother was lying on the sidewalk. I saw the blood under his head and immediately went back to my apartment to tell my girlfriend what I saw. I'm afraid your brother is dead, Miss."

Sarah felt an invisible knife in her gut. But she didn't believe this hopped-up guy at first.

"What? No. Wait. What did he do? Did you talk to the police?"

Sarah's eyes filled with tears. She always knew Geoff would be killed, but that didn't ease the pain.

"I'm not sure, Miss."

Oh, stop calling me Miss. My name is Sarah."

"Oh. Sorry. Yes, Sarah. Anyway, the cops kept everyone away from the scene. The next day, the cops came to our apartment and asked us about him. We didn't know anything except that he lived in the basement and liked to drink. I didn't even think about the number he gave me when the cops questioned me. I don't think they identified him. He was another street guy shot by the police when he tried to stab one of the officers. That's what the paper said, anyway. My girlfriend and I had a fight about a week later, and I left town. I found your number in one of my jeans pockets and decided to come look for the person behind the number."

Sarah sat stoned-faced.

"Geoff was my older brother. We didn't stay in touch much, but, I did miss him."

Chance knew his story sounded real. For some reason, the fact that the English dude was killed by the police didn't surprise her. He wanted to play her a little more.

"Yes, I'm so sorry, Sarah. Please call me Chance. If I can do anything, please let me know. But, I need a place to stay. I came in last night. I didn't think you would be the first person I talked to when I got to Tennessee. I'd call that fate. Wouldn't you?"

Sarah thought for a minute. She didn't know if fate was the word, but something was going on. First, there was Fiona's email asking about Geoff. Then some smelly random guy sitting next to her in Denny's tells her Geoff's dead. She knew she had to hear more about Geoff from this man. In a way, she felt sorry for him.

"I don't normally do this sort of thing, but since you knew Geoff and you were friends, come to my place. You can't stay long. Freshen up a bit and move on. My place is small, and mind you, a police officer lives across the hall. Since Geoff gave you my number, he must have thought you were okay. I am, or was, his little sister, you know. You can be trusted, right?

"Yes, Sarah I am trustworthy."

Sarah stared at him.

"Well then, you can freshen up and tell me more about my brother's last days. That would be a big relief."

"Oh, I don't want to put you out, Sarah. But that would help me a lot."

They slid out of the booth and walked out the door. Sarah stopped and pulled her phone out of her purse. She had to send the message she didn't want to send.

"Hi Fiona. I don't know how you knew, but Geoff is dead. How did you know? Sarah."

Chapter 15

I seem to have loved you in numberless forms, numberless times...
In life after life, in age after age, forever.

Rabindranath Tagore

Saturday, May 27th was a cloudy day in Nashville. Fiona felt the element of darkness surround her as she pulled herself out of bed and headed for the bathroom. Her mind was working in the present instead of the 1940s. Last night was another night in the Black Orchid Bar, and she remembered everything. She needed answers.

"Krabb's got to help me figure out this new dream world. I can't continue to live in these two worlds without knowing why. Maybe today will be the day I get answers."

Her mind was in full gear as the hot water started to bring her body alive. Morning showers were therapy sessions. She used them throughout her life to plan and debate her circumstances. She believed today might bring some closure. Krabb knew his stuff, and she believed him. The fact that he, as Myles, appeared to be romantically attracted to her, as Jayla, at the Black Orchid really set her mind in orbit. As she towel-dried her long hair she thought about Jayla and Myles.

"Was Myles different? Can this Myles influence Krabb? If so, then what will Krabb be in my life?"

The questions kept her busy as she put on her green and white Adidas T-shirt and khaki shorts. By the time she stood, her head and heart were pounding. But a quick bite of breakfast and a short visit to the orchid house made her relax a bit. Maybe her meeting with Krabb was more than she thought, but she threw that thought out as she got into the car and made her way to Belle Meade.

"Great to see you again, Fiona. Would you like some coffee?"

Krabb looked different than the first time she saw him.

"No, thanks. Thank you for seeing me today. I hope I am not ruining your weekend, Doc."

"No, I have some papers to write today. Seeing will help me in that endeavor. I don't usually see patients on the weekend."

Fiona smiled. Krabb was writing about her. She wondered if he knew what was going on in her mind.

"Thanks again, Doc. Seeing you today will help me more than you know."

"Yes, of course. Now what can I do for you. More or different dreams, I suspect?"

Fiona described her dream experiences, and Krabb sat and listened without moving. He stared at her and didn't change his facial expression. When she finished her story, Krabb reach for his pen and made a couple of notes.

"Interesting story, Fiona. Again, I'm flattered that you included me in your dream, but I'm not surprised. I knew we had some sort of connection after our first meeting, but in my mind, I couldn't place where."

"Please tell me why I'm having these dreams. I know I'm missing something."

Yes, of course you are. Let me explain. The dream world has its own structure. You can call it a molecular structure that takes up no space as you know it. Our dreams consist of dimensions that expand and contract. Those dimensions are related to ideals that have no familiar structure. Your intuition has more freedom in this structure. Your actions are more fluid. Images appear and disappear freely because value fulfillment has greater control. Molecules move around without restrictions. In other words, there are no patterns to follow."

Fiona looked around the office. She noticed the original artwork on all the walls. She recognized a couple of the artists. Plus, there were more orchids than she remembered on her last visit.

"Do you mean I act like an orchid in dreams? You know, do I drop all the ego related stuff in dreams?"

"Well, in a way. Let me say your psychic and mental structures do exist in your dream world, but those structures are not dependent on matter. The motion of your molecules is more spontaneous. In that regard, you might say you are like an orchid."

"What about meeting all these people in the bar? I know them differently here." And why are they black? Why do they look and talk differently? Why do I still know who they are and what they feel?"

Krabb smiled.

"It is interesting isn't it? First, let me say that dreams are a byproduct of the relationship between your physical being and inner self. Dreams are not reflections but byproducts of chemical reactions and a transformation of energy from one reality to another. The dream world is necessary for the existence of the physical being. Now, there are levels within the dream world. Science has identified one or two of these levels, but there are more. The rapid eye movement your experience in one level is not the level you are connecting with. You are connecting with a deeper level in your consciousness. Other elements of your soul are interacting with you in some fashion in this level.

"Do you mean my soul is in parts somewhere in some reality? It's not whole and unique to me?"

"Indeed. The soul is a multidimensional infinite act. This act of creativeness brings the slightest probability into actuality. The soul is a creative act, and it creates for itself infinite dimensions and aspects of consciousness in order to experience value fulfillment."

Fiona was following Krabb's thoughts, but she was struggling to keep up.

"So let me jump ahead a little. Is this soulmate thing real then? I read we all have soulmates. That means I have a soulmate, and you're it, right? Is that what you're saying? Or are you saying we are soulmates in the 1940s, and we chose not to be in this time period?"

"No, not necessarily. All of us have connections that exist in other time frames. I call them focuses or counterparts. The soul makes sure it experiences physical reality in an assortment of manifestations. We could be male in one time period, female in another, or transgender in yet another. Remember, consciousness of which we are a part and a whole of is essentially one. But we choose what time frame we want to experience, how we want to experience it, and then we begin to focus in that particular reality. When we make that choice, we forget the oneness from which we came."

"So let me think. Jayla, who is living in the 1940s, is part of my soul, and she chooses to live in the 1940s as a black woman. She is not me, but she is another part of me?"

"In a sense, yes. Here's what we do: We, as aspects of our soul, experience actions as we move along a single line of what we call time. Each dot in the line represents a moment in time. But at any of these points, your actions move out in all directions. Your actions, which contain your energy, form an imaginary circle with a particular point being its apex. In dreams, you are not traveling from that single point you call a moment. You are delving into the moment. You, Fiona, are feeling another part of your whole soul. Each part of your whole soul is an individual experiencing value fulfillment at a particular point in what we call moments in time. Remember, time is the duration of objects."

Fiona scrunched her face. She wasn't sure what Krabb meant.

"So you are saying I'm living the actions of another me in these points in my dreams?"

"Let me use a mountain as an example. Mountains, as you know, are composed of many layers of rocks that serve as its foundation. Let's say the top of the mountain is you now, and the rocks below it represent the past. The mountain is not any layer of the rocks below the top, but there is a relationship between the mountain and the rock layers. The mountains and all its rock layers exist at once in your mind, but if you examine each layer, you notice the sediment that was formed in the rocks. That sediment is from another time period. Of course, the rocks still exist or the mountain wouldn't have a foundation. You, Fiona, are experiencing one layer of rocks in your foundation."

"No, wait. What? Really? Are you saying I'm seeing a past version of myself, and she is black? In fact, all the people I know or have been close to me are black?"

"Like a mountain, you have a history of the past and you also have a history of the future. But let's just talk about the past for a moment. You are not the past self you see in your dreams, but she is a part of the history of your being. All of your selves exist in their own time and space. That's why I call them focuses. They exist simultaneously with your life; just like the rock layers live simultaneously with the mountain. In your dreams, you have tapped into that other layer of reality where these people experience life. And remember one thing. What happens at the top of the mountain affects the rocks below, so you have an impact of these other forms of your soul, and they influence your life too. There is constant interaction between you and the people you come in contact with. That interaction also happens while you dream."

"That's some crazy shit, Doc. How is that possible? I thought the soul was inclusive. You're saying my soul is divided between at least one other person, and if that's right, then there are more focuses of me around. Right?"

"Yes, Fiona. Please understand we are stepping on the toes of religion when we talk about things like this, so they are hard to believe. Although religion serves a purpose, it has brainwashed us in several ways. But we are in another mode of knowing now. We know your dreams bleed into your conscious life, but they also bleed into other probabilities. Each individual portion of your soul seeks new possibilities of development and many new dimensions of actuality in order to feel value fulfillment in different ways. Your greater personhood, which is actualized from the creativity of your soul, exists before you do, and it gives birth to a lot of . . . let's call them, 'psychic children' that become physical entities. Those psychic entities become physical at different points in time. Your attention can be shifted from any physical moment to any probable moment by what's known as a parallel thrust. Your ego has a lot to do with your feeling totally separate, but in dreams, the ego is not totally present.

"I waited to answer your question about the ego so you see why it doesn't enter your dream world. You are shifting to another dimension and feeling what one of the psychic children or entities of your greater personhood is feeling without actually looking like yourself. You are, in those dreams, the Jayla entity you mentioned, and I am Myles. Your sister is Amber, and Shorty is Flip. Jake the bartender is your brother Geoff, but we are also more than that, just like the mountain analogy. But remember this: Each individual is experiencing what you are experiencing in a different way. The relationships you see are soul arrangements so certain issues can be addressed. The reward for that interaction is expanded awareness of the individual, the soul, and all consciousness."

Fiona felt overloaded by Krabb's knowledge.

"Does that mean Geoff is dead now, since he was killed in my dream?"

"Not necessarily. But that's not to say he's alive in this life either. Geoff is still making his own choices somewhere. Those choices are not all Jake's choices."

"So does that mean you are not romantically interested in me, even though Myles is very romantically interested in Jayla?"

Krabb laughed and moved around in his chair for the first time. He looked at the clock on his desk. They had another 15 minutes left.

"Well, our relationship is different here. Right, Fiona?"

Fiona looked out the window. She wasn't sure what she felt about Krabb. She stood and looked at the man she linked to Myles.

"I don't know what I feel right now. My head is spinning. I guess the big question is how do you feel?"

Krabb looked at her. He felt his eyes move from side to side as he thought about her question.

"I guess all friendships have a bit of romance in them, Fiona."

"That's a cop-out, Doc, but I'll take that as a yes."

Krabb stood up.

"Why don't we talk about all of that next time, shall we? You're going to have more experiences in the Black Orchid Bar, and I want to hear about them."

"Well you can pled the fifth today, but I'm coming back and asking again," Fiona said. "To me, there's a difference between friendship and romance. And I'm still not sure what you just said about me and Jayla and the others. How is all that possible? Why am I learning about her for the first time, now?"

Krabb walked her to the door.

"Fiona, we are what we believe in this reality. We are taught not to believe in dreams or in reincarnation or anything that goes against our religion, whatever that may be. What I am describing is not reincarnation. It is the incarnate action of the soul. We'll talk about all this again. It is exciting and a little confusing, but it's real. See you next time."

Fiona's mind raced as she drove home. She didn't know why she'd asked Krabb the question about being romantically interested in her.

"Geoff is dead. I know he is, and why do I think I have a romantic interest in Krabb now? Is that where this therapy session is heading? Krabb isn't my type, but there is something about him. Maybe it's his brain, or maybe it's Jayla telling me she wants me to kindle a romance with Krabb."

Fiona went directly to her computer when she got home. The first message she read was from Sarah confirming what she already knew. Geoff was dead.

Fiona quickly answered.

"We must talk about this, Sarah, sooner than later, please."

Chapter 16

**And only the enlightened can recall their
former lives; for the rest of us, the memories of
past existences are but glints of light, twinges of
longing, passing shadows, disturbingly familiar,
that are gone before they can be grasped, like
the passage of that silver bird on Dhaulagiri.**

Peter Matthiessen

Jayla walked into the Black Orchid bar with Myles around
11 p.m. They both had a weird attraction to the place. The
lights were dim; smoke, as usual, hung in the air. It was
Sunday, and the jukebox lit-up as Billie Holiday's Fine and
Mellow filled the room. The bar was almost empty, and
Shorty was nowhere in sight. Five men sat at the table near
the rear door playing Mississippi poker, and the tall, dark-
skinned woman with the curly blonde wig who was at the
end of the bar the last time was tending bar. The five men
at the table were some of the same men who sat at the bar
last time. There wore the same clothes, but they all were
drinking beer with shot chasers this time.

"What's up, y'all? What you drinkin' tonight? The wigged
woman asked. Jayla smiled.

The woman behind the bar didn't give them a chance to sit
down. Myles pulled the bar stool out for Jayla and stood
behind her with his hands on her shoulders.

"Give us two Scotch and sodas, light on the soda."

Jayla watched as the woman, who looked like a mixture of different races, quickly poured their drinks.

"Aren't you Shorty's wife?" Jayla couldn't resist asking the intriguing bartender. She wanted to get to know this tall beauty. She certainly didn't fit the type Jayla thought would be with foul-mouthed Shorty.

"Yep. That yardbird Shorty Longsleeves and me have been together about a year. Can't say why I'm with that loser, though. Guess it's cause I like my baubles, you know what I mean? He's a no-good drunk and a liar, plus he likes to play with all these bitches round here. He don't think I know, but shit, I'm all over it. He ain't foolin' me, baby. I'm fixin' to leave his ass anyway. I have bigger plans, and Shorty's not in them."

Jayla smiled. She knew guys like Shorty. Jayla looked at Myles as he took his first swig of Scotch.

"So is your last name is Longsleeves?"

"Hell no, Sistah! I'm a Treegap. Holly Treegap. Mama was sort of a house slave, and daddy was Cherokee. He rescued her from some son-of-a-bitch who lived in Columbia, Tennessee, when she was 16.

"You must have some life story. I thought my life was something, but bet you have me beat, Holly. Can I call you Holly?"

Holly nodded. "You bet, baby."

Myles turned around and looked at the table in the corner. He bent over and whispered in Jayla's ear, "Let's go over there and chill, baby." He pointed to the empty table as she turned her head. It was right next to the card players.

"I want to ask Holly one more question. I don't know why I'm interested, but I am."

She turned and looked at Holly. "What happened to Jake? I know he's dead, but how?"

"Lord, child. Well, rumor has it Jake was screwing a young girl he met here. He was no good. Always in trouble. Always trying to play girls, but he was a good bartender. His wife, Amber, knew about his flings and hated him for them even though she was sleeping with Tyrone. It's a real sex circus 'round here. Jake didn't care that his wife was cheating because he said the young girl was better in bed. He didn't even hide it from nobody. He was giving the girl money, and that pissed off Amber. I heard Tyrone tell Shorty that Amber threatened to kill Jake because he told her he was leaving her for the girl. I think her name was Tonya or something, but she had enough of Jake's flaming temper and threatened to cut him off too. Lord have mercy! He was a crazy, man. Tyrone said Tonya stabbed Jake one night while he was sleeping at her place. He said Tonya had some nasty friends, and they made Jake's body disappear until the cops found it in the river."

"Did Tonya work here? Is Amber okay?"

"Tonya worked here for a while. That Amber Black will always be okay. She knows how to play the game." Myles jumped into the conversation.

"Isn't Jake married to your sister, Jay?"

Jayla frowned.

"I think that Scotch got to you, Myles. You mean Tyrone, not Jake, right?"

Myles and Jayla moved after that comment. They stood behind the men at the table instead of sitting in a booth. The five men were talking about the war. The guy with the high-pitched voice sitting on the first stool was talking. His black fedora was hanging on the back of his chair.

"Damn. This war talk got me thinkin'. Do y'all think the man is going to come after us? Hell, I'm damn near 24. I'm a lover, y'all know that. I don't want to kill nobody."

The large man sitting next to him was still wearing his Homburg with the black Petersham ribbon. The hat sat on the back of his head, and his accentuated forehead stuck out over the table.

"Shit, man. They're gonna call you, Sly. They don't care how old you are. They want Negro folks up there on the front line, even though they don't want us fighting next to them. They're scared, but putting us in the line of fire is the easy way to get rid of us and save their own asses. You hear me? Bet the first one to go is my 18-year-old brother. They'll get the one youngest ones first. I'm almost 25. I know I'll go too, but I'll go after the young kids. Now y'all don't get me wrong. I love my country, but my country don't love me."

Sly Gallo shook his head.

"I hear that, Cave."

Reginald "Cave" Jackson was Sly's best friend. They grew up together in east Nashville. They dated sisters. Neither had ever been in trouble. They went to church every

Sunday at the Eastside Baptist Church, and they sang in the choir.

"But Cave, remember we know how to fight for right. We all need to do the right thing about all of this. Maybe if we do, this racial bullshit will stop. This country got to wake up. This color thing got to stop. Maybe if we fight with these white church-going, two-faced brothers of ours, they will see that we are just like them. We just another version of them. The chocolate kind, you know. Everybody likes chocolate, right?"

The guy with the brown Porkpie hat and dark yellow complexion sitting next to him had a frown on his face.

"You two are jumping the gun. Hell, we don't need to get into something that is none of our business. That's white folks' business. They want war. That's all they know. They been fighting us for years cause we different. Y'all know that."

Cave smiled as he looked into Rocco's eyes. "You ain't been readin' the paper, Rocco. It's our business according to those Washington people. They been sending supplies over there, and they are going to send us once they figure out they can. Don't you remember Roosevelt's talk back in '37? This is his way to get us out of this damn depression."

The thin man with the pencil moustache and eyelids that never seemed to close had his hand on his chips and was sliding them from side to side. His white shirt cuffs were rolled up, and his bowtie dangled from his neck like a limp piece of bacon.

"Now wait a minute, boys. Y'all know we gotta do what we have to do for this country. I know y'all think we been dealt a messed-up hand being colored and all, but it ain't so bad. Look at those Jews, brothers. That prick is oven-roasting them, and we gotta help stop that. They may not be the same color as us, but they sure are part of us, and that no-good Kraut is coming after us next. I think we need to see this fight for what it is. We all could be in an oven someday if we don't stop this kind of shit."

He picked up his cigar and put it in his mouth. Sly and Cave looked at him, then looked at their cards. Sly looked up.

"I know, you're right, Murdock, but that don't make it any easier. I don't want to fight, and I don't want my brother over their either. That's all I'm sayin'."

Murdock Calvin nodded his head and then turned to the young guy who looked part black and part Arab. His thick black moustache was twisted at the ends. "What you think bout all this, Nigma? You got any kin in this fight yet?" That name of yours, Nigma… isn't that a French or Dutch name or something?"

"No, no. Nigma is a Hindu name. My father is from Pakistan and mom is African. They live in England."

Cave threw six chips into the pot in the center of the table.

"Me and my big dick call your bet, Murdock, and I raise two bits."

"What do your parents say 'bout this war, Nigma?" Cave asked.

"I got a letter from Mom six months ago. Her words are still fresh in my mind: 'Evil in the world is hard to ignore. We create it and then try to run away from it. Everyone has to accept what they create. There is no justice in ignorance. No faith in avoidance. We reap what we sow, and for some of us, the fruit from our harvest is the blood of our brothers. Tolerance has no home in hypocrisy."

The table was silent.

"Damn, Myles. I thought these jokers were just young guys drinking and having fun, but I was wrong," Jayla said. "I like these boys. They may be young and broke, but they have character."

Myles looked at her, and then tapped Nigma on the shoulder.

"I like what your mama said, man. I don't want to fight at my age either, but I don't see we have a choice. The man is gonna put us in the line of fire so they can get this country back in step with the times. They gonna use our color, once they figure out how they can without pissing off the bigots who want to kill us. That some screwed up shit, ain't it?"

The men around the table looked at Myles.

"I heard that." Sly was the first to acknowledge Myles. Cave nodded. "I know you're right, cat." "Not much we can do, but wait," Murdock added.

Myles took another sip from his half-full glass and shook his head.

"Well, I guess the big question is: Is the fucking worth the fucking?"

The table broke up in laughter.

"Yeah, I hear that." Murdock wanted to say something before Sly. "Guess we have to look at it that way. We can agree to fight or be put in the slammer. Either way, we gonna die of something. Guess fucking is a better way to go. What you think, Cave?"

"You got it. Guess will all want to go out, but not like Jake did. That's all I gotta say."

The table rumbled with "Yeah" all around.

Jayla stood in shock. She was experiencing the fear and the folly of war first hand. She quickly downed her drink and pulled on Myles's arm.

"Let's get out of her. All this war talk makes me want to puke. I want to help people. That's why I became a nurse."

"I know. Let's go to my place. We can help each other, right?"

Jayla smiled and gently tapped him on the face as they started walking toward the door. They dropped their glasses on the bar as they passed it. Holly looked at them and smiled.

"Goodness gracious. At least I know two people who can be in love without fighting. I reckon there's hope after all. It's too late for me, and I hate that."

Jayla stopped and grabbed Holly's hand as she picked up the glasses.

"It's never too late, Holly. There's always somebody out there to love. You just need to open your eyes and your heart."

"Good lord, child. You forgot something, girl. Someone needs to kill Shorty first!"

Jayla put her hand over her mouth and laughed.

"I think Shorty will help you with that."

Fiona's eyes opened, and she suddenly sat straight up in bed. She quickly pulled her T-shirt off. The bathroom lights made her squint, but she found her toothbrush. Her mind started to replay her latest dream. This segment revealed more secrets. She spit out the toothpaste and looked in the mirror.

"This is crazy!" she thought. "All those people are people I know! Sly is my high school boyfriend, Matt. I think Sly is gay too. Rocco is my first love, Jude Pringle. I could tell by the cologne he wore. It wasn't the same, but it was close. Murdock is Max Westwood. He's got that thrill-seeker frame of mind. I could tell by his lack of fear. Cave is Jesse Alterman – a big guy with the same hairstyle. One of the men said he had a big dick, and so did Jesse. And I really believe Ali Nigma is my father. They have the same mannerisms in a strange way. I must tell Krabb about all these men! My whole life is playing out in a different time and with different faces, but I know them all. It's not just those little things that make me think that way. I feel them inside of me somehow. They are familiar. I wonder if they feel the same way about me."

Chapter 17

All who live possess eternal life, and few would trade it for an immortal body, if they truly understood what it is to be alive.

Audrey Auden

Krabb was in another world when his intercom buzzed. He ignored the first annoying sound and kept reading Dr. Stanislav Grof's interview with the Institute of Noetic Sciences. Grof was one of his friends. Krabb tried to read everything Grof published. Grof's answer to a question about past life experiences really piqued his interest.

"Also some things that I have observed in my clients — past life experiences that could be verified, or out-of-body perceptions which were veridical — in other words, people experienced astral projection to other places and the accuracy of that perception could be verified. So the common denominator of all those stories is that they describe events that should not have happened if the universe were the way it's described by materialistic science. Those things would be, in principle, considered impossible."

The buzzer sounded again as he finished reading that paragraph. He picked up the phone.

"Yes?"

"Fiona's here, Doctor."

Fiona's salt-and-pepper hair was pulled in a tight knot, and her face glowed from the sunlight coming into the room from behind Krabb's desk. Her long, white cotton dress and white wedge sandals also caught Krabb's attention as she sat in front of his desk.

"Hello Fiona. How are you?"

Fiona smiled

"You know we had sex last night don't you?"

Krabb had a big smile on his face.

"Ah, forgive me. No I don't recall that. Must be a sign of my age, I guess. Are you sure? I know I would remember something like that."

Krabb chuckled.

"You're talking about another one of your dreams, aren't you?"

Fiona looked around the room and realized his office was filled with antiques. She recognized a couple of pieces from the 1940s. She saw similar items in her dream.

Fiona nodded and sat down.

"Right. Another dream. By the way, your office is filled with furniture from the 1940s.

"Oh, yes. I've been collecting antiques for several years. I'm not sure why I like the 1940s, but I think you're about to tell me."

186

Krabb subtly twitched when he noticed Fiona's facial expression "We are a dating couple in my dreams, Doc. Not only that, my sister committed suicide in this dream. Plus, all my former boyfriends are there talking about World War II. What the hell? Am I losing my mind?"

Krabb sat back in his chair.

"Well, let's recap this dream world before we go on. First, how do you know these people are people you know? They look different, so how can you know?"

Krabb knew his answer, but he wanted to know her answer.

"Well, I didn't at first. When my mind adjusted itself in this dream, I felt their relationship with me. I felt the same emotional bond I felt when they are who they are here, plus there were other signs like familiar scents and body gestures. Do you understand?"

Krabb nodded.

"You mean you recognized their energy. You felt an energy exchange that was similar to the exchange you have with them here."

"Yes. That's it. They are familiar in the same way here."

"Right. I understand. Now let me recap our last meeting."

Fiona listened as Krabb told her what she had told him on past visits. He was very precise. Her past as well as her dream world was front and center once again. She nodded as Krabb gave her his version of some of her dream events.

"Now wait, Doc Are you saying that my sister in these dreams is actually my mother in this lifetime?"

"Yes, it appears that way. Laquisha is Olivia. Not only that, but all the men at the poker table are men you know in this lifetime. Your feeling about them is accurate."

"How is that possible, Doc? Any how is it possible that you and I are lovers?"

"I know it sounds crazy when you think in material terms. You can't live in two time periods at once, or at least science tells us we can't, but I think, and other therapists do too, that we do live simultaneous lives. Here's why:"

"I think I mentioned that your dream world is as organized as your own. What you're able to do is tap into other particles of your consciousness that exist in other levels or planes of reality. These people are living in the 1940s, but the 1940s is happening simultaneously with this time period.

"How can that happen? That's crazy."

"Well, I told you about the soul last time, and it was somewhat confusing, I know. Let me try again. Maybe this time it will be clearer.

"When your inner self or soul enters this three-dimensional life from another reality, the energy waves that propel it break into a number of conscious particles. These particles spread out and form individual lives or focuses. Quantum physics tells us that's true. Some doctors call these conscious particles reincarnational lives, but they are really simultaneous lives. So you have counterparts of you — we all do, by the way, living at different points in time and in a different place. I call them different planes or levels of reality. In your dream, the city is the same, but the year is different. Your consciousness, without your ego, is able to cross into this plane and experience that particular reality in dreams. Others do it while meditating."

"Okay, but why are these other people there with me? Shouldn't different people be there?"

"Most of the people you know now play a role in other lifetimes as well. It's a psychic choice to share a particular reality, or more than one, with what I'm calling conscious particles or counterparts. You might say you made a spiritual or soulful agreement with them. These people have a psychic relationship with you in one-way or another. That relationship is all about learning lessons and value fulfillment. Each person in your dream is acting out a life in order to expand their own awareness and yours as well. They are learning lessons from their relationships."

"Yeah, but I just met you in this lifetime. We are in our mid-20s in this dream lifetime."

"Our soul expands and experiences lessons in different ways. All the people you made a psychic deal with don't come into your life at the same point in time every time. They appear when you're ready, and they are ready to learn from the experiences you have with them. We wanted to share the beauty of a love back then, and all the men in your life then played a role that supported other lessons you needed to learn. Their role, per your agreement, was expanded in this life. My role as your lover then has expanded to that of a teacher now."

Fiona listened with a frown.

"So what am I to you now?"

"Well, you are a teacher too. Not everyone has tapped into the area of dream consciousness where we can feel and see other agreements being played out in other realities like you do. There's no doubt you have more counterparts living at other times, and so do I, but this particular time period, the 1940s, is special to us for some reason."

"So is Jayla really me, or is she just a part of me? And what about the other people I interact with in these dreams?"

"As I mentioned before, some of our soulmates are the people we have made some sort of soul agreement with. You can look at Jayla as a soulmate. She is part of your soul, but she has her own identity and individuality. The same thing is true for all the other characters, but they may not be part of your soul, which is creative action. There are other creative actions or souls, so not all of them are soulmates, but they are connected to you through your soul agreement. You might call them observing energies. This psychic bond is formed at the soul level in a reality that we know but are not able to access because our focus is usually on this reality. But you have the ability to focus on more than one, thanks to your lucid dreaming. Most people interact with these counterparts in dreams, but they forget they do. I'm trying to connect to mine in dreams, but I'm not as proficient as you are."

"So if all that is true, it doesn't mean that you and I will end up as lovers in this lifetime?"

Krabb started to laugh, and the twitch was back.

"Forgive me, Fiona I don't mean to laugh, but it is kind of funny that we are connecting in this fashion now.

Fiona laughed.

"I know, Doc. We have lot in common."

190

Krabb grabbed a piece of paper and pen and made a note.

"No, but let's focus on you. We still have a little time."

"Right. One last question today. Why did my sister commit suicide, and if she is part of my mother, why did mum do the same thing? I thought they were learning, just like me? The same goes for my brother, although I can see why he didn't learn, I think."

"Your mother and your sister in your dreams haven't learned the lessons they came to learn. Fear or some other emotional situation keeps them from getting out of a particular life by means other than suicide. Committing suicide is a fear-related action in most cases. But other people kill themselves for the experience. It is a strange form of value fulfillment. The same is true for your brother. People like him are stuck in the middle of a psychic black hole, but they will pull out of it in another lifetime once they face the fear they avoid. By psychic, I mean an innate quest to repeat lifetime choices."

"One more thing. Why is everyone black in this dream?"

"Our counterparts choose skin color, time periods and the place to experience them. We are all more than one race, live in more than one time, and we all have lived in different parts of the world. I know that goes against popular religious teachings, but I'm afraid those teachings are not completely factual. Most of the religious dogmas we are taught have been altered for control purposes. We have chosen to live in this particular time in order to feel the anguish caused by these distorted facts and controlling tactics."

"So the people living during World War II chose that time to experience the war?"

"Yes, absolutely. Most of the world found out how devastating a world war could be from that time period. But some individuals still feel the thrill of war. They believe war is the only way to survive. Some scientists say this belief stems from birth. Birth is an aggressive act, and that aggression continues for some people throughout a particular time period. Other people just like to be aggressive. It is their learning tool."

"Thanks, Doc. That's more information than I can absorb. I'm coming back next week. I want to tell you what happens with us when I go back to the 1940s."

"Yes, please do."

Krabb walked around the desk and held out his hand.

"Don't worry Fiona. I'm here to help."

"I know, and I'm here to help you."

Krabb smiled and nodded his head. The urge to give Fiona a friendly peck on the cheek surprised him. He believed he would never do something like that.

As Fiona walked out of the office, Krabb went back to his 1940s walnut desk. He didn't know what to think of the session, so he opened a book called *The Unknown Reality*, which was part of a stack on his desk. The first paragraph he read hit home.

"Every person is involved in the art of living. That art can't be confined to one definition. People who commit suicides may have a great lust for life. They put themselves in suicidal mode to feel the life experience in an unusual way.

The risk of dying gives them an intensified version of life in a strange way."

Krabb thought about Fiona's mother. Perhaps fear wasn't the catalyst for her suicide. Maybe she was a genuine risk-taker who knew her life never ended. Her suicide, as well as Laquisha's death, was her way of testing what she believed to be true about death. If that is the case, then Fiona may be susceptible to risk-taking too. She might be a suicide candidate as well. Krabb made more notes before her continued reading. He was emotionally involved in this case. Fiona made him aware of one of his other lives, and that was an exceptional bit of information. The big question he had was why that particular time period was front and center in her dreams and in his current reality. There were other time periods and identities to explore, but this one stood out in her mind. He quickly did a Google search about WWII. The first search title perked his interest.

"Whether or not FDR knew about the Japanese plan to attack Pearl Harbor actually misses the larger and more important issue, which is the fact that the Japanese were provoked into attacking America at Pearl Harbor. The majority of Americans, and even servicemen, were unaware of what was going on behind the scenes, but not all were. FDR had been charged in public with agitating for war since 1939. FDR had to push the Japanese into attacking the United States because the overwhelming majority of Americans opposed getting involved in the war, and Japan itself had no intentions of attacking the United States. Its interest was Asia. Without FDR's antagonisms toward the Japanese, Congress and the American people never would have allowed FDR to declare war on Japan or Germany. FDR knew this, and he also knew how important

it really was that America join in the war against fascism and imperialism."

But Krabb didn't think that was the point of Fiona's interest in the 1940s and the war. Maybe the African-American issue was the real reason. He did another Google search. An article written in 1941 for the Louisville Courier Journal by David H. Bradford confirmed his thoughts.

"The treatment that the Negro soldier has received has been resented not only by the Negro soldier, but by the Negro civilian population as well. In fact, any straight-thinking person with a sense of justice and right, without any respect to color or race, must realize the dangers inherent in the evil practices that have been permitted to exist in the Army. It is not a pleasant thought for Negroes to ponder that their tax money is being spent to help maintain an army that has little regard for the real principles of democracy."

He quickly found another article online and was fascinated by the African-American connection.

International events replaced the Great Depression as the defining force in the lives of African Americans. In preparing for and fighting World War II, America finally emerged from the Depression and laid the basis for an era of unprecedented prosperity. Industrial and military mobilization resulted in the movement of millions of people, many of them African Americans, from agricultural areas into the cities. This population shift substantially increased black voting strength in the North and West, which — combined with a moral recoil from the savage racial policies of the Nazis — drove the issue of black equality to the forefront of national politics. Moreover, hundreds of thousands of black men and women learned new skills and ideas while serving in the armed forces, and many resolved to claim their rights. Events abroad and in the United States during the 1940s heightened black consciousness and led to a more aggressive militancy among local leaders and black citizens in southern states.

Before the war broke out, the government-funded training programs regularly rejected black applicants, often reasoning that training them would be pointless given their poor prospects of finding skilled work. The United States Employment Service (USES) filled "whites-only" requests for defense workers. The military itself made it clear that although it would accept black men in their proportion to the population, about 11 percent at the time, it would put them in segregated units and assign them to service duties. The navy limited black servicemen to menial positions. The Marine Corps and the Army Air Corps refused to accept them altogether. When a young African-American man wrote the Pittsburgh Courier and suggested a "Double V" campaign— victory over fascism abroad and victory over racism at home—the newspaper adopted his words as the battle cry for the entire race. Fighting this struggle in a nation at war would be difficult, but the effort led to the further development of black organizations and transformed the world view of many African-American soldiers and civilians. Embodying the spirit of the "Double V" campaign, African-American protest groups and newspapers criticized discrimination in the defense program. Two months before the 1940 presidential election, the NAACP, the Urban League, and other groups pressed President Roosevelt to act. The president listened to their protests, but aside from a few token gesture he responded with little of substance. A. Philip Randolph, who was president of the Brotherhood of Sleeping Car Porters called on black people to unify their protests and direct them at the national government. He suggested that 10,000 African Americans march on Washington under the slogan "We loyal Negro-American citizens demand the right to work and fight for our country." Many African Americans who had never taken part in the activities of middle-class-dominated groups like the NAACP responded to Randolph's appeal. Soon he alarmed the president by raising the number expected to march to 50,000. Roosevelt, fearing the protest would undermine America's democratic rhetoric and provide grist for the German propaganda mills, dispatched First Lady Eleanor Roosevelt and New York City Mayor Fiorello La Guardia to dissuade Randolph from marching. Their pleas for patience fell on deaf ears, compelling Roosevelt and his top military officials to meet with Randolph and other black leaders. The president offered a set of superficial changes, but the African Americans stood firm in their demands and raised the stakes by increasing their estimate of the number of black marchers coming to Washington to 100,000. By the end of June 1941, the president capitulated and had his aides draft Executive Order 8802, prompting Randolph to call off the march. It was a grand moment.

On the surface at least, the president's Executive Order 8802 marked a significant change in the government's stance. It stated in part,

I do hereby affirm the policy of the United States that there shall be no discrimination in the employment of workers in the defense industry or government because of race, creed, color, or national origin. The order instructed all agencies that trained workers to administer such programs without discrimination. To ensure full cooperation with these guidelines, Roosevelt created the Fair Employment Practices Committee (FEPC) with the power to investigate complaints of discrimination. The order said nothing about desegregation of the military, but private assurances were made that the barriers to entry in key services would be lowered.

Krabb started to write a mental note. The complete disregard and underhanded verbal and physical torture of blacks in America was a nationwide topic thanks to the war. Fiona was picking up the energy from this particular time now, but he wasn't sure what part the orchids played in this awakening. As he walked to the door, a thought hit him. The orchids represent unity, equality and beauty, and the 1940s was the time when Americans started to see they were not isolated from the rest of the world. The 1940s and the Second World War mirrored the folly of unjust treatment, one-sided equality, and a distorted view of human beauty. Even though the Civil War brought an end to slavery, blacks were still second-class Americans in the eyes of the government and in the minds of a lot of citizens well into the 20th century. The war intensified the notion that white America said one thing and did another. Black people were feared because they were different, not because of any lack of mental or physical capabilities to perform at the same or higher standards than their white neighbors

Krabb pulled out his phone and dialed Fiona's number. He left a message when her voice mail answered. *"Hi Fiona, This is Gabriel Krabb. We made progress today. I'd like to see you same time next week. I have some answers, and I know you have more questions. Call if you can't make it. Thanks, and see you then."*

Fiona listened to Krabb's message as she sat on her porch. He was pulling closer to her, and she knew why. He believed her. At this point, she knew she had to look through Jayla's eyes again to keep the information flowing between her two worlds. She was, in part, Jayla now, and because she was, she would never be the same Fiona.

Chapter 18

As a man, casting off worn out garments taketh new ones, so the dweller in the body, entereth into ones that are new.

Epictetus

"So Chance, you've been here almost six days, and you still haven't told me about your girlfriend. Do you still love her?"

Sarah thought Chance settled into Middle Tennessee like a bed bug on an old mattress. She let him stay in her small guest room, but she was getting tired of his lackadaisical attempt to find a place to live. Sarah wasn't particularly attracted to Chance, but that didn't stop her from being cautiously friendly. Sarah was standing at the kitchen window with a mug of coffee in her hand one morning, and Chance was sitting at the kitchen table in a white T-shirt and old jeans. His graying hair stood straight up, and his bare feet were stretch over one of the kitchen chairs.

"Nah, I never loved her. We had a working relationship. I guess you could call it that."

"Did she work in the same office?"

"Nah, she worked on the strip. Did your sister reply to your email?"

Chance wanted to change the subject. He knew he would have to lie his way through a conversation about Bitsy.

"Yes, I thought I told you, Chance. She wants to talk about Geoff. Maybe you should meet her and tell her about him. I really don't know enough to explain it on my own. It's so bloody annoying that I had to find out about it from my sister and, of course, you. Now, what about you and your girl? You didn't finish."

Chance pushed away from the table. His mind was in overdrive. How could he explain that relationship to a woman who had no idea what that kind of life entailed?

"Well, first let me say that your brother was trying to tell me about his situation. Why else would he have given me your number? I think he was too sick to call you."

"Yes. I think I see that now. He was ill wasn't he? Anyway how did you meet your girlfriend?"

"I met her on a business trip to Vegas. I was living in LA and selling real estate at the time. Bitsy was working for a business associate, and we hit it off as soon as we saw each other. The rest, I guess is history. We were together for three years. She fell in love with another guy with more money, so I was odd man out."

Sarah knew he was leaving out details, but it really didn't matter to her. She was taking her mind off of meeting Fiona.

"You must have had some money too. The real estate business in California pays well, I suspect."

"Yeah, I did make money for a while. Then the bottom fell out, and I was caught with too many loans and not enough cash to pay them all."

"So sorry to hear that, Chance. Did you sell homes in Las Vegas?"

"Yes, but that market was worse than California, so I had to find another source of income."

"What was that?"

"Drugs"

Sarah's mouth dropped open. She looked him in the eyes and knew he was being truthful. She suspected he used drugs, but selling them was another thing to her. She realized she was giving a drug dealer a place to stay, and that sent a bolt of fear up her spine.

"Oh my. Was Geoff buying drugs from you?"

Chance had intentionally trapped himself. He was sick of lying to this woman. He was sick of playing Mr. Nice Guy.

"Yeah, Geoff was doing a lot of drugs."

Sarah looked at the river and set her coffee down.

"So, let me think for a sec."

Sarah started to put the puzzle together in her mind. The story about the police finding Geoff in the street wasn't how it really happened. She had a feeling Geoff died doing drugs, and Chance was there to watch it.

"Wait! I think I've got it. You sold Geoff drugs, and he killed himself using them. Is that more like it, Chance?"

Chance didn't have much credibility to lose, but he didn't want to lose more with her, so he lied once again. He felt a little guilty when it came to the death of the old English dude, so he decide to transfer that guilt.

"No, not quite. He was high when he died, but he got the drugs from a guy on Freemont Street. That guy, Yam Kern, has a reputation for selling crack with an extra kick in it. He was the guy all the street junkies got their fix from. Geoff didn't have the money to buy my coke, so he bought a hit from Yam Kern. I think he's the guy that really killed him."

Sarah was lost when it came to the drug world. She didn't want anything to do with it.

"Why not tell me all this when we met at Denny's, Chance?"

"I didn't want to implicate anyone that night. Yam's a nasty guy with a wide reach. He's a dangerous dude, and I didn't want you to get hurt. Kern is crazy and doesn't like women."

Chance started to believe his lie. Yam Kern didn't exist, but the lie sounded so good that his guilt seemed to disappear as he watched Sarah's reaction.

"I must say I'm not happy. I would have never brought you home from Denny's if I knew you sold drugs. Taking drugs every now and then to ease some sort of pain is different to me. I'm not a drug lover, even though I have used prescription drugs to get through some rough times."

He knew that was a lie, but he didn't answer. Chance saw her drug bottles in the bathroom cabinet. He just nodded his head as he stood up.

"All right. Let's stop all this drug talk for now. I'm going to email my sister, and I think this would be a good time for you to start looking for another place to live. Nothing personal. I just want to live alone."

Chance shook his head. He knew it was just a matter of time before she would kick him out.

"Oh, right. I will. Tell your sister I will meet her if she wants to talk about Geoff."

"I will. Thanks, Chance."

Sarah went to her bedroom and started her Dell computer.

"Hello, Fee. I would like to meet so we can discuss Geoff's death. A friend of his is here with me now and offered to meet you. Would you like to meet somewhere in Nashville?"

She hit the send button and looked out the window again. It was a cloudy day, but a ray of sunlight was trying to break out of the clouds. The light was striking the river at an unusual angle. She immediately thought it was a sign that the darkness she felt toward her sister was about to be absorbed in this new light. It was, to her, the light of family redemption, but she thought again. Fiona didn't really understand her. She didn't know the real Sarah.

Chance made a few calls about an apartment while Sarah sent the message. He didn't know what he was going to do, and that was good with him. His life for the last several years had been hit and miss. More misses than hits, so he thought he was due a break. As he dialed the second number, he thought about his past and the people in it. He never had a close friend or a real love. He was a loner who found group love doing drugs. When he heard the recording, he ended the call and walked to the doorway of Sarah's bedroom.

"I want to thank you for all you have done for me, Sarah. I know you didn't have to take me in and treat me so well. I can't remember the last time anyone has been this nice to me."

Sarah looked up from the computer screen. She saw truth coming from Chance's eyes. She saw another Chance in that doorway. He looked like a lost boy rather than an aging drug dealer. A chime sounded from her computer, and she saw Fiona's email.

"Hey Sarah, so good to hear from you. Are you in Nashville? Yes, we can meet there, but I think you should come here. You know the place off Cotton Lane. Just Google for directions. Tell me when, and please bring the guy who knew Geoff. I must talk to him. Love, Fiona."

Sarah looked up. Chance was still in the doorway.

"Fiona just answered me. She wants to meet you. I'm going to her house tomorrow. Okay?"

"Yep. I'm with you."

Those words hit Sarah hard. Somehow, she knew Chance wasn't going anywhere without her. He was her rescue animal, but she didn't want to keep him. Death had brought them together. That connection was important to her, but she knew it wouldn't last long.

"Forget about calling to find a place. You've got a friend in me, Chance. You can stay here until we resolve this Geoff thing with Fiona. Why don't we go get a bite to eat? How about Denny's?

Chapter 19

Men must endure their going hence, even as their coming hither; ripeness is all.

Shakespeare

Fiona was about to call Krabb when Sarah's email arrived. She read it carefully and responded immediately. Then her mind took her back to the bar. She could almost go back at will now. All she had to do was sit quietly, close her eyes, and open her mind.

"Holly, we got to find Tyrone. Where is he?"

Jayla was sitting at the bar sipping a gin and tonic, and Myles was behind her gulping down straight vodka.

"Well hell, child. He's your kin. Didn't you see him at the funeral?"

"I did, but we couldn't talk. He left in a hurry. Laquisha always said that man couldn't sit still for nothin'."

"I'm sorry 'bout your sister, Jay, honey. Were you two close?"

"When we were kids we did everything together, but when I left home, we drifted apart. She got mixed up with some no-good men, and then she met Tyrone. I knew he was into some stuff, but she seemed happy so I gave her my support, you know?"

"She never came round here. Tyrone don't much either. He just collects the money and keeps a lid on my husband. Lord knows he needs one."

"Laquisha was a loner, Holly. She never liked to be around people. She told me one time that people gave her hives or something like that. She stayed with Tyrone 'cause he would give her medication, if you know what I mean."

"Lord, I do, child. Tyrone does have his hands in a lot of things. I like him, but Shorty thinks he's a bullshitter. I told him it takes one to know one."

Jayla and Myles laughed.

"All Jay needs right now is some closure," Myles said. I mean, she needs to know what happened to her sister, really. You know what I'm sayin'?"

"I hear y'all. I do know this much. Shorty has a meeting with Tyrone tomorrow night at 11. Y'all come back then. I think y'all can corner him then, but don't tell him I told you. He don't like people to know his business, you know?"

Jayla smiled and stood next to Myles.

"Thanks, Holly. You are a good friend, even though we just met a few weeks ago."

"Yeah. We're sisters from different mothers."

Myles liked Holly in a strange way. He and Jayla looked around the bar and saw the men once again.

"Let's go over and talk to them, Myles."

"All right, but I need another drink." He tapped his glass with one finger as those words left his mouth.

206

"You drinkin' the same or somethin' else?"

Holly was right on it.

"I think I'll switch. Let me have straight bourbon."

"What bout, you, Jay?"

"The same, please."

Holly poured and served the drinks. She noticed the five men sitting around the table and watched the couple walk in that direction. She liked them even though Shorty had a problem with Jayla. The two lovebirds came in almost every night and would exchange small talk with her before they found a booth where they could drink and cuddle together. Jayla stood at a booth and was about to say something to Myles when Fiona's phone rang.

Fiona snapped out of the 1940s and was in the present once again.

"Hi, Fiona here."

"It's Mimi, Fiona. How's it going?"

"Great, Mimi. I'm glad you called. I need to tell you about my dreams. But how's your prison reform proposal going?"

"Well those old suspender-wearing, high-waisted, pseudo holy rollers from Tennessee keep stalling me, but the suits in Texas are on top of it. The Texans have closed three prisons in the last year, and with our help, they'll close more over the next two years. They're focusing on rehabilitating the first offenders and spending money on chronic offenders, but it all takes time. State government moves almost as slowly as the federal government. They call it being fiscally prudent. I call it a covering your ass.

All I can say is we're making progress, and I feel good about it. How are you doing, Fiona?"

"Well, I've been better. Found out my brother Geoff is dead."

"Oh, my condolences. Was he sick?"

"You might say that. He was sick all his life. I don't know exactly how he died, but my sister is coming to see me with a friend of his, so I'll know more then."

"Right, well, if I can do anything. . . I"

Fiona cut her off.

"That's just the half of it, Mimi. My dreams have really taken a turn. In a recurring one, I'm living in the 1940s as a black woman. And Krabb is there, and all the men that were close to me are there too. Plus my mother, sister and you are there. We are all drinking in this bar called the Black Orchid."

"Well that's appropriate. Am I black too?"

"Yep. Black and Asian, I think."

"Oh dear."

Fiona laughed. Fiona put Nyla and Mimi together even though Jayla never had a conversation with her. Fiona got the connection from her dream about Myles and Nyla talking one night in the bar.

"Krabb says we're learning from these people. He calls them counterparts or conscious particles of the soul. Never heard that before. Even Schuler didn't get into that much detail."

"Wait! What? Schuler? Who is Schuler? And Krabb is black?"

"Yes, Krabb's black, and he's my boyfriend. Dr. Arthur Schuler is a long story. I moved to New York to be with him years ago. He was a shrink and my dad's age at the time. I fell in love with him. He helped me come to terms with my mother's suicide. I stayed with him for a couple of years. He died of a heart attack after we had sex one morning."

"Oh my God, Fiona! You must have been scared and completely devastated."

"Yes, I was. But I was ready to move on. His death, sad as it was, made that possible, so I guess Krabb does have a point. Krabb said everybody comes into your life at just the right time. Schuler was like that. You're not going to believe it, but he told me he was going to die a week before it happened. He said he was going to die in bed. I just didn't know I was going to be in bed with him. We talked so much about death that I wasn't afraid of death or dying. I understood the inevitability of it back then, and now I'm beginning to understand it from a different perspective."

"Crazy story. Is Schuler in your dream?"

"You know, he might be, but I haven't recognized him yet."

Mimi was silent for a few seconds.

"I don't mean to pry, but what does Krabb say about all this stuff?"

"He's very interested. In fact, I think he shows signs in his office of being alive in the 1940s. Have you ever noticed all the 1940s-style furniture he has there? Plus the orchids, and how about the photo of Carl Van Vechten on his credenza?"

"Who in the world is that?"

"Van Vechten was a famous photographer and writer during the 1920s. He was a proponent of the black civil rights movement back then. He donated a lot of his work to Fisk University. The Krabb in my dream, his name is Myles, is an artist who went to Fisk.

"Wow! That's amazing. Never heard of him, but I did see that photo in Krabb's office."

"Yes, and I'm Jayla. Your name is Nyla, and my sister is Jiggy but goes by Amber."

"Sounds like she's more than one person."

"You know, she is. She's the only one that seems like more than one person in my dream. I knew a Jiggy growing up in England. She was Sarah's best friend."

What is your brother's name in the dream?"

"His name is Jake, and he's the bartender. Guess what? Someone kills him in my dreams."

"No way. Oh my God! I never knew anyone who was killed. Maybe that's why I'm so scared of killers. God, things are starting to make a little sense. These fears have been with me all my life. Interesting stuff, Fiona."

"That's just half of it. I'm going back for another session after I meet with Sarah and her friend. She called me and wants to meet as soon as possible."

"Well, let me know. I want to know more about me in this dream. Will you keep me in the loop?'

Fiona pulled her mouth away from the phone and sneezed. She grabbed a tissue and sneezed again.

"Sorry about that, Mimi. Off course I will. I want to know why I know about them now, and I also want to know if they know about me. I think Krabb might have the answers."

Mimi felt the perspiration on her forehead and hands. "Thanks for sharing all of this. I think this is going to help me somehow. I would like to have a normal life. It's about time."

"Right. Me too. Maybe we can get over our hang-ups, if you know what I mean."

"Are you talking about your orchids? Or my fears?"

Fiona hesitated. She forgot for a minute that the dream wasn't just for her healing.

"Both. This dream is all about what I believe and what everyone in the dream believes. It's a snapshot of one section of our soul. That's what Krabb said. I'll call you in a couple of days, Mimi."

"Will you tell me if I die in that bar, Fiona?"

Fiona and Mimi laughed. Both realized that they were no longer just Fiona and Mimi. They were also Jayla and Nyla.

"I wonder if Nyla has dreams about me, Fiona."

"That's a question Krabb might be able to answer, Mimi. I think she does, but she may not remember them. You dream of her and don't know you do. Ask Krabb when you see him. He'll give you the scientific version of how dreams work."

"I didn't know science knew that much about dreams, Fiona."

"Well, maybe all this information is coming from Krabb, not science. I don't discount it because science can't confirm it. They can't confirm I've got a soul, but I sure know I have one. Don't you?"

"Well, yes I do, Fee. But I was taught there's only one person to a soul, not a group of people living at different times. That's what my church says anyway."

"Yeah, and therein lies the problem. We believe what they tell us until something like this happens. They can't explain it. They call it crazy or demonic and pray for us. We don't need prayers to confirm what we feel. What we need is acceptance and the truth. I believe that massive library over there in the Vatican has proof that people have known about other dimensions of reality for years. They just hid that from us in order to build a power-hungry political church."

Mimi coughed in the phone. "Excuse me, Fee. Well, the belief in reincarnation has been around for thousands of years, so I guess it's up to us to decide what to believe based on our imagination and intuition."

"That's the spirit, Mimi. You've hit on an important element in all of this. This is our reality, and we can build it anyway we want. Krabb said even though we are multidimensional, we still are individuals experiencing the life we imagine."

"True, Fiona. I can feel another part of me sometimes. When I do, I try to contain my imagination and make it conform to accepted beliefs rather than letting it wander through the corridors of my soul."

"Exactly, Mimi. And the truth is, we can wander all we want mentally and be other people because we are."

Chapter 20

It is, in particular, the phenomena of somnambulism, double consciousness, split personality, etc. ...   These issues have enabled us to accept the possibility of a plurality of personalities in one and the same individual.

C.G. Jung

"Do you have to water all these flowers every day?"

Chance was sitting at the old table in the orchid nursery with Sarah and Fiona.

"No, not really. Watering depends on their size. The ones in smaller pots can go four or five days without water. Larger ones need water every seven days or so."

Fiona wasn't sure about this relaxed guy with a small birthmark on his right cheek and a stubbled face. She wasn't crazy about his sort of beige hair that stuck out in all directions. His attitude seemed genuine, but there was something about him that put her off. Fiona turned to Sarah. "I wanted to bring you out here so we could talk while I tended to a few things. Hope you don't mind."

Sarah expected nothing less. When she and Chance arrived at Fiona's house that morning, Fiona was sitting on the porch looking into space. Fiona hadn't changed much since their last meeting, which was well over 20 years ago. She was older and a little heavier, but she still had that calm air about her. The first thing Sarah said to her sister when she saw her was: "I see you're still dreaming, Fee. Are you still dreaming about Mummy?"

Fiona remembered why she didn't stay in touch with her sister even though she loved her. There was always a dig of some sort coming from Sarah. Fiona jumped up and hugged Sarah, but she knew it was game on. Sarah always tried to stick a mental knife into her. The man behind her sister just stood there smiling, and so did Sarah.

"Oh, so good to see you, Sarah! Lord knows I've missed you much more than you realize."

Sarah wasn't swayed. Her sister didn't like her, and she would never change her mind about that.

"Do tell, Fiona. Losing sleep over my absence? I hardly think that's so."

Fiona sat back down without acknowledging Chance.

"I know. I haven't stayed in touch, but it does take two, you know. But I have been dreaming about you, not Mummy. It seems you're still the muffled one in the family. Of course, Geoff doesn't count."

"Do say, Fee? What sort of dreams? Oh this is Chance. He's the fellow I mentioned in my email."

Fiona smiled and put out her hand.

"Well, nice to meet you Chance. I'm Fiona. Are you working with my sister? How did you know my brother?"

She kept talking so Chance couldn't answer.

Sarah felt a strange vibe from her as Fiona stood and walked by her without touching her again. It was as if Fiona was scared to touch her. She also noticed the strange stare Fee gave Chance as she passed him. Sarah felt like she had lived this porch scene with her before someplace else, but she couldn't remember where.

"Well Fee, I must say this is quite impressive. I love all these orchids. Is business good, sis?"

Sarah looked at Chance as she touched a few orchids. She didn't think her sister was capable of having such an incredible array of orchid species, and she knew Chance didn't expect anything like this display of beauty.

Fiona continued to sip her tea. She stared at Sarah and then at Chance. Chance seemed nervous. His eyes were bloodshot, and beads of sweat formed on his forehead.

"Yes, but I didn't ask you here to talk about the flowers. I want to know about Geoff. Chance, what can you tell me about his death?"

Chance didn't want to lie again, but he had no choice. He began his tale as he told it to Sarah about Yam Kern selling Geoff a bad batch of crack. When he finished, Fiona looked at Sarah.

"Do you think he knew what he was doing, Sarah? He must have been high all the time. Was he, Chance?"

"I think so. He didn't do anything but go downtown and panhandle, then come back home and drink and smoke."

"Sounds like he hit bottom, or should I say, he never left bottom. When did he die, and how did you find my sister, Chance?"

Chance told her about the phone number, and he gave her a day of death that coincided with Jake's disappearance. Fiona nodded and listened. She looked at Sarah.

"You know, he didn't find you randomly, in my opinion. He found you because he knew you in another life. I think you two share a secret."

Chance and Sarah looked at each other. Sarah immediately thought Fiona was too far gone mentally to believe her, and Chance thought she might be using some wild drug. He wanted to ask her but stopped when Sarah said:

"Are you saying we had a past life together? Don't know I believe that sort of thing. Why do you think that, Fee? Those crazy dreams of yours must be frying your brain."

Fiona told the pair about her dream of the Black Orchid and the people in the bar. She could tell they both were captivated by the story but didn't believe it. Fiona made it personal. She told Sarah that she was a woman called Amber, but Amber was also Jiggy, and she was married to a guy named Jake, who was actually Geoff in this life.

The story sent Sarah over the edge.

"I don't believe I would have married Geoff in any lifetime, Fee, and that Jiggy thing just doesn't sound right. You're pushing it with that arrangement. But then, who is Chance? Is he in the bar scene too?"

Fiona looked at Chance.

"I'm not sure at the moment, but I feel like he is. I think Chance may be a guy named Tyrone. I sense something about you, Chance, that reminds me of him. I'll know more when I meet him tonight."

Chance looked at her.

"You're going to meet him tonight? Where?"

"At the bar."

Chance smirked, "Can I come?"

"No need. I think you're already there."

Chance looked at Sarah and began to laugh.

"I'm sorry, but this dreaming-to-be-someone-else business is not for me. I believe we only live once and die, so we might as well get as much in as possible. Live on the edge and feel the breeze of death as it goes by. That's my motto."

Fiona stood up and moved to a group of orchids a few feet away. Chance noticed that the flowers appeared black.

"Are those flowers really black, Fee?"

Fiona didn't like his using the nickname her family and friends used for her, but she answered.

"Orchids bloom in many colors, but they don't have the pigment to produce a true blue or black color. This Paphiopedilum Stealth is as close to black as they get. I have this group here because that's the orchid that is painted on the bar's front door."

Chance's face was emotionless, but when he went over and looked at this almost-black orchid, he started to daydream. His mind shot him a scene of a door with this orchid on it, but he quickly snapped back to the nursery.

"Wow. Something strange thing just happened to me. I was watching someone painting that flower on an old walnut door. That never happened to me before."

Sarah rolled her eyes. "Are you doing drugs again, Chance? You promised me you'd stop."

Sweat started dripping down Chance's nose "I'm sober, but I think all these flowers are making me a little drunk. I feel a little sick right now."

He had to lie once again. He knew he was too far gone to stop on his own, but he tried to pretend he could.

Sarah saw the fright in his eyes. She turned to Fiona.

"We must go, Fee. It seems Chance is ill for some reason. I'll call you in a day or two. We can continue our talk about this bar of yours, then."

Fiona was ready for them to go. She got what she needed from them. Geoff died around the same time that Jake disappeared, and she had the feeling that the new guy in Sarah's life was the same guy who is protecting Amber in her dream. Chance must be Tyrone. But all of that didn't help her shake the feeling that her sister was back in her life to verbally berate her for not being a real sister to her. She knew she wasn't always there for Sarah, but Sarah didn't want her. If she did, she would have told her she was living in Clarksville before she casually mentioned it in her last email. Fiona's mind re-read the email.

"Fee, I'm living in Clarksville now. Have been for several years. I'll see you soon. I have the address. I'll bring Chance with me."

The message still felt cold. And she thought Sarah's comments were cold today. Fiona knew she was self-absorbed today. It was all about her and her mission to solve the dream puzzle. Sarah was expendable now. There was no sisterly love in the meeting today. They were just two people trying to figure out why they were sisters. Neither really liked the other, but some internal magnetic bond held them together. Fiona thought, "I wonder if Sarah feels what I feel. I wonder if Amber feels it too."

The Discovery

Precautions to be taken in the case
Of freak reincarnation: what to do
On suddenly discovering that you
Are now a young and vulnerable toad
Plump in the middle of a busy road,
Or a bear cub beneath a burning pine,
Or a book mite in a revived divine.

Vladimir Nabokov

Chapter 21

One integrates life as story because one has stories in the back of the mind.

James Hillman

"You know the president needs this war! He ain't gonna miss the chance to make a big name for himself at our expense!" Myles was very animated when he continued his speech. "You know it's about money don't you? The war is going to put people to work building cars, trucks, ammo, and other stuff for the war. If he lives long enough, he'll be a hero. He's an opportunist who wants more power, and he's going to get it at our expense. I bet a year from now, we all be in trenches dodging bullets."

Jayla looked at Myles as he finished his rant. He took another sip of his Scotch on the rocks.

"Hell, Myles, you might be too old to fight. Besides, those white boys up there in Washington don't want colored men in the army, do they?"

"You better believe they do! Now that they're talking about passing that order or law Roosevelt wants passed, colored men will be right in the middle of this fight, and that's gonna happen for a reason. We will show the world that we can overcome injustice by supporting our race as well as our country. We'll go and fight with honor, even though we don't get any respect for being equal citizens. We'll show the world we are equal, capable, and respectable. Skin has nothing to do with character."

Holly couldn't hold her tongue.

"Maybe this country will wake up, and see that we get some of the same treatment as those poor people over there get. Only difference is our white folks keep their torture on the down-low, and they do it in the name of God."

Jayla and Myles nodded their heads.

"Yeah, heard that. I know that's true," Jayla said.

Holly didn't waste any time looking busy as Tyrone strutted through the door dressed in a full-length fur coat. His black fedora with a long white feather sticking up at a 90-degree angle was tilted to the right side of his head. Amber was on one of his arms, and Nyla was on the other.

Holly couldn't help herself.

"Hey Rone. You must be warm with that rug you got round your body. You sick or something? Guess the sisters are helping you heal, right?"

Tyrone wasn't laughing. "Guess the only thing you're sick of is that man of yours. I'm supposed to meet that chocolate shrimp tonight. Where is he?"

Holly was wiping the counter. "He's in the back doing whatever he does."

Tyrone frowned. "I don't pay that little shrimp to stay back there. He's about to find out he's not needed round here."

Tyrone didn't waste words. He was still talking as he grabbed a bottle of bourbon and three glasses from under the bar. He poured himself one, then two shots for the ladies. "I don't know why you stay married to that guy, Holly. You could do better. I'm single now."

"Hey Tyrone. I didn't get a chance to talk to you at my sister's funeral. Guess you didn't want to talk about what happened, right? It looks like you're ready to move on," Jayla said.

Tyrone scratched his full beard with his right hand. Jayla noticed a small dark birth mark on his right cheek. That was the only spot on his face that was not covered with hair. His birthmark rang a vague bell in her mind, but she didn't know why.

"You know, Jayla. I've been ready to move on. Your sister was sick. I mean really sick. I don't want to talk about it here, but we could go in the back room, and talk if that's what you want."

Jayla quickly left her seat and so did Myles.

"Okay let's talk back there, Tyrone.

Tyrone looked at Myles. "Just you, Jayla. Myles here can sit and talk to the girls."

Jayla and Tyrone went to the back room, leaving Myles with Nyla and Amber.

"Tell Myles what happened to Jayla's sister, Amber," Nyla said.

Amber started speaking slowly:

"I was at the house that night. Tyrone asked me to come over and talk to Laquisha. She didn't want to talk to me. She called me a whore and ran into the bedroom. She knew I was sleeping with Rone. When she told me to get out, but not in those exact words, she left me and Rone in the kitchen. It all happened so fast. I was talking to her one minute, and the next minute, she was in the bedroom with a gun to her head. I didn't know what she was doing until I heard the shot. Lord have mercy! I just couldn't believe she would do that, especially after hearing about Jake and all."

"What about Jake, Amber? I heard some stories about that. Some say he was cheating on you."

Myles wanted answers too.

"I can't talk about all that now. You know, it's complicated. The cops believed I wasn't involved."

Myles looked at Nyla. Her thin, light chocolate face was the perfect backdrop for her light green eyes.

"Nyla, did you like Jake?"

"Jake was messed up, so I stayed away from him. Jake and Amber were a thing. Everybody knew that."

Amber started to say something, but Jayla and Tyrone came back before she could.

"Did you talk to Shorty?" Holly was curious.

Tyrone shook his head from side to side and grabbed the bottle he left on the bar.

Jayla sat and thought about what Tyrone told her in the back room. She knew her sister had problems, but not serious mental problems. Tyrone said she wanted to kill herself long before she did. Jayla looked at both girls. Amber was smoking a Lucky Strike and talking to Holly. Nyla was on the other side of Myles, smiling and whispering in his ear. Jayla heard Nyla say, "Is she the girl you were looking for the last time I saw you?"

Myles nodded his head as he finished his third drink. Jayla turned to Tyrone.

"Thanks Tyrone. I know you tried to keep my sister straight. Guess she didn't want to live like a trapped woman anymore."

Tyrone looked at his drink and shook his head. His face moved close to Jayla's.

"Guess, me and life let Laquisha down," Tyrone whispered. "I picked this kind of life for me, but she wanted more. She wanted to be white, and that's what killed her. She read about some crazy shit called re-incarnate or something before I opened this bar. She said a guy by the name of Ed or Ted Cayce talked about people having other lives and shit like that. She really believed in that stuff. She started to believe she could come back as a white woman. I told her all that was crazy talk. We only got one shot at this life, and we have to take everything we can out of it. Being black is our way of telling the world beauty has no color. Beauty is our natural state. We don't need to be white to be beautiful. Take orchids, for example. Orchids come in all colors. That's why I painted that black orchid on the door of this place. Black orchids are the only flowers that show how beautiful black can be.

Jayla thought about her blackness for a second. No white person ever told her she was beautiful except a few men who wanted sex from her. Jayla thought about orchids. She always felt a strange connection to them, even though she never bought one.

"I've never heard of a black orchid. Have you ever seen a black orchid, Tyrone?"

"Well, no. But I had a dream about them after a night of drinking a lot of gin. I saw them in this place filled with orchids, but the ones that really stood out in this place were the black ones. It was if they were calling my name or something. I know the dream was weird, but do you know what the really weird part of that dream was, Jay? I was white in that dream! The people around me were white. I never had another drop of gin after that night. I'm not like Laquisha. I like being black."

Jayla smiled and looked around the room.

"Guess being white is enough to make anyone stop drinking gin, isn't it? Your business would go to hell if everybody was white, right Tyrone?"

"Man, I don't want to think about all this white business anymore. I got the best bar this side of the Cumberland River for people like us."

Myles couldn't keep quiet any longer. "And what kind of people are people like us?"

Tyrone finished the last gulp of bourbon before he answered. "We're the kind of people who are going to make a big difference in this world someday. I believe we're here to change the way people get along. You know, we love music, fun, good food, and family, but the world don't know that yet. They think we're products of dumb slaves or African natives. They think we want to force our lifestyle on other folks. We just want a voice. We want a balanced system of justice, but that ain't gonna happen any time soon. We are just like those poor suckers in Germany who are being burned alive. We are rebels who don't want to be rebels. But we have to show them that if you disrespect our right to be humans, your right to be human will be in jeopardy someday too."

The group was silent. They knew he was right, so they all nodded in agreement.

Myles was impressed. He held his glass to Tyrone.

"Wow, Tyrone. You must have been thinking about all that for a very long time. Here's to you!" Myles downed his drink. Tyrone did the same and then smiled.

"Yeah, you could say that, man. Bourbon makes me talk like somebody else. That's why I drink. I can't say all those things and make sense when I'm sober."

Holly poured Myles another drink, and she looked at Tyrone while she did. "Guess we all drink to be somebody else, Rone. We all want to be more than we are in a way. Look at me. I wanted to be more than I am, but I made some stupid choices. I let a bullshitter fill my head with crap, and here I am. I always wanted to be a model, but I didn't believe I could."

Tyrone took another sip. "Holly, you could have your own bar someday. You could be the boss. You got what it takes to be rich, baby. Don't sell yourself short because you're married to Shorty. You could throw him to the curb, you know."

Holly nodded her head. "I know I'm gonna be somebody even though my skin ain't the right color. I dream about running my own club and marrying a decent guy, but I always wake the hell up!"

Holly started to laugh, and the group laughed with her. Jayla raised her glass, and the others did too.

"Here's to Holly. May she never wake up from her dream!"

Holly frowned and Jayla saw it.

"Now, I don't mean you should die, Holly, honey. I mean you should start living your dream. I know I am, and I bet everyone here is too."

"Man, I have some pretty nasty dreams," Tyrone said. "That's why I don't sleep at night."

Myles nodded and looked at Nyla. "I'm living my dream right now, and I'm not waking up!"

Jayla saw Myles looking at Nyla and started to wonder about him. Jayla felt jealous for the first time. Nyla had her hand on Myles's arm, and she was putting her face close to his.

"You know I still want you to paint me, don't you?" Nyla asked Myles.

Myles turned his face so it was an inch away from Nyla's. "I want to paint you, baby. I'll call you."

"You used that 'baby' word pretty freely, don't ya Myles? I'm ready to get out of here. You coming, or are you too busy?" Myles felt Jayla's anger. "No, honey. I was just talking about painting her."

"That better be all you want to do to her."

Nyla tried to defuse the situation. "I'm sorry Jay. I know he's your man, I just thought he wanted to paint me, that's all."

"I've heard that before, Nyla. You coming, Myles, or are you in the painting frame of mind?"

Chapter 22

Great is the power of memory, exceedingly great, oh my God, a spreading limitless room within me. Who can reach its uttermost depths?

Augustine

Myles sat with the other men around the table. The war was the topic tonight. Jayla was standing behind Myles listening to the conversation. Nyla was standing behind Cave. Cave's voice was louder than usual.

"So what are we going to do? I just heard the NAACP pushed the government, and the government formed an all-black group of flyers," Cave said. "We can sign up and go down to Tuskegee for training if you want to do something 'bout this war. I gonna sign up, but I want y'all to think about it. I'm thinking we could all be together and get this thing over with quick. What do you think, Sly?"

Sly looked at all the men and then focused on Myles.

"Myles you got anything to say? Your girl is behind you. You think she would let you go?"

Myles turned to Jayla, and then Nyla. Then he looked at the five men around the table. "I gotta tell you, you guys have become a second family to me. Me and Jay have been coming in here a couple of nights a week, and we watched this war become real together. We've talked about the war over there and the war we fight every day in this country, and what we gotta do about it. Hell, this country is trying to fight the biggest racist in the world with a racist army! That don't make sense. We're all sick and tired of being third-class citizens. They got to hear our voices. It has to stop, but it won't till we do something about it. There's prejudice everywhere, so that's why I'm with Cave. I'll go fight if it means we get one step closer to showing this country that we want a balanced justice system. No, wait! We want a balanced view of what the people in this country looks like."

Ali Nigma was moving his chips up and down with two fingers as he listened to Myles. "I heard about that air group you're talking about, Cave. They want black pilots who can fly supplies to Africa and Europe. I'm no pilot, but I could work on the planes. Y'all know I'm a mechanic."

Murdock smiled. He knew about Nigma's talent as a mechanic first-hand. "Hell, Nigma can fix anything. He put my Dodge back together when the damn thing blew up on me last year. Shit, I'm no mechanic, but I can type and do paperwork. I did graduate with some sense. Y'all know that?"

Rocco broke-up in laughter. "Hell, you call that typing, Murdock? I saw you write something on that machine last week, and it looked like you were a chicken pecking bugs."

The table broke up. Myles got up and gave Jayla a hug. He glanced at Nyla and smiled. Then he said: "I don't know about all of you, but I'm going to that building on Broadway and sign up."

Sly pushed his hat back on his head and stubbed out a Camel cigarette. He pointed his finger at Myles. "I'll go. What time you going?"

Cave threw his cards on the table and roared, "Shit! Let's all go when Myles goes!

The others at the table nodded their heads

Jayla and Myles finished their drinks standing at the bar. Jayla was worried about the man she loved. She didn't know what she would do without him. Jayla kissed Myles's cheek. "I know you want to help this country, but do you want to risk all you've got to do it?"

"I don't have much, baby."

"You got me."

"Yeah, and I know that's worth more than money. And I have my art. That will be around long after I'm gone. I'm not signing up to prove anything to anybody. You know colored soldiers in the First World War were treated like dogs by their own country. I don't want that to happen this time, so I'm going to act and speak my piece like any other tax-paying citizen in this country."

"Well you know what, honey? I just may sign up as an army nurse then. What's that Alabama group called, Myles?"

"I don't know, but I'd like to call the group the Tuskegee Colored Eagles."

Jayla rolled her eyes, and her lips came together in a full circle. She turned to Holly and smiled. It was Holly's turn to talk. "Lord have mercy, child. That don't sound like any kind of name the government would use. Anything to do with a color other than white sends shivers up the backs of those crazy fools in Washington."

Holly liked to talk. It was a slow night. Shorty was gone. Tyrone fired him the night he went to the back room to talk to Jayla. He found him getting a blow-job in the men's bathroom.

"Shorty didn't even say nothing when Rone made me manager. I've been putting up with that guy for a long time, and he don't have the guts to look me in the eyes and congratulate me. Lord knows I hope he signed up to fight, and I hope his balls turn blue and his pecker falls off."

Holly poured herself a drink. She downed it in one gulp and continued. "I haven't talked to Shorty in weeks. He's been living with that small bitch with red hair. I hope she gives him the crabs. She never keeps her legs closed. You know who I'm talking about. She was Jake's girl."

Myles chuckled and said: "Guess Shorty likes to live dangerously."

Jayla laughed. "Shorty is one guy I'll never like. It's like he wants everybody to notice him for doing nothing."

Nyla walked to the bar. "I saw Shorty the other night, Holly."

"Oh you did? And where was that, Nyla?"

"Well he was over at that place on West End called Jimmy Keely's. He was waiting tables. All they have is Negro waiters in that place. I know he saw me, but he didn't say anything to me. But I called his name as he walked by me."

"What were you doing over there, Nyla? That place is for white folks."

234

"I know, but I was with Jimmy, the owner. He wants me to go to work for him as a hostess. Don't know if I want that since Myles is painting me and all. Just might not have time, 'cause after he's done, I'm going to Alabama and work in an ammunition factory. My cousin, Willie Mae Govan, wrote me and said I could make good money and help end the war at the same time. She said there was a spot for me at DuPont. That's the company that makes bullets and secret projects to end the war."

Holly put a drink in front of Nyla.

"Here, child. This one's on the house. You deserve it. I didn't know you was so damn interested in helping fight like that."

Myles and Jayla toasted Nyla. Myles wanted to say more, but he stopped himself. "Nyla, I wish you nothing but the best. I know you will come out of this thing a better person."

Nyla took a sip of her martini. "I'm not going' yet, Myles. You gotta finish with me, right? I want to see what I look like to you."

"Oh yeah. We are gonna finish. You know it's becoming one of my favorite pieces."

Jayla was sick of the Myles and Nyla charade. "Here we go again, Myles. You and Nyla again? You know I like both of you, but don't try to fool me."

Myles downed his drink and smiled at Holly. Then he smiled at Nyla. Trying to keep two women happy at the same time was taking a toll on him.

"I gotta go, Jay. I'm going downtown in the morning. I want to check out that air corps thing. Are you coming with me?"

Myles was almost out the door before Jayla answered. "No. I wanna talk to Nyla and Holly. The idea of making bullets sounds like something I'd like to do, but if I did, I might use them in the wrong way, especially if you are around."

"No. Now wait, Jay. I'm sorry, but I had a little too much tonight. I need some sleep."

"That's not all you need, Myles, but I'll stop there. Maybe I'll see you tomorrow, but for now we're done."

Nyla walked toward the door with Myles. "I've got to go too. Bye for now, y'all."

Jayla watched them moved toward the door together. She was jealous, but she acted nonchalantly and said, "You two have a good life down in Alabama."

Jayla didn't know why she said that, but Fiona did. For the first time, Fiona realized she had the power to plant suggestions in Jayla's mind, and that scared her. If she could do that, Jayla could as well. She realized that her thinking process was not only influenced by the world she lived in. Some of her thoughts could be the work of counterparts living in another time. She had to call Krabb.

Chapter 23

We travel with the same clan over and over again, from one life to the next, until some ultimate purpose is fulfilled and we no longer need to return.

Raquel Cepeda

Krabb sat behind his desk reading an internet news site when he began to think about the one patient who changed his outlook toward patients. When he first started seeing her, it was a very professional relationship. He went through his usual introduction with her and listened as she described some of her dreams and how she interpreted them. As his mind took him through his recent past, he smiled and started a dialogue with himself.

"I really can't have these thoughts. But there is something about her that feels familiar."

Krabb snapped out of it when the intercom buzzed.

"Yes?"

"Fiona's here for her appointment, Doctor."

"Give me five minutes, then send her in."

Krabb wanted to finish reading the notes he made about Myles and Jayla. He did some research and discovered Jayla Thackeray was a nurse who lived in the 1940s. She died in 1962. He turned to Fiona's file and noticed Fiona was born in 1962. He also searched for Myles Dunbar and found that he did serve in WWII and was killed in 1945. That was the year he himself was born. He thought about the connection, but he didn't want to share it with Fiona on this visit. Something told him to wait until their next meeting. Krabb pushed the intercom button.

"Send Fiona in, please."

Fiona walked into Krabb's office and immediately noticed the new painting of a naked black woman.

"Oh, I love the new painting, Doc. Who's the artist?"

"My friend Paul Harmon painted that one. He calls the work, "La Revue Nègre." I fell in love with it when I went to his studio the other day."

Fiona nodded in agreement, but she didn't say a word.

"I have some information for you Fiona, and I'm sure you have more to share about your dreams. Let me tell what I've discovered about your return to the 1940s."

Fiona wanted to go first, especially after seeing the new painting, but she patiently listened to Krabb.

"The bar and the people in it are giving you a glimpse or a snapshot of how the soul expands through contrast, and in this case, war. You are watching the life of a woman who makes a contribution to the advancement of blacks in America by experiencing and participating in the war. You are making a somewhat similar but radically different contribution with your work with orchids. Jayla is showing you that racial discrimination is a tool for the expansion of thinking. You and Jayla are experiencing your own creative challenge, and each of you learns something from your experiences."

"Okay, but why are all the other men and women in the bar people I know now or have known? I don't get it, Doc. Why are these people still playing a role in this life of mine?"

"You made an agreement with certain souls. Those souls project basic units of consciousness — we call them individuals — into our material reality at the same time your soul performs that creative act. The individuals involved learn lessons from each other and help each other experience mass events. You must realize we are experiencing a mass physical dream in one point in time, and other individuals from other souls experience the same dream in other points in time. But there are many dreams for souls to experience, and we creatively choose which souls to experience them with. The fact that they play different roles in these dreams is the result of individual choices. If they played the same role, there would be no expansion of the soul."

"So the soul does all this to experience expansion?"

"Precisely! The soul or creative action knows itself through experiences. My definition of the soul is creative action. My definition of God is the eternal expansion of consciousness through basic units of consciousness, of which we are one."

Fiona was going deeper into this Krabb hole of information than she expected. Her view of the soul and God was nothing like his. All she really wanted to know was why she was living as a black woman in the 1940s.

"Does that mean my soul is allowing me to see other individuals whom I have a pact with?"

"It's not a question of allowing, Fee. You are choosing to tap into the fertile field of consciousness that exists in all aspects of time. You just happen to be focusing on the 1940s in order to help you with the challenges in your life. I think that challenge includes your relationships with men, your fear of black people, and your close connection to orchids. In your dreams, you have a relationship. You see blacks as caring, honest members of society, and you are watching them help the black movement as it takes shape before the war. You see how black people can impact beliefs in this dream. Those individuals in those roles are helping you deal with your fears as well as your passion, which I think is flower awareness. By that I mean the orchids' ability to feel, communicate and to be sexually active. People don't understand orchids, and they don't understand the incredible persecution and traumas that blacks have gone through."

Fiona thought for a second. She did fear blacks because some people thought she was black. She feared being called black because of her own dark skin color. Her father taught her that behavior. He would always say, "My skin may be dark, but it's not black like those savages in Africa." Both sisters thought blacks were mean humans, and they avoided them until they came to the United States. Sarah's fear of blacks was greater than Fiona's because Sarah's skin was almost as dark as African skin. Sarah verbalized her fear to her when she was younger, but she hid her fear from others. Krabb's statement started to make sense to Fiona. But, she never looked at her relationship with orchids as a tool for expansion of her awareness. She knew she loved them, but she didn't think she would impact the masses in terms of how they felt about orchids. But now that Krabb mentioned it, she started to understand her mission in life. She could turn her fear into a productive difference, and she could turn her passion into a focused awareness of what life truly is.

"I'm starting to get it, Doc. I did fear blacks, and my passion is untapped, so to speak. But I also get the feeling that you and I are in some sort of transition in my dream."

"Can you elaborate on that a little, Fiona?"

Fiona told him about her latest 1940s dream, and how she thought she was the catalyst for the breakup of Jayla and Myles. She told him about Nyla, and how she thought Myles was doing more than painting her.

"I see. So you got the impression that Jayla actually felt your thoughts about Myles?"

Krabb looked over his notes and then looked up.

"Now tell me who you think Nyla is in this life?"

"Nyla is Mimi. You know Mimi. Of course you do. She's the one who told me about you. She knows your background pretty well, I might add."

Krabb quickly looked out the window, and then he wrote a note before he answered.

"I don't like to talk about other clients, Fiona. You understand, don't you? But I do know Mimi."

Fiona saw a little nervous twitch in his right eye, just like she saw in Myles's when he was talking to Nyla. Myles's twitch was in his left eye, however.

"You know, Doc, Myles is painting Nyla in the nude, and I think he's having sex with her too. I'm beginning to understand all men a little better, thanks to Myles. He's a typical playboy who uses woman for his own sexual pleasure."

Krabb thought for a minute. He had to choose his words carefully.

"Not all men are playboys, as you put it, but there are many that want to experience sex with more than one woman at a time. This is not accepted behavior, but some men — and women I might add — want sex with more than one partner. That behavior has been going on for centuries. I'm not condoning it. We call it a sin, but it is a fact of life."

Fiona paused.

"Why do you think you bought that new painting of the nude black woman, Doc?"

Gabe gazed at the painting for a few seconds. He remembered how quickly he decided to buy it. He didn't usually buy things impulsively.

"If I'm honest with myself and you, I would say I had help making that choice. Now where that help came from, I can't be sure. But my quick purchase may be the work of your Myles. Is that what you think?"

Fiona smiled. "If I can influence a choice in a past life, why can't people in the past influence a choice in the future?"

"No doubt they do. I may be more like Myles than I realized."

"Do you screw more than one woman at a time? Is that what you mean, Doc?"

Fiona suddenly realized she was projecting her beliefs about Myles on to Krabb.

Krabb looked surprised. He didn't answer.

"Sorry, Doc. Guess I'm letting my dreams bleed into this reality."

"Well, let's get back to the real question, Fiona. Do you think Jayla is going to forgive Myles for his misdeed, or is she going to hold it against him as he goes off to war? Perhaps he believes he is not coming back from the war and wants to experience the beauty of love with two women before he goes."

"Is that a message from him, or are you posing that question?"

Krabb laughed. He liked his client's sense of humor and poignant question.

"Remember Fiona, I'm not dreaming your dream. You are, so you tell me. Is Myles talking for me?"

"I don't know, Doc. Guess I must go back to the bar and find out."

Fiona immediately had a frightening impulse.

"But what if these people are gone? What if I go back, and all of them have moved on? Can I still be in sync with their reality?"

"As I mentioned before, Fiona, you will be able to connect with Jayla and the others if you keep your inner channels open. If you begin to doubt yourself, or if you begin to fear the outcome of these episodes, you may cut off your connection. So I would suggest you keep an open mind and let them live their reality. Now don't get me wrong. Your thoughts will still influence them, but not always. It depends on them. Be assured they are living their experiences. You are only observing them. Don't worry. I'm sure you will have more interaction with that group, so why don't we set an appointment for next week?"

Fiona flashed back to Schuler, who encouraged her to live in the present. Krabb is saying live in more than one reality at a time. Therapists are a strange group, she thought.

"Thanks, Doc. I get it now. I do need to find out what happens with Myles and Jayla. I can't let my thoughts tarnish theirs."

"Well, I'm afraid it's not that easy, Fiona."

"Maybe if we became lovers, we'd solve the problem between Jayla and Myles."

Krabb laughed.

Fiona suddenly thought about Mimi. Mimi was a part of this dream and her bar dream - a very important part.

"You know, Mimi knows about my dream, but not all of it. I didn't want to spoil her idea of God too much."

Krabb nodded his head.

"I didn't know you believed in God, Fiona."

"I didn't until you explain that mystery to me. I think there's no better proof than watching the orchids express their expansion in the eternal energy of creativity."

"Well said, Fiona. You have been listening."

Chapter 24

**When it's all over and the dust from our
Ancestors bodies and our own settle from the
four winds only then will we see that we were
here!**

Stanley Victor Paskavich

The sweat dripping down her forehead was a typical
morning occurrence. The agony of watching her brother
live in a basement, drunk and high on drugs, was an
insidious dream now. For years, Sarah had nightmares
about her father and his demanding disposition about some
of her childhood habits, but those dreams seemed to be
abating now that Geoff was gone. For the last few months,
her mental health seemed to be deteriorating. Sarah wasn't
sure why she felt sick all the time, but she suspected some
of her issues were caused by Chance, the last person to see
her brother alive. Sarah pulled herself up from bed using
the antique wooden nightstand she kept from her
childhood. She sat up.

"My God, why can't I forget the way he died and move
on?" she wondered to herself. "And that sister of mine
doesn't even care how hard it is on me. She's like a damp
squib that corrupts my story. I don't know why I got her
involved in my life at all. All she cares about is her
dreams."

Sarah's family issues were taking a toll on her coping skills, and she knew it. Years of mental abuse from her husbands and lack of confidence from her father were back in her life. She had to do something before it was too late, but she couldn't wrap her mind around forgiving her father for her skin color or her lack of confidence. She also wasn't about to forgive Fiona for being Fiona. She managed to drop her legs over the side of her sleigh bed and stand. She looked at her phone. It was 10 in the morning. She had been in bed for more than 12 hours. The smell of coffee danced through her nostrils, and that waltz sent her mind into hunger mode as she put on her red velvet robe and Ugg slippers. She made a bathroom stop, then walked into the kitchen. By now, the voice that snapped her out of her ravenous state was all too familiar.

"I thought you were dead, Sarah. I was ready to call 911. Are you all right?"

Chance seemed genuinely concerned about his platonic roommate of two months. She was an important but wobbly crutch for him. He managed to wean himself off the drugs after his meeting with Fiona. The thought of being someone else and the image of the black orchid inspired him to get rid of his stash. One late night visit to Denny's took care of that. Dori and her friends bought what he had left. He had enough money to last him for a few weeks, thanks to Sarah's rent-free generosity and the money he got for the crack. The most important lesson, he thought, was Sarah's depressed state. He saw an old version of himself in her. He knew Sarah was on the verge of a breakdown because she couldn't let go of the past. He wanted to help, but he knew he couldn't. She didn't want his help. He sensed her animosity through her conditional kindness. He knew, in some way, she held him responsible for her brother's death. And he knew he was partially responsible. He still wanted to help, so he put a cup of tea in front of her as she sat down. He was still holding his coffee mug.

"Here. Maybe this will help get the cobwebs out, Sarah."

Sarah didn't like talking in the morning.

"Thanks. Don't have any cobwebs, Chance. I just have a lot of unanswered questions."

Chance didn't want to get into another conversation about her brother. They had many of those over the last couple of months. They talked about why Geoff was the way he was and why she was so devastated by his death. Chance listened and understood more about her and her brother, but all the conversations ended the same way. Sarah couldn't stop blaming herself for not getting get Geoff help. She couldn't forgive herself for not telling her father about Geoff's behavior, and she couldn't come to terms with the fact that her mother knew about Geoff holding Jiggy captive for a few hours back in England. Her mother never told anyone she knew until the night she committed suicide.

Chance was tired of her pity party. "You know, I can't give you answers, Sarah. The only one who can is you." You need to talk to someone about these mind troubles of yours."

"You sound like my sister. All this dream business, and now talk about my sanity. I can't handle much more of it, you know."

"I think you're trying to make sense of something that doesn't make sense. And I also think your brother wanted to die, and he did it the best way he could. I think we all pick how we want to die. I was using drugs because I wanted to die. You are depressed because you want to die. We all die, but we fear the thought and the act. One thing your sister showed me in that flower house of hers was that life and death are a continuous cycle. We should live to the fullest like the orchids and celebrate death as another chance for life. Fiona wasn't the reason I changed. The orchids helped me change, and I'm surprised I'm telling you that."

Sarah took two small sips of her English tea. She listened but was turned off when she heard her sister's name.

"Well, here we go. Fiona, once again, is influencing the people around me in some way. I must say, I'm sick of it. If you're so bloody convinced that she has all the answers, go live with her. In fact, I would like it if you would pack your things and leave. We don't have anything else to talk about if that is the way you think. As you know, my sister and I don't see eye to eye and never will. You know that, Chance. Please do us both a favor and leave as soon as you can."

Chance wasn't surprised that she snapped at him. He knew it was time to go.

"I'll pack now and will be out of here within the hour. But first, let me say I appreciate all you've done for me, Sarah. You helped me more than you know. I guess the only way I can return the favor is to leave. Please know I will always be grateful for your kindness."

Sarah's eyes filled with tears. She was done with anyone who knew about her family or had any sort of contact with her sister. She wanted to be alone. Then the thought of Jiggy ran across her mind. "No, wait," Sarah thought to herself. "I don't want to be alone. I want to be with the only friend I ever had, Jiggy." Her lips unlocked as she looked at Chance.

"Thank you for your kind thoughts. I wish you luck or whatever it is that makes you happy."

Chance stood and extended his hand.

"I don't believe in luck, Sarah. I believe in myself.

An hour later, Chance had a bus ticket in his hand. He was on his way to Nashville to start over, and Sarah was on the computer Googling Jiggy Didi.

*****

Her last meeting with Krabb left Fiona confused and exhausted. When she arrived home, she napped, and a few minutes later, Jayla was sitting alone at the bar. Tyrone and Holly were behind the bar, and the men who were regulars weren't there. The bar was empty. The Billie Holiday song drifting from the jukebox was barely audible. She sipped her gin and tonic and looked at Tyrone.

"Where is everybody?"

"All the men are gone, Jay. And no men means no women"

Tyrone pointed at a sign on the wall. Uncle Sam donned his red, white and blue hat and pointed. "We Want You For The U.S. Army!" Jayla fought the tear rising in her right eye. Tyrone handed her a tissue and said, "I didn't think my Black Orchid would be a victim of this war, but look at it. The big question is what are you doing here?"

Jayla looked at Holly. Holly still represented a powerful presence, even though no one was around.

"Holly, what are you going to do? Are you and Tyrone keeping this place open?"

Holly smiled as she moved closer to the bar.

"You know, these men will need a place to drink and talk when they come back, so hell yes! I'm going to be here. That's what I can do for this country. I'll listen to stories of pure hell, and I'll sympathize with the broken men who return. There may be comfort in a bottle, but there's compassion in a set of ears and an understanding mind. I know what it's like to be broken, to be beat down until the last drop of hope spills out on the floor. So hell yeah! I'm going to be here for them, Jay. You can take that to the bank. My word is gold, Jay."

Tyrone shook his head in agreement.

"Shit. I got enough money put away to carry the note on this place and keep it open. This place means a lot to me. I learned who I am here. Holly did too, so I'll let Holly do her thing, and I'm going to help my brothers get a fair shake another way."

"How you going to do that, Tyrone?"

"I'm going to join the NAACP! They need guys like me. I'm a solid citizen and a straight shooter. I'll help my people by representing them."

Jayla finished her drink. She saw another side of Tyrone, and it surprised her.

"Very noble, Tyrone."

"What you gonna do, Jay?"

"I'm going to join the Army Nurse Corps. My friend Mabelle Keaton Staupers sent me a note and asked me to join. She's involved in the National Association of Graduate Colored Nurses. She said the Army Nurse Corps has 48 colored nurse positions open, and she wants me. I wrote back and told her I would serve if she needed me. She knows I worked at the Harlem Hospital. She worked for the Harlem Tuberculosis Committee when I was up there. I miss nursing. My sister Laquisha's suicide, and my love affair with Myles have kept me away from my passion. I care for people, especially colored people, so I'm going to try to help the cause by using my nursing skills."

Holly smiled and lifted a glass.

"Yes, girl. All the boys, including Myles, are on their way to Alabama. I told them all to write me, and they better if they know what's good for them. I'll be right here ready to answer any of them. You know that."

Jayla pulled a piece of paper and fountain pen out of her blue clutch.

"Write down your address, Holly, and put Tyrone's address down too. I'll let you know what happens. I promise."

"You better do that, Jay, or I'll come back and haunt you in your next life."

Tyrone laughed. "I will too, and I might be white, so be careful, Jay. You're the only family I got now."

Jayla reached over the bar and hugged both of them.

"Family sticks together no matter what, y'all. Time doesn't matter, does it?"

Chapter 25

Love for the beauty of the soul. I shall love you always. When the flower of life has gone, ever I shall find you. When all is lost and winter comes, I shall be your springtime. And memory fades and wilts then, I shall always find you . . . I shall always find you . . .

Laurel A. Rockefeller

In his dream, Krabb's khaki shorts and favorite T-shirt were drenched. It was one of those humid summer days In Nashville. Half the charcoal in his Weber grill was bright orange, and the other half was cold black. The main course burned above the orange coals as Krabb wiped his forehead with a wet towel.

"Here, I'm not a chef. See if you can save these poor things."

Mimi agreed and yanked the burgers to safety with the spatula she pulled from Krabb's moist hand.

"Thank God you're a good shrink, Gabe, because you're a dud when it comes to grilling."

"I know. I don't know why I try. I guess it's because the food tastes so good when I get it right."

"You do try, but it's painful to watch."

Krabb started to toss and turn as Krabb heard himself say:

"I almost told Fiona the last time I saw her, but I decided it was not a good time. Fiona told me about "the Nyla in her dreams, and I think that prompted me to ask you here."

Krabb watched Mimi transferred the hamburgers to a platter and set them in the center of the table.

Her voice was low when she said: "I know you can't tell me about her sessions, but do you really believe she is seeing another part of herself in these dreams?"

Krabb sat on his weathered oak picnic bench and pulled the cellophane off cartons of potato salad and slaw. He looked at his patio furniture and how it matched the ranch-style home he'd lived in for 15 years. He loved his location. He was 15 minutes away from his office on a good traffic day, and his section of Tyne Boulevard was considered one of the prettiest in Belle Meade. He felt a gulp of beer go down his throat.

"I do believe Fiona is seeing part of herself just as clearly as she sees me. Her story is fascinating, and I'm writing a version of it."

Mimi voice was softer this time.

"A novel or a journal paper?"

"Both. I need more information. I'm sure she'll have more information to share about the bar."

"Well, at least I'll be able to read about it at some point. Fiona told me about Nyla."

"Yes, indeed. Even though the characters are drinking in a bar and have little in terms of worldly possessions, they all have rich intentions, and most of them seem to have outstanding moral character."

"Wow. Has that one beer loosened you up, Gabe?"

Krabb laughed and put his arm around Mimi.

"I'm just trying to be polite, Mimi. I can't answer all your questions, but I will say I'm glad we are having an affair." You do know working in an ammunition factory during the war didn't suit you, right?"

Krabb watched Mimi's face turned pale.

"Gabe you're not going to believe this, but I have a serious fear of bullets. I dream about bullets and bombs, but I've never told you about those dreams. I thought my fear was a product of some of the TV shows I watch, like Blue Bloods or NCIS. I absolutely hate bullets, bombs, guns, and violence, and now I think I really know why. You're telling me I made bullets for big guns or bombs, and that makes me sick."

"I thought the part about us having an affair would make you sick, not the bullets. You know, just talking about it will help you understand that not all of our fears come from this life. Once we know where our fears originate, we can address them and transform them into something else. Fear is negative creativity, and we can change that behavior once we understand it."

Krabb watched himself touch her hand and reached for a burger at the same time.

Mimi looked puzzled as she finished her sandwich.

"Do you think we just had an affair back then, or did we live together or get married, Gabe?"

Krabb heard himself again.

 "I have the feeling we just had a fling. Myles was on his way to fight, and you were on your way to make bullets or some weapon. I don't get the feeling they ever saw each other again, but I'm sure Fiona has that information."

Krabb looked into Mimi eyes and saw someone else.

"Mimi let's not think about what was. Maybe we had a short romance back then to show us how compatible we really are. I'm not Myles, and you're not Nyla, but a portion of them is still alive in us. You might sense the Myles in me and be fearful of my intentions. I can assure you I learned what I needed to learn from him, and I make my own decisions. I never married because I never felt what I feel now. I know my age may be an issue, but I want to spend the rest of my life with you, if you want me. I don't know how long that might be, but I know we'll make the best of our time together."

"Have you had dreams about Myles too, Gabe?"

Krabb suddenly woke up. His shirt was soaking wet and he felt sick to his stomach. For the first time, he allowed his inner feelings to manifest in one of his dreams. He could never have burgers with Mimi or Fiona. Their relationship was professional and nothing more. But deep down in the heat of another era their relationship was personal. He felt it. He was Myles, and Fiona and Mimi were Jayla and Nyla. This dream convinced him of that. He was part of Fiona's dream now, and he was excited beyond words. Krabb suddenly remember what he read in the book, The Unknown Reality. Energy never dies. It transforms itself as consciousness expands. Krabb realized Fiona and Mimi were catalysts for his expansion, and he appreciated them for showing him that everything is connected in one way or another. Krabb smiled as he remembered another thought in the same book. Life is not about years. Life is like an energetic pulsating wave that moves through people and shows them the value of their experiences.

*****

Fiona walked through the familiar glass door 30 minutes early and quickly noticed the receptionist was gone. But she did see Mimi standing in the lobby with Krabb. They were just finishing a work session.

"Hey, y'all I'm a little early. You know what they say: Dreams do come true. Don't you think?"

Krabb smiled and walked closer to Fiona, and for the first time, Krabb thought about hugging her, but he didn't. "Yes, I'm ready. Let's go in. Mimi, see you next time."

Fiona gave Mimi a hug.

"I call you later."

"Please do, Fee. I have questions for you about Nyla.'

"I bet you do. Don't worry. We'll figure it out, Mimi."

Krabb and Fiona walked into his office. Fiona noticed nothing changed from her last visit.

"Please sit, Fiona. Where do you want to begin?"

Fiona told Krabb about Sarah and Chance. The visit was not one of her best moments, and Krabb sensed that as she told him about Sarah's comments and her comments to Sarah. Fiona told Krabb that Chance was in her dream, but he didn't understand what she was talking about. When Sarah and Chance left her, Fiona felt like she failed in the sibling relationship department.

"Remember we are here to have experiences," Krabb said. "Not all our experiences are good. We act like fools at times, and at other times, we don't have compassion for people or the situation we find ourselves experiencing. So it is okay to respond to situations in an unusual way. Even those actions bring awareness to the soul."

Fiona nodded. "Let me tell you about the dream. Jayla, Tyrone and Holly are talking in the empty bar. I think all the men have signed up to fight, Doc. The dream is changing again, and I want to know more."

She talked about Holly and her desire to keep the bar open. She mentioned Tyrone's interest in NAACP and how she thought about him now.

"You know, Tyrone is really a good guy with a few bad habits. I think he's going to make a difference. I think Laquisha's death changed him."

Krabb opened his computer while he listened. He wanted to share his research.

"Somehow Sarah thinks I was the star child, and Geoff and she were just afterthoughts. I guess being the youngest, I got most of the attention. At least, they thought so, but I don't know why she blames me for their actions."

"Yes, I'm sure the suicide changed Tyrone. It changed you, too. In fact, your mother's suicide and Laquisha's suicide had a big impact on how you perceive yourself. From what you told me about your sister, she is handling all these challenges in a completely different way. She feels betrayed and lost, and in a way, she blames you. People rationalize things to suit their reality. Sarah's reality is much different than yours. She needs to blame you for thinking the way she does. She can't deal with what she did in the past."

"Do you mean in our childhood? Do you mean the disappearance of Geoff?"

"Yes, I believe so. She feels innately responsible for Geoff's death because she played a part in his life. Her part may or may not have been the reason for his disappearance, but she holds herself responsible. Sarah also feels responsible for your mother's suicide. Somewhere in the back of her mind, she thinks she could have averted Geoff's fate, and your mother's as well."

Fiona sat straight up. He eyes were fixed on Krabb.

"So why is Amber so important? She has other counterparts, according to you. I'm sure some of them were more stable. Am I wrong about that?"

"Well, my belief is Amber is Sarah's closest counterpart in terms of lessons. She has many counterparts, as we all do, but Amber is influencing her the most right now. That's not to say the others don't play a part."

"Is that the same for everyone?"

"Not necessarily. It depends on the life lessons that pertain to the desires of the individual. You know we all have similar desires, but not all our desires or beliefs are the same, as you well know."

"Okay. Got that. One more question, please. From what I told you about Violet, Holly, Flip and Shorty, can you tell me why they are in my life? None of them really influenced me. Although Violet, and to a lesser degree Flip did in a way. I guess Shorty did make Jayla mad so that may count too, I guess. Is that why?"

"Yes, the people whom we make agreements with don't always teach us lessons in a kind and gentle way. Some of the people in our lives want to disrupt us. They want to cause us some kind of pain. Those people teach us the greatest lessons, because they always show us something about us that we fail or don't want to see in ourselves. They show us the duplicity of being human and the folly of being set in our beliefs about who we really are."

"So I should look at all of them the same way and appreciate them no matter what, Doc?

"You always have a choice. You can avoid these people, but the lessons still must be learned. You can be discerning and accept what you want from them and discard the rest. Remember, you never get it wrong, and you never get it done."

Fiona looked confused.

"Get what wrong and what done?"

Krabb smiled.

"Your life, Fiona. We are in a continuous stream of energy that expands from our experiences. The knowledge we absorb becomes part of the wisdom of our soul."

Chapter 26

Whenever I hear old chronicles of love,
It's age-old pain,
It's ancient tale of being apart or together.
As I stare on and on into the past, in the end
you emerge,
Clad in the light of a pole-star, piercing the
darkness of time.

Rabindranath Tagore

The black Lexus SC 430 raced through traffic on Broadway. The driver, Flip Pooker, just left the Tin Roof on West End after drinking six shots and four beers. He was zooming toward Second Avenue. As he closed in on Eighth Avenue, he vaguely saw the light turn yellow, then red. It was almost 8:30 p.m., and he worried that his new girlfriend would leave him if he didn't get to the Wild Horse by 9 p.m. He pushed his right foot down on the pedal as hard as he could. Pooker didn't see the man on the old bike crossing Broadway on Eighth. He didn't hear the sound of the bike hitting the front fender. He didn't notice the loud thump the 200-pound man made when he hit the hood of his car, and he didn't see the inflated airbag before he came to a stop. The airbag hit him so hard he had a heart attack.

The biker and Flip died on the scene. When Fiona turned on the TV the next morning, she couldn't believe her ears.

The reporter said the man on the bike, Chance Hansen from Nevada, was helping the homeless. He was carrying bundles of newspapers across the street for two homeless men who would sell them on the adjacent corners the next morning.

Fiona immediately thought the man on the bike might be the guy named Chance whom she met when Sarah visited. She knew Flip was Violet's son and the counterpart of Shorty. Fiona quickly texted Sarah.

"Did you hear about Chance and Flip? I can't believe it. Was that your Chance?"

Sarah responded quickly.

"Seems like you always contact me when something horrid happens. I heard about it, and yes. It was. I'm sick about it."

"It's not your fault, Sarah. You tried to help him."

"It is my fault. I threw him out. He had no place to go. Now this."

There wasn't anything she could say that would make Sarah feel better, but she tried.

"If I can help please let me. I want to be close to you."

Sarah's response was quick and to the point.

"No need, Fee. Jiggy is here with me now, and all is spot-on. I love her."

Suddenly, Fiona's current dream made sense. Her mind started to draw some rapid conclusions.

Shorty and Tyrone hated each other, and in this lifetime, they die together. Sarah and Jiggy were both Amber in my dreams, and now they are back together as lovers. Sarah loved Jiggy from the start of this life, but she had to go through men and a lot of pain to realize it. Sarah hated herself, not because of her skin color, but because she is gay. She tried to deny it until Geoff's death. Chance made her realize what she really wanted.

Fiona pulled into Krabb's parking lot an hour later, for her last session with him. The receptionist asked her to take a seat. Fiona's red sleeveless T-shirt, khaki shorts and flip-flops made the receptionist look twice at her.

"I want to make sure I have your correct address, Miss Mistry. The doctor is updating his client list. "

Fiona confirmed her address with Krabb's young assistant, and then she started to daydream. She was back in England playing football with Geoff and Sarah. She watched as she kicked the ball and hit Sarah in the face. Sarah fell to the ground in pain. "You are such a damp squib, Fee. That hurt, and I'm never going to forgive you!"

"I'm so sorry, Sarah. It was an accident. I would never hurt you!"

Sarah stood and wiped the mud off her shorts.

"I don't care. I'd rather have Jiggy as a sister, if you want to know the truth."

The receptionist's voice snapped Fiona back into the moment.

"Dr. Krabb will see you now."

Fiona walked through the door and smiled at Krabb.

Krabb stood up as Fiona rattled off her first question.

"Did you hear about the accident last night on Broad?"

"Yes, I saw the news. Why?"

"Well, the driver of the car was Violet's son, whom you know as Shorty in my dream, and the guy on the bike was Chance, and he is Tyrone in the dream. Shorty and Tyrone hate each other in the 1940s, and they died together in this life. I think I know why now! No one would understand the importance of that meeting except me, and you, of course."

"Yes. Situations like that happen all the time. We just don't use the insight to put the pieces together. Let me interject something here. I did a little research and discovered that Jayla died the same year you were born. She died in August, and you were born in September that same year. And Myles died in 1945 — two months before I was born!"

"Wow! We are so connected with these people, Doc! All the things you said about the soul must be right. I can just imagine my counterparts whom I haven't connected with. You too, Doc. But never mind them. What else do you have, please? Tell me more about us now!"

Krabb looked at his computer, then started to type.

"Okay. Here we go. Let's start with Jayla. I found this article the other day. Let me read it to you." Krabb cleared his throat. "This is a 1942 editorial in The Crisis Magazine:

'The role of black women in the struggle to desegregate the military has often been overlooked, but their militancy contributed to the effort. The colored woman has been a more potent factor in shaping Negro society than the white woman has been in shaping white society because the sexual caste system has been much more fluid and ill-defined than among whites. Colored women have worked with their men and helped build and maintain every institution we have. Without their economic aid and counsel, we would have made little if any progress.'"

Fiona nodded.

"Wow. Black women have always been underestimated, and they still are, in my opinion. I'm not sure where Jayla served while she was an Army nurse, but she was a hero in every regard as far as I'm concerned."

Krabb continued reading from his computer.

"Now this article was told by Virgil Patterson, a Tuskegee Airman. Patterson told historian Ben Vinson III this story. It's about the boys in the bar. You mentioned they joined the Tuskegee Airmen in some capacity."

'Unlike all other units in the Army, the 99th Squadron and the 332nd Group, made up of the 100th, 301st, and 302nd squadrons, had black officers. The 99th went to North Africa in April 1943 and flew its first combat mission against the Italian island of Pantelleria in the Mediterranean on June 2. Later, the squadron participated in the air battle over Sicily and supported the invasion of Italy. The squadron regularly engaged German pilots in aerial combat. General Benjamin O. Davis Jr. commanded the 332nd Group when it was deployed to Italy in January 1944. In July, the 99th was added to the 332nd, and the group participated in campaigns in Italy, France, Germany, and the Balkans. The Tuskegee Airmen gained an impressive record. They flew more than 15,500 sorties, completed 1,578 missions and escorted 200 heavy bombers deep into Germany's Rhineland. They accumulated 150

Distinguished Flying Crosses, a Legion of Merit, a Silver Star, 14 Bronze Stars, and 744 Air Medals. The Tuskegee Airmen and the black ground troops who looked after their planes had to overcome more than the racism that cast doubt on black soldiers' ability to fight. They also had to master the technology of complex machines. The 332nd Fighter Group flew more different kinds of fighter planes than any other group of pilots during World War II.'"

Fiona was silent. Then she looked at Krabb.

"I knew it! The boys at the bar knew what they had to do. They accepted the challenge and went above and beyond. I hope I find out what happened to all of them!"

"Me too, Fiona. I also found an article on DuPont. Nyla may have worked for a short time in an ammunition factory, but I have a feeling she went to work for DuPont's Savannah River Plant in South Carolina. That facility helped create the hydrogen bomb."

"Wow. That is amazing, Doc!"

Fiona remembered her telephone conversation with Mimi. Mimi told her about her insane fear of bullets, guns and bombs. She thought Krabb could be right.

"Funny, Doc. Mimi told me she was deathly afraid of bombs the other day."

"She told me the same thing, Fiona." Krabb didn't tell Fiona how Mimi told him, however. "It's amazing, Fiona.

We pick up feelings, lessons and information from our counterparts, and we don't know it."

Fiona shook her head again in agreement.

"I know, but I still don't know why I found you. I think I know about the others, thanks to you. They are all taught me something about me, even though they didn't know me that well. But Myles didn't teach me anything in my dreams except that he was a two-timing flirt who liked to drink and paint. Do you think Myles is trying to tell me something else or teach me now through you?"

Krabb moved to the chair next to Fiona. He wasn't sure he could answer her question. He took a deep breath and sat silently beside her.

"Are you okay, Doc?"

"I think Myles wants to apologize for hurting Jayla. Somehow, he knows what he did to her, he did to you. You carried the pain of Jayla's rejection through this life, and it impacted your ability to have a fulfilling relationship. He knew Jayla was more than he could handle. He didn't think he was capable of giving her what she needed because of his insecurities. He showed his insecurity in a very typical and negative way. He never told Jayla his true feelings, and by me telling you, you might be able to pass them on to her."

Fiona closed her eyes, and as she did, she saw the image of Jayla. Jayla was alone, lying on a bed with her eyes closed. She appeared to be asleep, but her lips were moving. Fiona couldn't hear what Jayla was saying, but a strange feeling ran up and down her body. Jayla's thoughts and body seemed to be tangled with hers.

Fiona quickly opened her eyes and looked around the room. She stared at the nude painting on the wall. Then she focused on the orchids below the window as if she was seeing them for the first time. Her eyes met Krabb's. In a way, he looked different. He was white, not black. Her mind told her he was always white, but she questioned herself. She felt an impulse and then said, "Myles is that you? It can't be. You're white, but I feel you, and I see Nyla's painting. Where are you? And where in this dream am I?"

Krabb held Fiona's gaze, but he didn't say a word. Fiona slowly got up from her chair and moved toward the back wall of Krabb's office. A big gold-framed mirror hung at just the right height for her to see her head and torso. She moved closer to it. Fiona suddenly stopped a few feet from the mirror and looked straight into it. The words came out slowly.

"Lord have mercy! I'm a white woman! I know Tyrone and Laquisha said they might be white someday, but me? Jayla? Lord, what a dream!"

Fiona's fingers touched her face as she mumbled those words. She looked at Krabb who was standing behind her.

"Myles, honey, are you really here? Guess Tyrone was right. Maybe we all live as white folks, black folks, China folks and all. I feel so strange in this body, but is it me? I know it is. Myles, you do like being white, don't you? I'm not sure about it. And these clothes! It looks like someone took all my dresses and left me with nothing but my underwear!"

Fiona felt her T-shirt and shorts as she continued to channel Jayla.

"Don't like my clothes, but the hair and eyes aren't bad. In fact, it looks like my skin still has some black in it, but you, honey, you're milk white. Did you really want to look like that in this dream?"

Krabb was alarmed. "Fiona, Are you okay? Do want some water? Please come sit down. You're moving your mouth but nothing is coming out of it."

He gently took Fiona's arm, and she immediately felt her body react to his touch. Her glassy eyes closed, then opened. Perspiration oozed from her pores.

"Fiona, please sit down and let's figure this out."

"Okay. Wait, Doc." She put her hands to her face. "God, Jayla was just here. I felt and heard her talking to you. She was dreaming, and she was here in that dream. She was talking to you and looking at herself. When she saw herself, she saw me. And she saw you and knew you were Myles. Did you hear her, Doc? She couldn't believe she was a white woman, or that Myles is white too."

"No, Fiona. I didn't hear a word, but I could tell you left your body, and that someone was taking your place for a few minutes. I must say, I never thought I would get that close to Jayla, but I think I just did. What else can you tell me about the encounter? Did she feel afraid? Was she nervous?"

"I don't think so, Doc. She knew she was dreaming. I could sense that, but I also sensed that she thought the dream was real. I don't think she realized who I am, and I don't think she knows what the connection means."

Krabb nodded.

"Yes. That would be unusual for her to understand given the time period and her beliefs back then. But she may want to know more about this life. Now that she had this dream, perhaps she'll try to come back."

Fiona glanced at the painting on the wall.

"Perhaps she will, but what about the others, Doc?" Are they going to let me in now that Myles is gone?

"Well, perhaps you'll find out, now that this dream world is open at both ends."

"Maybe. I now know we all live to dream and then dream to live. It's all one big dream isn't it? We are either dreaming with a body or without one, right?"

"Yes, that is the nature of consciousness. We dream and then live our dreams in an ever-expanding stream of dreams. We pick which ones to focus on, and that makes this energy we call life so powerful. Life is the stepping stone that brings us to the epicenter of all dreams."

"Yes, I see what you mean. We are like clouds that move through the air. We take shape from the people that see us. What I see in me and what you see in me blend in the memory and the future of all that dreams.

"Fiona, I think you've got it!"

"Thanks, Doc but what is 'it'?"

Krabb smiled. "Well Fiona, let me quote Motown: 'You don't have nothing until you feel your soul.' Soul is that indescribable beat that you hear as your mind connects to the tempo that carries you through the unchartered world within your dreams."

Fiona looked at him and wondered about that statement. Then it hit her.

"Doc, let's just say, our souls are like a song that hits the high and low notes of life with the rhapsody of a fine-tuned piano in a dream machine."

"I like it, Jayla."

"Me too, Myles."

Epilogue

For a long time, my subconscious rested in a dark place, ticking through memories like a jukebox selecting a record . . .

Chelsie Shakespeare

"It's been almost two months since we talked, Fiona.?"

Mimi was curious about Fiona. No one had seen or heard from her in a couple of months. She was happy Fiona picked up the phone.

"Oh my God! I have been busy traveling, Mimi! I went on an orchid buying spree last year. I had a dear friend look after the orchids while I was gone."

Fiona was in the nursery when she answered the call.

"I still wonder about you and your dreams. I remember you told me about your last meeting with Krabb and how you acted like Jayla. Have you had any closure since that meeting?"

"No, I haven't had any more dreams involving Jayla, if that's what you mean. And I haven't been back to the Black Orchid either. For some reason, I can't go back. Something in me is blocking my ability to return for the closure I desperately need."

"Maybe you should talk to Krabb again. He might help."

Fiona was silent for a minute. Her phone chimed with a text message.

"Jiggy and I are leaving Tennessee. Going to a state that will marry us. No need for you to know where. I'll send you a message when we get settled."

Fiona answered while Mimi waited.

"I wish our relationship was different, Sarah. I am sorry for the part I played in distancing us. At any rate, congrats to you, and give my best to Jiggy."

"Mimi, are you there? I just got a text from my sister. She's leaving the state to get married. I'm a little sad about that. Let me call you back."

"Yes, I'll be here."

"Thanks, Mimi."

Fiona walked to her porch. Her sister finally put the final nail in their relationship. She felt alone as she looked at her message again. Fiona told herself she had her orchids, and they were her family, but she felt the void left by her birth family.

Fiona moved to her porch swing. She watched two bluebirds play in the open field behind her house. The birds were free. That is true love, she thought. She closed her eyes. Within minutes, she was back in the Black Orchid. She saw the faded black orchid on the door as Jayla entered. The room looked different as she watched Jayla take a seat at the bar. The booths were gone. Red and white checkered tablecloths covered the small tables. The walls were now white, not black. The old jukebox was still there, but the lighting was different. It was no longer a dark smoky hangout. It was now a small restaurant. The people were different too. Men wearing black leather jackets and white T-shirts crowed the bar. Jayla felt out of place until she heard a familiar voice.

"My Lord! Is that you Jay?" I thought you were long-gone like the others."

Jayla looked at the smiling gray-haired woman behind the bar. She didn't recognize her at first with her wrinkled face and sagging eyelids. She noticed the woman's red tank top. The woman quickly poured Jayla a drink.

"Here, Baby. It's been a while. You still drinking gin and tonic? Are you doing okay?" The bartender slid the drink to her.

Jayla suddenly recognized her old friend. Jayla looked around the bar again, and then she looked into the mirror. She had aged too. Her faced looked fuller, and there were creases around her eyes and mouth. Her black hair was short and mixed with gray. She had a slight scar on her left cheek. Her short black dress covered the bottom half of her neck. Jayla took a sip of her gin and tonic.

"The place has changed, Holly. How are you doing, and how's Tyrone."

Holly served two beers to the burley young white men at the bar, then poured herself a shot of bourbon from the bottle she kept under the bar.

"You know, Jay, I'm surviving. It's been 20 tough years since I saw you. Been like that for everybody, I guess. At least I kept this place open. I told you I would, but it wasn't easy. Had to find a new partner after Tyrone left it to me.

This new guy is white, and he rides a motorcycle. You can tell, can't you?"

Jayla sipped and nodded in agreement.

"Is Tyrone dead, Holly?"

"Fraid so. Poor fool did join the NAACP, but some white trash drunk shot him one night in front of the bar just after he started his third year with that group. He did some good for folks around here while he was alive. He said he would help us get the vote, and I guess the white folks didn't like that much."

Jayla ached with loss.

"I hate that, Holly. After all, he did try to make something of himself before he got shot. When did that happen?"

"Well, I think it was 1949, I'm not really sure, but it sounds about right. You know how time is . . . you never know where it goes. Where were you in '49, Jay?"

Jayla push her glass away.

"I was still in Europe. I was sent to Greennock, Scotland, with my group of Army nurses in 1944. I stayed there for a few months, and then I was transferred to England. I stayed there after the war was over because I met a wounded officer and fell in love. But, I found out it wasn't love. He just wanted someone to take care of him while he ran around like a tomcat. For some reason, I always pick guys who can't be faithful. Anyway, I worked as a nurse until the end of 1949. I came back to the States and moved to Chicago. Been there more than 10 years working as a nurse at the Northwestern University Hospital off Michigan."

"What brings you down here, Jay? I did get your letters. Thanks. But then everything stopped. Thought you might be dead or something."

Jayla's glass was half-full, but the lime still hovered on the edge.

"No. I just stopped writing when I got back. I was trying to understand all this killing. I still see death, Holly. Seems like it follows me. I didn't think I would live past 40, but here I am. Something told me I should try to find out what happened to the old group. I never stayed in touch with any of them, including Myles, but I did see him recently. Did the boys stay in touch with you?"

Holly finished her shot before she answered. "You bet they did, girl! Do you know they all stayed together in that Alabama colored group? Myles became a pilot. Cave and Sly became gunners or something on one of those planes, and Rocco was a navigator. Nigma was a mechanic. They were called the "Black Bird Men." They all stayed in touched with me until the end of 1944. Then in 1945, I got a letter from Nigma. I still have it. You want me to read it to you? I keep it in my purse. It's a little beat-up cause I read it every now and then. Those boys were special, you know."

Holly fumbled through her oversized black purse under the bar, and pulled out the well-worn letter, which was still in the original envelope. She cleared her throat.

"Hi there Holly,

I wanted you to know how brave our friends were. I found this article in an Army newsletter and wanted you to read it, so I copied it. I think I got all the details right, so here it is.

'In 1945, the 332nd Fighter Group (that was the boy's group) was awarded a Distinguished Unit Citation for "outstanding performance and extraordinary heroism." Here's what happened to all of them.

Army pilot Myles Dunbar spotted a string of BF-109s heading toward a crippled B-24. Dunbar turned into the German formation. He gave the leader a burst with his .50 calibers, and the plane went hurtling down to the ground. Dunbar radioed the others in his flight crew and heard, "I'm right behind you." But when Dunbar looked back, all he could see was the gun of another German BF-109, pointing right at him. Dunbar slowed down, and the German plane overran him. A few more shots, and Lt. Dunbar had another kill of the day. Two more Germans were still in view and seemed like easy pickings, but another German was on his tail. Dunbar was shot down. The plane was never recovered.'

"The other three were shot down over Sicily that same year. In fact, they died a couple of months after Myles. They all got medals for bravery. I didn't know how to tell you, so I just thought I would send you the whole story. All our friends were heroes. They served their country the only way they knew how — with courage, conviction and the will to win. They did win, Holly. They won for all of us who have colored skin. Don't know if I'll ever get back there. I'm in India now, but y'all are in my thoughts. Take care, Nigma. April 15, 1945."

Jayla's eyes filled with tears. Makeup ran down her face. She wiped it with a napkin.

"God, I knew it. I've been avoiding that awful news. What about Nyla? Any news about her or Amber?"

Holly wiped her face with a bar rag. She poured another shot and downed it. A man at the end of the bar called for a refill, but she ignored him.

"Nyla's alive. She's living in South Carolina or somewhere. Think she married a doctor she met while she worked in a factory. He's a not a regular doctor. He's a scientist or something. And that damn Amber? Well, that bitch is living with Shorty. Don't ask me how that happened because I don't care. All I know is she and Shorty have a place over on Fourth Street. Shorty can barely walk and Amber has a bad heart."

Jayla looked around the bar again. It wasn't the Black Orchid anymore. The cool jazz was gone. Hillbilly rock took its place. She watched Holly while squeezing the lime into the rest of her drink.

"How long you gonna stay here, Holly? This place has changed. You don't look right here anymore. Can't you do something else? You want to come back to Chicago with me?"

Holly pushed her gray hair back behind her ears.

"You said you saw Myles, Jay. How come you said that? He's been dead for a while now."

Jayla hesitated. She wasn't sure how to tell Holly about her dream. She looked around again.

"Remember when Tyrone was talking about Laquisha wanting to be white, and him not wanting to ever be white? Just the thought made him mad. Well, I had this dream a few nights ago, and I know you're not going to believe this, but Myles was in it. He was white. He was sitting next to me in an office. He didn't look like Myles, but I felt him somehow. His painting of Nyla hung on his wall, and orchids were all around. When I looked into the mirror in his office, the face looking back at me was white. The name Fee or something was in my mind, and Myles had another name too. Holly, when I woke up, I sat in my favorite chair and just looked at the Chicago skyline. As I did, the thought came to me that we all must live in a dream, and that dream is in another dream of some kind. I remembered Tyrone saying Laquisha talked about that guy Edgar Cayce, so I went to the library and read about him. He had dreams like the one I had, Holly, but he could heal people while he was dreaming. He said our soul lives as many people, but we only remember the one we live. I know this all sounds strange, but it's true. I haven't had another dream like that one. I needed to come here first and see where all this stuff started. Somehow, the dream and the bar are related."

Holly stood frozen. Then she leaned over the bar so her face was inches from Jayla's.

"Jay, What if I told you I saw myself as a white woman with a son who was a white version of Shorty? I can't tell you how scared I was. I woke up before I saw any more in that dream. That dream almost made me stop drinking. Guess that's why I woke up."

Jayla laughed.

"I believe you, Holly. The more I read about this dream world, the more I believe in it. Why don't you try to dream that dream again? There is a message in it for you. I think the message I got was Myles is okay, and if he is okay, then all the boys are doing real good."

"Thanks, Jay, but no thanks, baby. I reckon I'm going to drink myself silly in this place. No more dreams for me. I've lived all of mine. I'm a bar girl, and always will be. I don't know nothing else and don't want to know. But I'll write you if you want."

Jayla saw fear in Holly's eyes. She knew Holly was at the end of her long road of drinking and that she wouldn't stop until she reached the end of that road. She knew she was living her own dream.

Fiona was back on the porch, and her phone was buzzing.

"Hello?"

"Hi, Fiona, I just spoke to Mimi. She said you might want to talk. Are you okay?"

"Oh, hi Doc. I just came back from the bar. It's all changed. The bar's a hangout for motorcycle dudes, now, but Holly is still there. Bless her heart. I think I'm seeing the bar in the 1960s now. Jayla returned, and Holly told her the whole story. The men, except for Nigma, died in the war. Jayla told Holly about her dream, and Holly said she saw Violet and Flip in a dream, but she didn't know their names."

Fiona took a deep breath.

"What year did you say Jayla died? It was 1962, right? Well, I think I saw Jayla around that time, Doc. She was telling me something, but she didn't know it. I think she died right after that, but I don't know how.

"You know, Doc, I think I know why I'm the way I am, now. Jayla was like me. All the relationship disappointments in my life and in hers made us fear relationships, and I need to change that somehow. I turned to my orchids for solace, but I needed to do more. I also know Sarah didn't care much for family or friends when she was Amber, and that attitude followed her into this life. Shorty and Flip had that same attitude about respecting friendships and family. Holly loved the spontaneous actions and challenges that happen in a bar and the comfort of her bar friendships. Violet brought that with her in this life. And my dad (or Nigma in my dream) loved life. He stayed alive through the war. All these people repeated their behavior in a different way. What they didn't learn then will be lessons for their counterparts. You know what I mean? If lessons aren't used to increase awareness, they will repeat themselves in some form in other lives."

Krabb was quick to answer.

"Very insightful, Fiona. But what do you think about the boys and Myles?"

"I think the men in my life used the lessons they learned from them. But the black men have a stronger message, I think. They lived and died doing what they believed. They lived to experience the challenge of being judged inferior. They lived in a bigoted and judgmental time and rose above it. They showed the world that the instability of feeling separate and different leads to violence and war. They proved that distorted and one-sided power creates mistrust and unrest. Misguided power changes the face of humanity, and that face turns half-truths and untruths into truths. I learned so much from them. I believe their beauty lies with the orchids now."

Krabb couldn't respond at first. He knew she was speaking from a place deep inside of her.

"Are you putting Myles in that group too, or do you have something more to say about him? After all, I am him."

Fiona didn't hesitate.

"Right! You know you are Myles, Doc. I know what I learned from him. But the real question is what do you learn from him?"

Krabb smiled.

"I feel like I'm the patient now."

Fiona laughed.

"You know what I mean, right? You're still living his lessons, just like I am living Jayla's. We are learning to be mindfully flexible and astutely aware that what we do and how we do it is not just because we learned it here. Some of what we do and believe is buried in the creases of our soul. We use buried beliefs as tools to fulfill our dreams and the dreams of our counterparts."

Krabb nodded. "I couldn't have said it better myself, Fiona. Do you think Jayla will be dreaming of us after her death?"

Fiona nodded her head. She listened to Krabb's voice as she sat down on the swing and looked at the river, the trees and the rocks. She looked at her nursery as if she saw her orchids for the first time. The voice belonged to Krabb, but she knew she was listening to Myles.

"Fiona? Are you still there? Hello?

Fiona and Jayla's future counterpart felt Fiona hold the iPhone tightly to her ear and thought:

Those damn phones were primitive in 2012.

Fiona smiled as the inner message danced through her mind. Another story was about to begin. Fiona was back in her body, and Jayla and somebody else were there too.

"Doc, you're not going to believe this, but I think I just heard from the future Jayla and me. But I'm getting the feeling that I'm not a woman in this future reality. I'm a man!"

Krabb laughed.

"Does that must mean I'm a woman in that time period, Fiona?"

"God, this gets complicated doesn't it, Doc?"

"That's why most of us only want to know about and live one life, Fiona."

*****

About The Author

Born in Philadelphia, award-winning author H.T. Manogue spent the first twenty-one years of his life conforming to logical beliefs and rituals. He spent the next twenty-six years of his life rebelling against those beliefs and rituals in one way or another.

For the last fifteen years, he has been studying and writing about consciousness. His journey has taken him through the history of religious thought and the intricacies of philosophy as well as other associations and influences that impact the human belief system.

Retiring from the shoe industry after 35 years of "sole" searching, Hal discovered his real soul when he started writing poetry in 1996. His first book, *Short Sleeves: A Book For Friends*, was self-published in 2003. His second book, *Short Sleeves. A Book For Friends 2006 Collection*, and his third book, *Short Sleeves: A Book For Friends 2007 Collection*, were published in those years. *Short Sleeves: Spirit Songs*, his most recent book of poetry, was published in 2008.

Essays from his book, *Short Sleeves Insights: Live An Ordinary Life In A Non-Ordinary Way*, published in May

2009, have been republished in other books and newsletters around the globe.

Manogue's third novel, *Bed Bosh & Beyond*, addresses the afterlife through the eyes of none other than George Carlin, one of the funniest men of the 20th Century. *Bed Bosh & Beyond* is now in print. His 2013 award-winning novel, *The Butterfly Ball,* and his 2012 award-winning novel, *Living Behind The Beauty Shop*, continue to inspire people around the world.

All Manogue's paperback and eBooks are available on his Website: http://www.shortsleeves.net/ as well on Amazon and all bookstores.